HIGHLAND VAMPIRE

HIGHLAND VAMPIRE

HANNAH HOWELL

ADRIENNE BASSO

DEBORAH RALEIGH

KENSINGTON BOOKS

KENSINGTON BOOKS are published by

Kensington Publishing Corp.
850 Third Avenue
New York, NY 10022

ISBN 0-7394-5838-8

CONTENTS

Kiss of the Vampire

Hannah Howell

One

Scotland—Spring, 1478

The sun would set in a few hours, Jankyn thought as he crouched inside the narrow, deeply set stone arrow slot. When the sun was at this particular spot in the sky, he could safely view the gardens below. He grimaced as he thought of the teasing he would have to endure if it was discovered that he had a liking for flowers. A MacNachton liking flowers? Jankyn could almost see his kinsmen rolling on the floor, weak from hilarity.

It *was* rather pathetic, he mused, even as he took a deep breath, savoring the scent of primroses, bluebells, and musk roses. A garden flourished in the sun. He lived in the shadows. Perhaps it was more envy than appreciation. There was a part of him that hungered for a chance to turn his face toward the sun, to revel in its warmth upon his skin. It would be the last pleasure he enjoyed if he was mad enough to try it, but there were times when he was sorely tempted.

There was a soft rap upon his door and a woman called his name, but he ignored her. Something else that would both surprise and amuse his kinsmen. When he had first arrived at the king's court, he had freely indulged his lusts with the women gathered here, but that game no longer interested him. They no longer interested him. He was weary of being the dark, mysterious lover the women could brag about to their friends. There was a danger lurking in such excess for it stirred not only curiosity, but jealousy. He was also simply tired of fleeting, empty passion, of bedding down with women who did not really care to know him well, or would run screaming from his embrace if they did.

It was time to leave, but he could not give in to the urge to return to the comforting, shadowy depths of Cambrun. He had not yet found a suitable mate for his son David or finished his own work. Born of an Outsider, David could live a near-normal life, and Jankyn was determined to give him as rich a one as possible. There were also strong indications that it was here he would discover why he did not seem to be the pure-blooded MacNachton he had always thought he was.

"Are ye sure she will come here?"

Jankyn frowned down at the young man who had spoken, interrupting his peace and his thoughts. He recognized the elegantly dressed man as Sir Lachlan Armstrong, an impoverished young man with a small, poor holding. His companion was Thomas Oliphant, the youngest son of a laird with a lot of sons and little money. It was widely known that they would make any woman a poor husband. Jankyn tensed for there was something about them that made him think they were on the hunt, and he wondered which poor lass was their prey.

"Aye, Tom, she will," replied Lachlan. "I had Eleanor tell her the roses were in bloom. The lass loves flowers."

"Och, aye, she does that, but it doesnae mean she will come to have a peek at them now. Could be she willnae come until the morrow."

"Nay, 'twill be soon. Ere the sun sets. Eleanor told her that Old Rob, a mon weel kenned for his skill at foretelling the weather, had talked of a fierce storm coming, one that would be sure to damage the flowers. The lass willnae want to risk missing a chance to see them in full bloom."

"Clever."

It was and Jankyn had to wonder why Eleanor would help these fools. Since the two men could give her little save a rutting, he had to think Eleanor did not like the lass she was sending into this trap. There could be many reasons for that, but knowing Eleanor as he unfortunately did, Jankyn suspected the chosen victim was young and beautiful. Eleanor did not like it when some other woman drew men's interest away from her. The intended prey must have arrived recently, during the last two weeks in which Jankyn had cut himself off from the intrigues of the court, both political and sexual. And dear Eleanor was one of the reasons for that self-imposed exile.

"O'er by that rowan tree would be a good place to await her," said Lachlan even as he strode toward it.

"There is one wee problem with this plan," said Thomas as he joined his friend. "Which one of us gets to have her?"

"We will both *have* her, but the first to draw blood will be the one to wed her."

"Which will still leave one of us with an empty purse, little or no land, and the need of a weel-dowered wife."

"Nay, nay. This lass has enough for us to share a wee bit, just enough to make it easier to get that rich bride. Agreed?"

"Agreed."

Swine, Jankyn thought. The rumors that said these two hid a callous brutality beneath their fine clothes and bonnie faces were obviously true. Glancing toward the sun, Jankyn knew he would not be able to perform any daring rescue. The best he could do was call out a warning, letting the rogues know that their perfidy was not unwitnessed. There would be little glory in it, but the ones in the garden would see nothing wrong for none of them would expect a man to leap from where he now perched and live.

It was not long before both men tensed and shifted deeper into the shadow of the tree. Jankyn knew their prey had entered the garden and he waited with them. When the woman entered his line of sight, Jankyn nearly fell from his perch. He easily recognized that lithe shape and the sensuous way the young woman moved. Her long, thick, honey gold hair swayed with each step she took, adding to her allure. Although he had seen little of her in nearly three years, he had obviously recalled Efrica Callan very well indeed. The two men lurking by the rowan tree intended to attack his laird's sister by marriage. His shock had also stolen away the chance to warn her, and he cursed softly.

His first inclination was to roar out his fury and attack, but he forced his rage back. Efrica was no fool, nor was she helpless. There was also the sun to consider. Fists clenched, he waited.

"Weel met, m'lady," said Lachlan as he moved to stand in front of Efrica, Thomas slipping around behind her.

"Mayhap I misjudge ye, but I dinnae think ye are here to join men in admiring the flowers," Efrica said.

Jankyn saw her sleek body subtly move as she prepared herself for an attack.

"We would rather show *ye* our admiration."

"Another time, if ye please."

Efrica felt fear chill her blood, but forced herself to ignore it. Fear stole one's wits and she would have need of hers now. Somehow she was going to have to slip free of this trap yet not do something that might raise too many questions. She could smell the lust in the men. It sickened and terrified her. Their plot was easy to discern. Rape, then a forced marriage. It was a ploy she should have considered when she had seen their anger over her rebuffs of their attentions, polite though those had been.

Just as she moved to leave the garden, Lachlan grabbed her by the arm. "Release me," she hissed, and saw both men look at her curiously. "Now."

"So fierce," drawled Lachlan. "Do ye bring that fire to all ye do?"

"And do ye always bring another fool with ye to subdue a lass so much smaller than ye are?"

Insulting the man had not been wise, Efrica decided as she watched his face redden with fury. She had sensed the brute hidden beneath the courtier's finery shortly after meeting both men. Although it was pleasing to have her judgment proven correct, she would have preferred to savor the small pleasure within the safe confines of her chambers or safely hidden within a crowd.

The only way to adequately protect herself now would be to toss aside the mask she wore at court. The genteel, polite lady she portrayed before others would gain her nothing now. Unfortunately, revealing too much of her true nature could rouse a curiosity that held its own dangers.

"Ye greet a mon's wooing with cold scorn," said Thomas. "Tisnae wise to lash at a mon's pride so."

"I doubt what ye plan now could e'er be called wooing," Efrica said, turning slightly in the small hope that she could keep either man from getting a firm hold on her. "Best ye pause a moment to consider the consequences."

"The consequences will be that ye will marry one of us. There is nay more to consider."

"Nay? How about the anger of my kinsmen?"

Lachlan snorted, the crude sound heavy with scorn. "The Callans? An unimportant clan who hides away upon their lands hording their coin. Weel, 'tis time that largesse was shared by ones who ken how to use it."

Efrica hastily swallowed the low, feral growl that crowded

into her throat at this insult to her clan. "On useless finery and jewels for adulteresses and whores? Better it was pitched into the sea."

"Ye have been here for ten days searching for a husband. Weel, we have decided 'tis past time ye got one."

"And ye have tossed a coin to decide which of you will be that mon, have ye?"

"Nay, lass, we mean to toss you and the prize goes to the first mon in." Lachlan smiled coldly as he tried to pull her into his arms. "In truth, it goes to the first to draw blood, my sweet."

"Och, aye?" Efrica flexed her fingers. "I believe that will be me."

Jankyn winced as he watched her rake her nails across Lachlan's face, for he could remember how sharp those long elegant nails of a Callan woman could be. Lachlan was lucky he still had his eyes. In fact, Jankyn suspected Efrica had tempered her blow, only lightly raking Lachlan's skin, for there was not that much blood, nor did Jankyn think the furrows running from check to cheek were that deep. Jankyn felt an ancient hunger stir within him as the scent of fresh, warm blood mixed with the light perfume of the flowers, but he forced it aside, keeping his full attention upon the ensuing battle below.

A part of him still wanted to bellow in rage, to put an immediate halt to this assault upon Efrica, but he continued to hold silent. It would be best if she handled the men in her own way. Efrica had agility, strength, and cunning. Perhaps even enough to get free of this trap. The last thing she needed was to draw too much attention to herself, and she had the wit to know that. If she freed herself, no one would hear of this confrontation. The two men intent upon rape would certainly not be talking. If he interfered in any way, this outrage would no longer be completely secret. There was even the chance the men might try to use his knowledge of it to force Efrica into a marriage she quite clearly did not want.

With a sensuous agility that impressed Jankyn, Efrica managed to elude the grasp of both men. It was quickly evident, however, that she had not really escaped them. For two men who seemed to do little but indulge themselves in every available vice, Lachlan and Thomas proved to be swift and cunning. Jankyn had the uneasy feeling they had played this cruel game before.

Even as he tried to think of a way to put an end to this without revealing too many of his secrets, or Efrica's, Jankyn watched the tide of the battle turn against her. His anger grew each time they chased her, each time they thwarted her attempt to escape, and each time they touched her. This was no way to treat a woman. The fact that this woman was connected to his clan through her sister's marriage made it a personal insult as well as a crime. Jankyn was not sure why, but the fact that it was Efrica seemed to make his anger all the fiercer.

Then they threw her to the ground, Thomas pinning her hands down as he crouched by her head. Lachlan quickly got the rest of her held firmly beneath his body. Jankyn forgot all about secrets that needed to be protected, and all about the chance that Efricia might be humiliated by being seen in such a degrading position. He even forgot about the sun. A soft growl rumbled deep in his throat as he leapt from his perch.

Efrica hissed a curse as Lachlan evaded her kicking legs and used his body to hold her down. Fear was a bitter taste in the back of her mouth, but she twisted her body, continuing to struggle. Although both men had made her uneasy from the beginning, she had never suspected they could be capable of this sort of brutality. This might be a callous attempt to force her to marry one of them, but she had no doubt at all that both men intended to violate her. She suspected they had made some pact between themselves as to how to share her rich dowry once one of them got her before a priest.

"Weel, lass, it looks as if I will win the greater prize," said Lachlan as he began to push up her skirts.

"If ye do this, all ye will win is a deep grave," she snapped. "Ye will die for this."

"Aye, lass, they will."

Her attackers had just begun to tense in surprise at the sound of that deep voice when Efrica suddenly found herself free. She lifted her head to see Lachlan, then Thomas, hurled across the garden to land hard against a tree. It took her a moment to recognize the man striding toward the dazed, softly groaning pair. Jankyn MacNachton was really there, was not some dream, and he was furious. Recalling what that emotion could do to a MacNachton, Efrica leapt to her feet and ran to him just as he grasped each stunned man by the front of his doublet and lifted him up.

"Nay," she said, slipping beneath his arm and placing a hand upon his chest. "Ye must nay kill them."

Jankyn looked down at her and she inwardly shivered. His elegant features had sharpened into a look that was chillingly feral. His golden eyes were those of a predator. He held each man several inches off the ground as if they weighed nothing. Then, slowly, his fury began to fade, his features softening slightly, and the snarl that had shaped his sensuous mouth receding.

"Best ye put them down ere someone sees. Aye, and ere they gain enough wits to open their eyes."

"*That* is a problem easily solved."

Efrica winced as he knocked the men's heads together and tossed them back on the ground. A quick glance at her attackers revealed that they would probably not be seeing anything for quite a while. She was turning back toward

Jankyn, prepared to ask him what he was doing there, when he staggered.

"What is wrong?" she demanded, wrapping an arm around his waist to help steady him.

"The sun hasnae set yet," he replied in a weak voice.

It took Efrica a moment to understand the implications of that. She cursed and started moving him toward the castle. Once within its thick walls, Jankyn recovered enough to respond to her demands and tell her where his chambers were. By the time they got inside his rooms, she was supporting nearly all his weight. He whispered a request for wine as he collapsed upon his bed. One sniff of the wine as she poured him a tankard was enough to tell her why he wanted some. It also reminded her, very strongly, of exactly what the MacNachtons were.

After downing a second tankard of wine, Jankyn fell asleep. Efrica stood beside his bed holding the empty tankard and studied him. His color had improved a little, and asleep, he was once again the darkly beautiful man she had known for three years. She sighed and shook her head. The man who had so swiftly appeared to rescue her, who had tossed her assailants aside like cushions, and who had been ready to slaughter the two men, had been laid low by the soft light of a setting sun.

"My hero," she muttered and went in search of a chair so that she could watch over him until he recovered.

Two

Efrica smiled faintly as she watched Lachlan and Thomas help each other stand up. They both looked frantically around the garden, then ran as if the devil himself were nipping at their backsides. If they knew the truth about the man who had tossed them around so effortlessly, they would probably be even more terrified. She just wished she could be certain this was the end of the trouble she would have with them.

Leaving the window, she poured herself a little of the untreated wine Jankyn obviously kept on hand for guests, and returned to her seat by his bed. David had briefly appeared and, after hearing what had happened, had offered to sit with his father, but she had sent him on his way. He had clearly wanted to return to the great hall for food and company, while she was content to remain out of sight for a while. The very last thing she wanted was to confront her attackers again. David had taken a note to her cousin Lady Barbara Matheson so that woman would not search for her or worry.

As she sipped her wine, Efrica studied the tall, slender man sprawled on the bed. It annoyed her to discover that her infatuation with the man still lingered despite three years of strangling it. His looks made such feelings understandable, for he was a beautiful man with his deep black hair and creamy skin. A long straight nose, high cheekbones, and a firm jaw gave his face an elegant, aristocratic look, whereas his thickly lashed golden eyes and sensuous mouth gave his face the warmth such perfectly carved features often lacked. In looks, he was all any woman could ask for. It was his nature that had made her so determined to kill all attraction to him. That was obviously going to take a lot more work.

She should have realized she had not cured herself of her fascination with Jankyn. From that first meeting at Cambrun when she was just a girl of sixteen, he had entered her dreams and stayed there. When she had arrived at court, she had learned of his reputation with women and the pangs that had roused should have warned her. If he had not exiled himself from those at court, she would have seen him with one or more women and ruefully admitted she would have undoubtedly suffered far more than a pang. It was unacceptable, but she was not sure what she could do.

Finishing her wine, she settled herself more comfortably in the chair, resting her feet on the edge of his bed. She would stay with Jankyn until she was sure he had recovered, and then she would do her best to stay far away from him. She refused to allow her heart to be held captive by a licentious rogue who lived in the shadows. Closing her eyes, she carefully listed all of Jankyn's faults until she fell asleep.

Jankyn slowly opened his eyes to a room lit only by a nearly burnt-out candle set near his bed. A moment later, he recalled why he was lying on his bed and feeling a little weak. As he started to look around, his gaze settled on a pair of small, stockinged feet resting on the edge of his bed.

After an appreciative study of the slender legs exposed almost to the knee, he looked at the woman sleeping in the chair and grinned. For a tiny woman, Efrica was taking up a lot of the large chair she was sprawled in, her slim arms dangling over the arms of the chair. Even so, the heavy, ornately carved seat accentuated her delicate build. He wondered how she had managed to move it, then recalled the strength she had revealed as she had helped him to his chambers.

Careful not to jostle her, he pulled himself up into a seated position, resting against pillows someone had obviously plumped up behind him. Although she still looked very young, her features had lost the last of the childish softness she had still possessed at sixteen. Her thick, honey gold hair hung in tangled waves to pool around her slim hips upon the seat of the chair. There was a faint touch of gold to her beautiful skin. There was also a slight feline cast to her delicate, fine-boned features, except for the full, tempting shape of her lips. Even at sixteen her mouth had been one to turn a man's thoughts lustful. Of course, right now, that tempting mouth was slightly open and emitting a faint snore. And that long, beautiful neck of hers was cocked at an awkward angle that could probably cause her a twinge or two when she woke up.

Telling himself he was only doing it for her own good, to try to save her from a little discomfort, Jankyn nudged her foot with his until she started to wake up. When her eyes opened, the clouds of sleep that lingered there turned them a warm amber color. It made him think of how her eyes might look clouded with the heat of passion. It was a dangerous thought.

"Ye have your feet upon my bed," he said and relaxed a little when the softness in her eyes was rapidly replaced by a look of irritation.

"I took my shoes off," she said even as she put her feet on the floor and began to stretch, trying to rid her body of the various small aches caused by sleeping in a chair.

Jankyn wondered how she could make such a simple act look so sensuous. "I thank ye for stopping me from killing those two fools, though they weel deserved it."

"Aye, they did, but twould have caused trouble, raised questions neither of us could afford to answer. And I thank ye for coming to my aid." She frowned a little. "I am a wee bit surprised ye were so close at hand whilst the sun was still in the sky."

"I was in the window. Tis shelter enough late in the day. I simply leapt down when it became clear that ye were losing the battle."

Efrica looked at the window, recalled how far above the ground it was, and looked back at Jankyn. "A bit dangerous."

"Nay. The sun was a far greater threat. Tis why I was slow to interfere," he admitted. "I had hoped ye could deal with it on your own."

"They were weel practiced in such games, I fear." She scowled. "Mayhap I should have let ye rip their throats out. Now they can recover and repeat their crimes against women."

"Twill be a while ere Lachlan dares show his face. Those scratches ye marked him with will take time to heal." Hating the lingering weakness that necessitated it, he asked, "Could ye bring me another tankard of my wine?"

Efrica nodded and went to get him his drink. She silently cursed her keen sense of smell, for it made it impossible to ignore the fact that his wine was enriched with blood. His need for it was one of the reasons she fought her attraction to him so vigorously. She never ceased to be amazed that her sister Bridget, married to the laird of the MacNachtons, could be so happy in a place where the sun never cast its warmth or light and among a people who required such a gruesome sustenance. It was because Bridget loved her laird, of course. Efrica was determined not to fall into that trap, but her heart appeared reluctant to heed good sense.

Jankyn's hand shook slightly as he took hold of the tankard, and Efrica moved to help him. She put one arm around his broad shoulders and placed her other hand over his to steady it as he drank. Being so close to him had her heart pounding in her chest and her blood running hot. Telling herself it would be humiliating to suddenly pull away and flee the room, she silently prayed Jankyn could not sense her reaction and would finish his drink quickly.

The drink rapidly revived Jankyn, but that made him all too aware of the slender, warm female so close at hand. As he sipped the last of his drink, he slowly inhaled her scent, an intoxicating blend of clean skin, woman, and a hint of lavender. He had been attracted to Efrica from the first moment he had set eyes on her, and that attraction was rapidly breaking every bond he had placed on it.

Just one little kiss, he mused as he slipped his arm around her small waist. Just one little taste of what he had long wanted, but knew he could not have. And he would have to steal it, he thought, for she was already tensed to leave his side. He finished his drink, tossed the tankard aside, and tugged her down onto the bed beside him so swiftly, she had no time to flee.

"What are ye doing?" she demanded, sternly telling herself to pull free yet discovering she was unable to heed that sensible command.

"Should ye nay thank your gallant rescuer with something a wee bit warmer than words?" he asked.

"I think that may be verra unwise."

"Ye are probably right."

Instead of releasing her, however, he wrapped his other arm around her and kissed her. Efrica's resistance to the embrace lasted barely longer than a heartbeat. His lips were so enticingly soft and warm. Just one little kiss, she told herself. Just one little taste of what she had so often dreamt of. When he nudged at her lips with his tongue, she parted them, welcoming the deepening of the kiss. With but one stroke of his tongue, the heat of desire raged through her veins, burning away all common sense and resistance. A little voice in her head warned her that now she had been embraced by him, one kiss would never be enough, but she ignored it.

It was not until he had shifted their bodies around on the bed until she was sprawled beneath him that Efrica regained a sense of the danger she was in. For one brief moment, she savored the feel of his lean, highly aroused body pressed against her. It was so tempting to take what he offered, what she wanted so badly, she ached with the need. She knew, however, that if she became his lover, it would bind her to him in ways she might never break free of. That thought gave her the strength to shake loose of desire's tight grip, and scramble free of his embrace. As she stood by the side of the bed struggling to regain some sense of calm, she was happy to see that he was as flushed and breathless as she felt.

"I am nay one of your *ladies*," she said, pleased with the cool steadiness of her voice.

"I have no ladies," he said.

"Ha! I have heard all about ye since coming here. Weel, *I* have *no* intention of joining your stable."

He inwardly cursed, all too aware of what was said about him and the women of the court. It annoyed him that he felt a sudden need to explain, even excuse, his earlier excesses. He was unwed and unpromised, had simply taken what was offered, as would any man. The look of something akin to disappointment in her eyes stung him nevertheless.

"Gossip and rumor are nay fact." He did not blame her for rolling her eyes over that pathetic response.

When she realized she wanted him to tell her that what she had heard was all lies, that he had been as chaste as a monk, Efrica decided it was time to leave. "Ye should be careful about disdaining all I have heard," she drawled, "oh great *dark stallion.*" She had to grin at the way he blushed, then scowled at her.

"Now I am certain ye have heard naught but whispered lies. And just what are *ye* doing here?"

"My cousin Barbara brought me. I am nearing twenty. Past time I get a husband."

The thought of another man touching Efrica, claiming her as his own, stirred a rage in Jankyn he fought hard to hide. "Barbara doesnae appear to be a verra good chaperone."

"She is the best. She doesnae cling to one's side, but is there when needed."

"Such as in the garden?"

A telling point, but she just shrugged. "Twas still daylight. It should have been safe. I will be more wary now. And may I now ask what ye are doing here? Aside from rutting yourself blind, that is."

Jankyn ignored that last remark. "I seek a wife for David. He is more Outsider than MacNachton, and I thought I could arrange a profitable marriage for him."

"Ah, of course. Twould certainly serve the clan weel if ye succeed."

"Aye, if only because it would allow us to point to one of our own who isnae so, weel—"

"Odd?"

"As good a word as any." He looked her over, then quirked one brow. "Do ye plan to keep your secrets from a husband?"

Efrica wished she had an easy answer for that question,

one she continuously asked herself. "I believe my secrets are easier to keep."

"True. Save for that noise ye make when your blood runs hot," he murmured, feeling his tamped-down desire stir at the memory of that low, throaty purr she had made as they had embraced. "Wives shouldnae purr, I am thinking."

"And I am thinking I had best leave ere I give in to the urge to strangle ye," she snapped, embarrassed that he had obviously known exactly how much his kisses had stirred her.

"Alas, so easily does the purring kitten become the hissing cat."

Opening her mouth to retort, Efrica quickly shut it again, swallowing the insults crowding her tongue concerning blood-drinking men who swooned like frail maidens when touched by the sun. "Nay, ye willnae goad me into trading insults." She stared toward the door. "I have grown beyond such things," she announced loftily. "Maturity, ye ken. Ye should try it."

A solid blow, he mused and grinned. That grin widened when she slammed the door behind her as she left. Maturity obviously did not stop her from indulging in that show of pique.

He sighed and stared up at the ceiling. It was then that he realized that the candle had flickered out quite a while ago and the room was almost completely dark. Efrica had not even realized it. He idly wondered if he should tell her that most people could not see so well in the dark, that a husband would surely notice such a skill and find it odd.

The thought of Efrica with another man banished his amusement. What a woman did before or after him had never troubled him before. He had, of course, never thought of Efrica with a man. In his mind she had always been that innocently sensuous young lass, sister to his laird's wife, and forbidden fruit. It had never entered his mind that she would not be forbidden fruit to every man, nor that she would not wish to be. Worse, now that he had had a taste of that forbidden fruit, he craved more. He wanted to hear her purr again, and he wanted to be the only man who heard her make that intoxicating sound. Jankyn had the sinking feeling that stealing a taste of that forbidden fruit was the biggest mistake he had ever made.

Three

"Ye kissed him?!"

Efrica scowled at her cousin, a little surprised that Barbara's words were not echoing throughout the great hall and turning all eyes their way. "Mayhap we should just hire a herald to ride o'er the land announcing it. Twould save your voice."

Barbara ignored her muttered words, but lowered her voice. "What was it like?"

"Barbara!"

"Wheesht, dinnae go all pious on me. The mon is a near legend amongst the women here."

"Aye, I ken it. Tis one verra good reason why I should ne'er have allowed it."

"The other being that ye liked it too weel."

There was little reason to deny that. Not only had thinking about that kiss kept her awake late into the night, but she had woken up several times all asweat and aching for the man. Her maidenly dreams about Jankyn were no longer maidenly.

"Weel, he wouldnae be the best catch ye might make, but—"

"I dinnae want to catch him." The look her cousin gave her told Efrica that the older woman did not believe that any more that she herself did. "Come, Barbara, ye ken what he is, what the MacNachtons are."

"It suits your sister verra weel."

Efrica sighed and slumped against the cool stone wall, staring at the brightly clothed courtiers filling the great hall. "She loves her laird. I refuse to love Jankyn. I love the sun, flowers, and songbirds. To live with a mon who can ne'er leave the shadows, who dwells mostly in the dark bowels of Cambrun castle? Twould smother me, I think. And he will long outlive me, will probably still look a young mon as I wrinkle and gray." She caught sight of Jankyn entering the great hall only to be immediately approached by a fulsome redhead. "And he is a lecherous bastard," she hissed, feeling a strong urge to break the hand the woman was caressing his arm with.

"My dear child, he is an unwed mon. Unwed and unpromised. He is also beautiful, a sleek, dark mon who can stir any woman's blood by simply walking into a room. From what I have heard, the women here set after him the moment he arrived. Show me a bachelor who claims he refuses such freely offered sweets, and I will show ye a great liar."

That was a truth Efrica preferred not to think about. Men started to seek such experiences the moment their voices deepened. It was one of those hypocrisies that often so irritated her. Men grabbed as much bedsport as they could, but considered any woman who did the same a whore. They strove to cast aside their virginity as quickly as they could, but demanded their chosen wives still have theirs.

"Tell me, who does Jankyn claim David is?" she asked Barbara.

"His son. He says he was wed, briefly, at but thirteen."

"Ah, clever. Gives David legitimacy and keeps everyone believing Jankyn is but thirty and a bit. Just how old is he?"

"I have no idea, except that he is at least ten years older than his laird."

"Oh." Barbara grimaced. "I think that would trouble me as weel. Aging is hard enough, but to do so whilst your husband remains strong and untouched by time would be verra difficult. Of course, there could be some verra delightful advantages to that."

"Wretch. Who *is* that woman with him? She looks like the one who directed me to the gardens."

"Ah. Tis Lady Eleanor MacBean. She isnae to be trusted. Sly, vicious, and has no morals at all. Last year, she tried to seduce my husband. Worse, she battered me with sly words, whispered lies, and spread gossip until I began to believe it."

"Nay, Barbara, your husband would ne'er—"

Barbara silenced her with one sharp gesture. "I ken it. E'en as jealousy began to gnaw at my innards, a sane part of me kenned it was all lies. Fortunately, my mon was rather flattered by my jealousy and was quick to bring me back to my senses. I tell ye this to give ye a warning. Tread warily round that one." She frowned as she watched Jankyn shake free of the woman and move toward them. "Ye might warn that bonnie lad, too. Both of ye have far too many secrets to protect. Ye dinnae need the trouble that vixen could bring ye. Aye, and we both ken her part in that attack upon ye may nay have been so innocent."

Efrica smothered the urge to flee before Jankyn reached them. Burying the feelings that kiss had caused would be difficult if he thought to pursue her, but she refused to run and hide. There was also the chance that such cowardice would tell Jankyn far too much about how she felt. A woman immune to his allure did not flee from him. It was difficult to remain calm, however, when Barbara slipped away soon after greetings were exchanged.

"I am pleased that ye havenae allowed what those two fools tried to do to ye to make ye hide yourself away," Jankyn said as he leaned against the wall by her side.

It did not please Jankyn that he had felt so compelled to see her. Nor did it please him that he had felt no inclination to answer Lady Eleanor's less-than-subtle invitation to indulge in a night of lechery. His body ached for a woman, but he had the feeling it now hungered for just one. He needed to cure himself of that affliction, but he was not sure how to do so. Just standing near Efrica had him taut with need.

"I refuse to let them think themselves of any importance to me," replied Efrica.

"But ye *will* avoid them, aye?"

"Like the plague."

Jankyn nodded, thought about what he should or should not say, then decided that being direct was best. "I think we need to talk about what happened last eve."

"Ye rescued me and then I rescued you." She tried not to blush beneath his stare but suspected she was not completely successful.

"Ye ken what I refer to, lass. We need to discuss what stirred between us when we embraced."

"Twas but a kiss, Jankyn. I have been kissed before."

For a brief moment, Jankyn almost believed she had felt little, had not experienced the depth of hunger he had, but then he noticed how she avoided his gaze. "And did ye let any of those men get ye beneath them? Did ye purr for them, Efrica?" He nodded with satisfaction when she glared at him. "We both felt it. We both felt the heat, the need."

Efrica refused to be flattered by his admission that the kiss had stirred him as well. "Lust. Tis no great thing. I am nay a child now so 'tis no surprise a skilled mon might stir a lusting within me. And from what I have heard, stirring a lusting in ye just requires a woman to give ye a smile."

"Curse it, Efrica, cease condemning me for taking what was freely offered, as any mon would do. I am without bonds and owe no one any explanation or apology." He sighed and rubbed the back of his neck, wondering how she could make him feel so guilty, even ashamed. "Aye, when I first arrived here, the interest I drew was a heady thing. I have ne'er left Cambrun save to go to some kinsmon's lands. It was a pleasure which waned verra quickly for I soon realized it wasnae truly a simple giving and taking of pleasure."

Although she truly hated hearing him speak of the other women he had been with, curiosity prompted her to ask, "What else could it have been?"

"The scent of new prey? The scent of mysteries and secrets? I was the dark, dangerous lover, the mon of shadows. A bold dare accepted. A challenge. Who could uncover my secrets? I was but another pelt to collect."

"Ah, I see. The women treated ye as men so often treat women."

That was an uncomfortable truth he had faced himself just recently, but refused to admit it. "I thought I had slipped into this life with ease, had become one of them, but realized that wasnae so."

"Is that one of the reasons ye came here? To see if ye could become one of them?"

Jankyn shrugged. "The thought had crossed my mind. Ye ken Cathal's plans to bring the MacNachtons out of the shadows," he began.

"Aye, he plans to breed the MacNachtons out of their caves." She forced herself not to blush with guilt beneath the condemning glance he gave her.

"Ye ken as weel as I that Cathal and Bridget are true mates, bound by vows and their hearts." He briefly smiled.

"And your sister, having just gifted our laird with a second pair of bairns, is doing more than her share of the work. Willingly and joyously."

Thinking of her new niece and nephew, Efrica had to smile as well. Bridget would have her hands full with those two, as she did with her twin sons now two. Then Efrica thought of her other niece and nephew, children bred when her brothers had dallied with some MacNachton women during one of their visits, women they had not married, and she frowned at Jankyn.

"Have ye come here to breed?" she asked.

"Of course not," he snapped, then sighed. "Since I first became a mon, I have hardly been a monk, have I?—yet the only child I e'er bred was David and I asked that lass to marry me. She decided to stay with her own kind. So, nay, the thought of breeding didnae bring me here. Since the outside world is creeping e'er nearer to our sanctuary, I thought it might be wise to let them ken a MacNachton or two, to set the image of a mon in their minds instead of naught but dark rumor. Tisnae working out quite like I planned, although I have made a few good friends amongst the lairds. Unfortunately, the explanations for why I am ne'er about in the day make that a difficult task."

"What explanations do ye give?"

He grimaced. "That I cannae abide the sun or verra strong light because it hurts my eyes and my skin is quick to burn." Jankyn scowled at her when she giggled. "It makes me sound a most delicate flower, I ken it. I had to make sure a few saw me practicing some of the more monly arts with David to soften the shame of it." He suddenly turned, resting his shoulder against the wall so that he could watch her more closely as he spoke. "And we have veered widely from the matter I thought we should discuss."

Efrica crossed her arms over her chest. "What needs to be said? Twas just a kiss."

"Lass, trust me to ken about such things. Twas nay *just a kiss*. Ye ken it as weel as I do. The heat, the need, came upon us fast and hard. We need to be honest about it or we cannae fight it."

"I am nay some wanton lass who—" The touch of his finger upon her lips silenced her as warmth flooded her.

"Aye, 'tis there," he said softly, forcing himself to remove his finger from her far-too-tempting mouth. "I dinnae imply that ye are wanton, lass. This isnae about morals. Tis about passion, the passion that stirs within us for each other. Unless we accept that truth, we could easily fall into its trap."

"Then dinnae kiss me again."

"I willnae. We are going to keep a verra respectful distance between us as of now."

It was exactly what she wanted. Efrica wondered why she felt irritated and hurt that *he* would suggest it. That was dangerously contrary of her. She was obviously going to have to give herself some very stern lectures once she was alone.

"That would probably be best," she forced herself to say, pleased by how calm she sounded.

"I will make that easier by getting back to work on one of the reasons I came to this cursed place."

"And that was?"

"To find out more about my own heritage." He stood up straight and gave in to the temptation to kiss her cheek. "Burying myself in dusty scrolls and ledgers should cool my blood."

Efrica watched him walk away and sighed. He was such a beautiful man, one who moved with a grace that drew and held the eye. If he had not been a MacNachton, she knew she would have been making a fool of herself trying to draw his interest her way. She had a strong inclination to do so now. The light touch of a hand upon her arm startled her, and she turned to face a concerned Barbara.

"Ye look verra troubled and sad, lass." Barbara watched Jankyn stride out of the great hall. "Mayhap ye should—"

"Nay." Efrica glanced around to be sure they could speak without being heard. "He is a MacNachton. I have naught against them. I ken they arenae creatures from a nightmare, soulless undead demons who see the rest of us as naught but food. Howbeit, *what* he is makes him unsuitable. Barbara, he cannae e'er join me in a walk through a garden to watch the morning sun dry the dew upon the flowers. He is already nearly thirty years my senior and e'en he cannae say how much longer he will live, but 'tis surely a verra, verra long time. We willnae grow old together. He is the only one born amongst the Purebloods for more than two score years. Tis clear the seed of a Pureblood is weak. Aye, despite his lecherous ways, Jankyn has bred but one child and that upon an Outsider, a MacMartin. A mon now and one who must still be cautious about how long he stays out in the sun in the full light of day. I want children, Barbara."

"Your sister—"

"Her husband isnae a Pureblood." She shook her head. "I weel understand the curse of ancient bloodlines that mark one as, weel, different. The Callans have dealt with it for generations, aye? Jankyn can toss grown men about as if they weighed nay more than a cushion. Those teeth he is careful to hide would make a wolf envious. He can rip a mon's throat out and drink deep of the blood that flows from that mortal wound. Aye, the MacNachtons have strict rules about such things now, saving such savagery for thieves, murderers, and enemies. He would have done it to the men who attacked me if I hadnae stopped him. The urge was there. To recover from being in the sun even that short while he needed to drink wine enriched with blood." She nodded when Barbara frowned. "Aye—*too different.*"

"It does make our ancestress seem nay so bad," murmured Barbara.

"Aye. Better a cat than a wolf. And the Callans have worked hard to breed it out until there is naught but a shadow of her left. The MacNachtons have only begun to do the same. Twill be a long time ere many of them can walk freely amongst us."

"I understand all ye say, but I think your heart doesnae completely agree with your head."

"Nay, it doesnae, but I will make it do so."

"E'en if he returns your feelings?"

"Aye, tempting as that may be. I might be able to accept all the other things, but when I waver, there is one thought, one hard cold fact, that always stiffens my spine."

"And that is?"

"I may be able to condemn myself to living in the shadows, but I willnae condemn my children to doing the same."

Four

She did not care that she had not seen Jankyn for a week, Efrica told herself firmly as she left the garden and entered the castle. The fact that she had spent a large part of her time in the garden looking up at the window to his chambers was just a matter of curiosity. It was a huge lie, but she clung to it. It was best to remind herself that the time she had just spent in the sun, enjoying its warmth and savoring the scent of roses, was exactly why Jankyn was not the man for her. He could not have even looked out upon the garden if the sun was shining in the window.

"Greetings, Efrica."

Startled, she looked around and saw David sitting on the floor, his back against the stone wall. That was odd enough, but looking more closely, she realized he looked pale. As she stepped closer, she also noticed that he trembled slightly. Quickly kneeling by his side, she lightly touched his face, wondering if he was fevered.

"Are ye ill?" she asked.

"Nay, only weakened." He smiled faintly. "I took Mistress Fiona for a stroll in the gardens and lingered longer than was wise. Twill pass. I can abide the sun, ye ken, but must be wary when 'tis at its strongest, and I forgot that for a wee while."

Efrica sat down beside him. She wondered how long he had sat here, for she had not seen him or Fiona in the gardens. He had the look of his father despite his dark red hair. The purity of his features, his lean, graceful body, and his dark golden eyes marked him as a MacNachton. Obviously there were other less welcome similarities as well.

"Do ye need anything? I could help ye to your chambers."

"Nay. Och, aye, a wee bit of Father's wine might speed my recovery, but I try to resist that cure. I wish to marry, ye ken, and that sort of thing can alarm a wife."

"Aye, but do ye mean to ne'er tell your wife about the MacNachtons? Ne'er return to Cambrun?"

He shook his head. "Nay, I willnae live a lie nor scorn my kinsmen." He sat up a little straighter. "I want to wed Mistress Fiona, and it appears her family welcomes my wooing of her. I have begun to carefully prepare the way for the truth, though it may need to be hidden from her kinsmen, at least for a while. Howbeit, I cannae hide all that I am from my wife, can I?"

"Nay, ye cannae. Especially if ye feel the need to, weel, mark her as your mate."

David nodded. "I feel it. That will be the hardest thing to explain. I fear I could lose her because of it, but I *will* have to tell her ere we wed. I but hope to make her love me enough to accept it all."

Thinking of how the dainty, brown-haired Fiona looked at David, Efrica smiled. "I think she does care for you."

"I think so, too, but it needs to be deep and strong. Father warned me that some women cannae accept it all. Aye, my mother couldnae. Tis why she wouldnae marry him. That and the fact that she foresaw how he would look as she aged, that he would soon look more like her son than her husband."

Efrica knew that feeling. "That could also cause ye some trouble, I suppose."

"I dinnae think I am of that ilk. I have aged as I should thus far. I dinnae heal as easily or as fast, either. Most of us who are bred of both worlds do live long lives, but nay so long as to raise much more than admiration in others." He started to stand up, smiling when Efrica moved to help him. "My strength is returning. Since meeting Fiona, I have occasionally cursed my heritage, but there are some verra good things about it, too."

When he took a step, he was a little unsteady, and Efrica quickly linked her arm through his. "Do ye want to go to your father now?"

"Wheesht, nay. I just need a bed to lie on, and mine suits as weel as his. He isnae in his chambers now, anyway, but in the ledger room, or whate'er it is called. He has been hard at work in his search this last sennight."

Efrica ignored the curiosity in the look he gave her as she walked with him. "He said something about researching his heritage, but exactly what does he search for? I thought the MacNachtons had already gathered all that was kenned about their heritage yet he apparently has some questions about his own."

"He does. We dinnae ken it all. Tis difficult for a MacNachton to travel in search of information, aye? Dangerous, as weel. Not long afore our laird wed Lady Bridget, one of ours was caught whilst aroaming and brutally executed. The priest of a village declared him a demon, ye ken."

"Ah, of course." It was yet another reason to tame her infatuation with Jankyn. If they wed, when she traveled to see her kinsmen, she would undoubtedly do it alone or risk losing her man to a hastily built pyre in some village.

"Father has discovered a few missing pieces in his lines, a few mysteries. He looks for answers. He begins to wonder if he is truly as pure-blooded as he was told. One thing that stirred his curiosity was how I am—more Outsider than Pureblood. Tis true that a mating of the two produces varied offspring, but I am more akin to my mother than my father in too many ways. That is unusual."

Efrica was unable to stop herself from being intrigued. Was Jankyn not a full MacNachton? Could he be more akin to his laird than to the ones who spent most of their long, long lives in the caves beneath Cambrun? It did not matter, she told herself firmly. He was more one of the cave dwellers than his laird was. More feral, more a creature of the night. There may be more Outsider blood in him than he thought, but it had obviously been well cowed by that of the pure-blooded MacNachtons. David may be more like his mother, but he still suffered some beneath the sun and still had a taste for blood, even a need.

Once she had left David at his chamber, Efrica sought her own. She was a little surprised to find Barbara there. Although they shared the chamber, Barbara was more often out than in.

"Looking for me?" Efrica asked as she moved toward the basin of water to wash her hands.

Barbara turned a little in the chair she sat in, warming her feet by the fire. "Nay, although I did wonder where ye had gone. I but grew weary of listening to the gossip of women, useful though it can be."

"I think ye begin to miss your husband." Efrica poured herself a tankard of cider and sat in the chair facing Barbara. "We *can* leave, ye ken."

"Nay. I *do* miss him and my bairns, but we shall linger here for a while longer. The finding of a husband for ye isnae something one can do quickly. Ye have stirred interest. Best to give it more time."

Efrica grimaced and drank some of her cider. "I could weel do without some of that interest." She brushed a clinging rose petal from the skirts of her elaborately embroidered blue gown. "Those two swine who attacked me are out of hiding again."

"Have they troubled ye?"

"Nay, save that they make my skin crawl. They humbly begged my pardon, blaming drink for their crimes against me, and I gave it. A quick exchange of lies and polite smiles. E'en Lady Eleanor has begged my pardon, proclaiming herself appalled that her innocent, friendly suggestion caused me such trouble."

"How did she ken it caused ye trouble?"

"A good question. I ne'er told anyone save ye and ye would ne'er tell. Nor would Jankyn." Efrica stared into the fire. "I believe she aided those two, was fully aware of their intentions."

"Best to avoid all three."

"I try. Lachlan and Thomas I can avoid without raising questions. Tis a little more difficult to avoid Lady Eleanor if she doesnae wish to be avoided. Whore she may be, but she is a verra highborn, rich whore who has many a powerful friend. Most of them men, of course. She willnae trick me again, howe'er." Thinking of how the woman had questioned her about Jankyn and the MacNachtons, Efrica frowned. "Her interest in Jankyn is verra keen."

"I believe they were lovers for a brief while, but nay since we arrived. Indeed, nay since a long time before."

That was something Efrica wished her cousin had not told her, although she had suspected it. "She obviously doesnae consider the affair over. Judging by some of her questions, she is also wondering if I am to blame for Jankyn's sudden loss of interest. Then again, from what ye say, 'tisnae sudden." She shrugged. "It doesnae matter. She need but look about and she will see that I have naught to do with it."

"I dinnae like the sound of that. Be verra careful around the woman, Effie. Verra, verra careful."

"Oh, I intend to be. She chills my blood. I had the passing thought as to how she would react if she saw Jankyn at his most feral, and got the feeling that would stir her lusts."

"Because of his strength?"

"Oh, that is astonishing and it can be, weel, exciting to see him so. What woman wouldnae be stirred to see a mon so valiantly and impressively deal with her enemies? But nay, I was thinking she wouldnae have stopped him from killing those two pigs, even though it could have put Jankyn in serious danger. Nay, I think she would have encouraged it, reveled in it, had her lusts roused by the bloodiness of it."

"Oh dear."

"Exactly. I think that, within Lady Eleanor, is a beast more feral, more bloodthirsty, than any MacNachton e'er was. They at least can be excused because of their nature, their need, their breeding. One they have worked hard to control. Lady Eleanor has no such inclination. As we cannae completely shed the nature of the cat bred into us from that ancient Celtic priestess, thus the MacNachtons cannae completely shed that nature of the predator, the wolf, from their bloodlines. Ah, but Lady Eleanor holds a true darkness of the soul, I think."

Barbara slowly nodded. "It would explain a lot. And ye are right. As with us, what is within the MacNachtons is the spirit of the beast. It has naught to do with morals or inclinations. It is what it is. But if what ye sense in Lady Eleanor is truly there, that *is* a sickness of the soul, a dark, hellish thing, and nay natural."

"I could be wrong," Efrica felt compelled to say.

"Ye rarely are and I saw it, too. I just couldnae name it as ye have. So, where *have* ye been?"

"The gardens." She told Barbara about her meeting with David.

"Ah, so the threat of the sun doesnae completey fade in all the children of mixed blood. A shame. Howbeit, David's bairns may nay suffer that weakness. And Fiona would be a good choice of bride. I think that beneath that sweet, shy exterior lies a strong heart, too. If the lad wins it, I think all will be weel."

"I hope ye are right. I think he has already lost his heart. He said he feels the urge to mark her as his mate."

Barbara smiled faintly. "Fair caught then. I must say, I was appalled when Bridget told me of it, but she said it was naught. A wee sip, she said, and only the once. Somehow I think Fiona willnae balk. Now, about this search Jankyn is on. Ye must direct him to our cousin Malcolm."

Efrica's eyes widened with surprise. She had completely forgotten about Malcolm. He was an odd little man with a voracious appetite for gossip, rumor, tales of the past, and any written record of any clan he could get his ink-stained hands on. If any clan had a secret, Malcolm probably knew it and had recorded it. He also lived close at hand. She realized she was eager to tell Jankyn and frowned. Honesty compelled her to admit to herself that one reason she was eager was because it would allow her to see him again.

"Mayhap ye should tell him, Barbara."

"I fear I cannae," Barbara said as she stood up and brushed down her skirts. "I am to meet with the ladies Beatrice and Margaret in but a few minutes. Come, Effie, ye cannae hide from the mon forever. If naught else, he abides in the same keep as your sister. There is a great difference between telling him something useful, mayhap escorting him somewhere once, and *keeping company,* so to speak. And mayhap 'tis best to see if ye can keep something this simple from becoming complicated. If ye cannae e'en take the mon a message, mayhap ye ought to think hard on why he afrights ye so."

Before Efrica could respond to that, Barbara was gone. While all Barbara said was true, Efrica had the feeling there was far more to the woman's insistence that she be the one to tell Jankyn about Malcolm. Efrica hoped her cousin was not matchmaking, had not decided that her infatuation with Jankyn ought to be fed instead of starved.

Once out of her chambers, Efrica had to find someone to tell her where the records were kept. It did not surprise her to find herself heading down into the bowels of the keep. It certainly seemed most fitting to meet Jankyn there. As she walked along a torch-lit passage, she sternly reminded herself of all the reasons she could not give in to her attraction to Jankyn. She must greet him as a kinsman, with no more than a gentle amiability. She would be strong, stalwart in her defense of her own heart. She was a woman now, not some heedless girl who had no control over her emotions.

Efrica stepped into the room where the records were stored, saw Jankyn studying some large book, and nearly cursed out loud. Her heart clenched at the sight of him. Her pulse grew a little faster. For some odd reason she felt inclined to sigh as she studied his lean form. Her mouth suddenly warmed with the memory of his kiss. For a brief moment, she wanted to flee, then her cowardice shamed her. Efrica straightened her back and moved toward him. She refused to run.

Five

He knew she was there before she spoke. There had been no sound, no hint of her approach, but Jankyn was not surprised. As her sister did, Efrica walked silently. Even his keen ears had difficulty hearing her move. He knew she was there because of her scent, one as recognizable to him as his son's. Jankyn took a deep breath, filling himself with the pleasurable scent of her, letting it warm him. Slowly, he turned to look at her, finding that the sight of her warmed him even more. Staying away from her had obviously done nothing to cure his wanting, but then the heated dreams he had been tormented with over the last seven days had warned him of that.

"What has brought ye here, lass?" he asked, then tensed. "Trouble?"

"Nay, no more than one usually finds in such a place, I suspect," replied Efrica. "Nay, I met David today and he happened to mention what ye were searching for." She stepped around the table to stand at his side and look at the book he had been studying. "Find anything yet?"

"A few glimpses, hints of something which may be important, but little else. The ones who compiled these records were more concerned with what a mon had in way of lands, wealth, and fighting men than in who he was or his blood-lines."

"Weel, I may have a better place for ye to look. My cousin Malcolm."

"How could he help?"

"He collects information."

"I ken the Callans are as interested in their ancestry as we are, but—"

"Nay just the Callans. Malcolm collects whate'er he can on everyone he can." She nodded when his eyes widened slightly. "He ignores naught, from the smallest whisper to church records. He continues the work of his father, grand-sire, and great-grandsire, all of whom were greedy con-cerning such information. If Malcolm was a woman, he would be reviled as the worst of gossips. As a mon, howe'er, he can excuse it all as a need to take careful note of the peo-ple of this land so that the ones who come after us can find the truth if need be. He tells any who claim the memory of elders is good enough that it takes but one plague or one battle to see all that knowledge buried and lost forever."

Jankyn felt the beat of anticipation in his veins. "He has a lot?"

Efrica laughed softly. "More than ye can e'er imagine, and his three sons travel far and wide to get more. He will ask a fee. Tis one way he can afford to continue his work."

"That is acceptable. Where does he live?"

"I fear ye will have to let me take ye to him. Malcolm may like to ken all about everyone, but he isnae so fond of meeting any of them. If we leave as soon as the sun sets, I can take ye to him this verra night."

"Shall we meet at the stables after the sun has set then?"

She nodded and hurried away to find Barbara and let her know what she was going to do. There was the thrum of excitement in her veins, and she knew it was because she was helping Jankyn in his search. She ruefully admitted to herself that it was also because she would be spending time with him, could enjoy the sight of him and savor the sound of his deep, smooth voice. Maybe Barbara was right. Maybe it was time to ask herself some hard questions.

Jankyn stood by the two horses he had chosen and waited for Efrica. Glancing up at the bright, full moon, he felt an ancient urge stir to life within him. His kindred would be out on the hunt tonight. It had been a long time since he had participated in one, and he found himself wishing he were back at Cambrun, racing through the hills and woods alongside his brethren.

Coming to court had, perhaps, not been wise. David may well have found himself a wife, but being among these people made Jankyn all too aware of what he was, and what he could never be. He did not think he had ever felt so alone. Not one of the women he had bedded had eased that feeling. The fact that, even in the throes of passion, he had to closely and continuously guard his secrets had only added to that sense of utter solitude. He suspected it was one reason he was so strongly attracted to Efrica. She knew what he was. He could be free with her.

His dissatisfaction had begun to grow a long time ago, however. Watching Cathal and Bridget, seeing their family grow, had bred it. This journey had honed it to a sharpness he could not easily shrug aside. He did not want to spend his long life alone, taking a lover now and then among his own kind, and doing little more than existing until, one day, he ceased. A piece of him would continue on in whatever children David bred, but in all other ways, he would leave no mark upon the world. It was a sobering, even chilling, thought.

Seeing Efrica hurrying toward him, Jankyn silently cursed. She made it even harder to shake free of the somewhat maudlin humor he was sinking into. He ached for her, hungered to smell the sun upon her fair skin and in her glorious hair. Jankyn had the feeling she was his mate, but he could never claim her. The blood of his ancestors was strong within him, which made him a creature of the night. Efrica was a creature of the light, more so than her sister. The shadows he had to cling to in order to survive would slowly smother her.

As he helped her mount, he let his hands linger upon her small waist a little longer than was necessary. Jankyn ignored the frown she gave him, mounted his horse, and silently signaled her to lead him to her cousin's. He knew he should not take full advantage of the attraction between them, but decided the occasional, small, stolen delight could do no harm. Except to make his dreams even more of a torment, he thought ruefully.

The house Efrica led them to was on the far southern side of the town. Set behind a thick, high wall, the main part of the house looked like many another. Here and there, however, someone had stuck a room on the side. The gates that led into the courtyard in front of the house stood open, only a scowling, white-haired man silently watching them.

"Efrica? Be that ye?" demanded the man as Jankyn helped her dismount. "I was about to lock the gates."

Efrica gave the man a hug and a kiss. "I ken it. Tis why we hurried. I apologize for coming at such a late hour, but 'tis impossible to come during the day." She hastily introduced Jankyn to her cousin, not surprised to see Malcolm's sharp green eyes narrow in thought. The man was already searching his keen memory for some information on the Clan MacNachton.

"Come in. Come in and tell me what ye seek."

Following Efrica and her somewhat ill-natured cousin, Jankyn listened to her explain why they were there. Malcolm kept looking at him, curiosity warring with fear in his eyes.

Somehow this man knew about the MacNachtons, at least enough to make him feel uneasy. As they walked through the house, Jankyn could see that almost every conceivable place had been turned into storage for books, ledgers, and scrolls. The man kept the main living areas relatively clean, simply lining the walls with shelves where he could, but most of his home was dedicated to his work. Somewhere in this warren was a tale or two about the MacNachtons, and this man was even now recalling them.

The next time the man looked his way, Jankyn gave him a wide smile. Malcolm's eyes grew very wide, and he paled slightly before turning his attention back to Efrica. She obviously noticed her cousin's upset, and frowned at Jankyn, suspicion glinting in her eyes. Jankyn gave her a sweet smile and was not surprised when her look of suspicion only deepened. Then Malcolm drew her attention as he led them into what had clearly once been the great hall. Jankyn stood and looked around in awe at all the shelves and tables so filled with things that people employed to record information they felt was important that the wood should have been groaning and buckling beneath the weight of it all.

"Ye will find the MacNachtons on the shelf by the window," Malcolm said. "Far end. On the left. I will get ye some wine and food, aye?"

Before Efrica could reply, Malcolm hurried out of the room. She turned to cast another suspicious look at Jankyn, but he was already striding toward the shelves Malcolm had indicated. Efrica was sure Jankyn had done something to make Malcolm so nervous, but since they had not been immediately turned out, she decided to ignore it and hurried to his side. A little voice told her that she ought to leave him here, that spending time alone with him was not wise, but she silenced it. If nothing else, she was intensely curious about what information Malcolm may have gathered on the MacNachtons. She silently helped Jankyn look for anything with the name *MacNachton* and place it on one of the several large tables scattered around the room.

"Ah, good, good," Malcolm muttered as he returned and set a large tray of wine, bread, cheese, and oatcakes on the table. "Ye may see a wee notation or two in places. Twill direct ye to another wee bit of information. Many clans are connected, ye ken, and the tales of one clan will oftimes slip into the tales of another."

Efrica frowned and stared at her cousin's neck. A glint of something shiny showed beneath the tousled locks of white hair and the neck of the ink-stained shirt. She reached out to touch his neck and gasped when she tapped her fingernail against metal.

"Malcolm, what do ye have upon your neck?" she demanded.

"Naught!" He covered his neck with his hands.

"Dinnae lie to me. Oh, Malcolm, ye have put some sort of neck ring on. How could ye insult a guest so?"

"Effie, he is a MacNachton." Malcolm whispered.

"Aye, and his laird is wed to my sister Bridget. Do ye see me wrapping metal about my neck? I think ye have heeded too many rumors, forgotten how to separate gossip and whispers from fact. I also think ye owe Jankyn an apology."

"Sorry," Malcolm muttered even as he started toward the door. "Many pardons. Let yourselves out when ye are done."

Keeping her gaze fixed upon the door Malcolm had shut behind him as he fled, Efrica said, "Ye showed him your fangs, didnae ye, Jankyn."

"They may have peeked out when I gave him a friendly smile," Jankyn replied.

She shook her head and moved to pour them each some wine. "That mon spends far too much of his life lurking about within this house reading about the past." She frowned when Jankyn studied what looked to be a brief letter, a faint smile curling his lips. "What have ye found?"

"The answer to the puzzle of how your brother kenned so much about us. He would only say that he had a knowledgeable friend. I believe I have found that *friend.*" Jankyn handed her the letter.

" '*Bridget has wed Cathal MacNachton, laird of Cambrun,*' " she read. " '*Who is he? Need to know immediately. Duncan.*' Rather abrupt. Howbeit, I suspicion my brother softened his lordly demands with a heavy purse. I wonder why he ne'er told ye about Malcolm."

"He had only just met us and kenned how closely we guarded our secrets. We ne'er thought to ask again, after he had come to ken us better." Jankyn sipped at the wine she had served him. "Still, I am nay sure I like the fact that someone outside Cambrun kens so much about us."

"Malcolm is verra careful about sharing this information. He kens all about the Callans, too, ye ken. Being one of us, he weel understands the value of secrecy. I will, however, tell him to put *your* secrets away with ours."

Jankyn glanced around the room. "The Callans arenae to be found in here?"

"There will be a listing, a few tales and innocent letters, but nay more. Malcolm carefully takes out all hints of our true ancestry. The full tale is more precisely recorded and tucked away in a verra safe place. Since your clan is now tied to ours, 'tis far past time he did the same, er, cleansing of the MacNachton information."

"Aye, that might be best. Tis troubling to think of our secrets written down here where, nay matter how careful Malcolm is, someone could see them. Rumors and dark, whispered tales of the past are difficult enough to fight. Set down in a book?" He shrugged. "Too many would see that as irrefutable proof."

Efrica nodded. "The verra fact that someone would take the time to write it all down gives it weight. So few have the skill that it gives it a great deal of power. Magic, e'en," she added as she returned to the shelves.

When Jankyn watched her bend over slightly to sort through several scrolls, his mind was immediately filled with several lecherous thoughts and he inwardly cursed. It was tempting to tell her to leave, that he did not need help, but he could not bring himself to do so. She was offering him help, had brought him to a treasure trove of information, and he would not insult her by curtly sending her away. He was a man with many years of experience, he reminded himself as he forced his attention to the book in front of him. He ought to be able to curtail his lust for a woman, for *any* woman.

That control grew harder to grasp than he liked as the hours passed. Far too often he would catch himself looking at her, thinking of all the ways he wanted to make love to her. She was proving to be an incurable fever in his blood. The fact that she was a pleasant and efficient assistant only made it worse. A simple lusting could be conquered in time, no matter how fierce it was. Lust mixed with respect and liking was very hard to shake free of. It was settling deep into his heart, and that could cause them both a lot of trouble.

It was Efrica who called attention to the swift advance of dawn hours later. Jankyn pulled himself free of his fascination with his research and looked longingly at several large books he had unearthed from Malcolm's vast collection. He looked at Efrica and caught her setting a letter on the tray Malcolm had brought the food and wine in on.

"Tis but a message for Malcolm telling him that we have taken a few things back to the castle with us," she explained.

"Will he allow that?" asked Jankyn.

"Nay if we ask him directly, I suspect. Thus the message and a quick escape."

"And this." Jankyn set a small purse upon the tray, the weight of it and the sound it made hinting at a sizable sum of money.

"That will certainly soothe him," she murmured as she followed Jankyn out of the house.

After carefully placing the books into his saddle packs, Jankyn noticed that Efrica had felt no need to wait for his help in mounting her horse, and so he mounted his. "Is anything wrong?" he asked when he caught her frowning.

"Actually," she replied, nudging her horse into motion, "I was but wondering where Malcolm got that thing he wore about his neck. Tisnae something one has just lying about the house."

Jankyn laughed softly as he rode beside her. "I suspect he had it made when word came that a Callan had married a MacNachton. Dinnae scowl. I took no insult."

Efrica was not so sure she believed that, but did not argue it. Malcolm's reaction to Jankyn only reaffirmed her opinion that she was a fool to be so attracted to a MacNachton, to even consider a future with the man. If even members of the Callan clan could not be at ease around Jankyn, how could she ever hope to have a normal life with the man?

Six

"It wouldnae hurt ye to spend a wee bit more time at court."

Jankyn looked up from the writings he had been carefully reading to frown at Malcolm. For the past four nights he had spent long hours searching through Malcolm's research, meticulously recording each and every mention of MacNachtons, including a few old, dark tales very similar to the ones whispered in the villages near Cambrun. It appeared that, back in the far, misty past, MacNachtons had found a way to travel farther afield than they did now. Malcolm had grown more at ease in his presence, although he still wore that odd piece of armor around his neck. Obviously Malcolm had read one too many of the tales of dark, wolf-eyed men riding through the night and leaving death behind them.

"Why?" he asked. "I cannae find the answers I seek there."

"I would have thought a mon of your ilk would have learned to keep his ear to the ground."

"What do ye mean?"

"Whispers and rumors, laddie. Whispers and rumors."

"Such things have always swirled about the Mac-Nachtons."

"Aye, and nay heeding them has sent more than a few of your clan to their deaths. Hard, gruesome deaths and unblessed graves."

Jankyn tensed. "What have ye heard?"

"What do ye think, eh? That ye ne'er show your bonnie face when the sun is up, that ye have an unnatural strength, that ye—"

"Enough. I ken it all, but I wonder how ye hear such things when it doesnae appear that ye e'er leave this house."

Malcolm sat on a bench across the table from Jankyn and crossed his arms. "Everyone who comes to me for information about their clan, or the bloodlines of someone who wishes to marry into their clan, gives me the promise that they will inform me of *any* news they can, rumor or fact. Tis rare that a day passes which doesnae bring me a missive, some messenger, or e'en some copied book, scroll, or ledger. There are several people at court right now who visit me from time to time to tell me all the news. Aye, things such as how two cruel bastards stalk my wee cousin Efrica and how there is a woman who is determined to have ye crawl back into her bed. Indeed, a woman who grows angrier each time ye shun her welcome."

Between trying to keep a safe distance between himself and Efrica and becoming engrossed in his research, Jankyn had not realized that Lachlan and Thomas had renewed their pursuit of Efrica. Given what those two men were capable of, Efrica could still be in very real danger. Her cousin Barbara was a good woman, but little protection. Lachlan and Thomas just needed to catch Efrica alone once, and Jankyn did not feel very confident that the opportunity would never present itself. Just thinking of what they had already tried to do to her made him furious.

Then Jankyn saw Malcolm's eyes widen and realized his

fury was revealing itself in his face. He struggled to control his anger and watched Malcolm visibly shore up his courage. Jankyn suspected it was only the man's concern and affection for Efrica that kept him from fleeing the room.

"I dinnae think ye ought to go racing back and toss the bastards round the garden again," Malcolm said.

"Did Efrica tell ye about that?"

"Nay. Ye were seen that day. An old friend of mine saw her peril and rushed from his bedchamber to go to her aid. He arrived in the garden just as ye rescued her. As he told me, ye threw the men aside as if they weighed naught."

This was alarming news. "He is the one spreading the rumors?"

"Nay. I convinced him that, e'en though ye are a slender mon, ye are a strong one. Can win any caber toss, and all that. Also said the MacNachtons can oftimes be spurred into a fierce rage when one of their own is threatened. Explained about the laird of the MacNachtons being wed to Bridget and all that. He still puzzled o'er how ye could pick each mon up, one in each hand, and mentioned how he had caught a fleeting glimpse of a verra alarming look upon your face." Malcolm nodded when Jankyn cursed. "I finally managed to get him to believe that blind rage had given ye such power, and weel, wasnae it shown by your near swoon afterward that ye had used up all your strength and may have e'en injured yourself a wee bit."

"Ye feel certain he willnae be telling that tale to anyone else?"

"Aye, e'en if he thinks on it all again and begins to doubt all my clever explanations. I made it verra clear that I wouldnae be pleased to hear such tales spread about the clan my most beloved cousin is now a part of. I didnae threaten to retaliate by revealing a few embarrassing truths about his family, but he understood the implication. The important question is, is he the only one who saw ye that day? He believes 'tis only those two men and the lady who whisper about ye, but one hopes there is no one else who saw ye and thus can affirm those spreading rumors."

After cursing again over that dire possibility, Jankyn hastily finished the work he had been in the midst of when Malcolm had arrived. The moment he was done, he collected up his completed work and started out of the room, Malcolm at his heels, obviously intending to tightly lock the gates after Jankyn had left. Jankyn knew he was close to unlocking a few secrets about his bloodlines, but the security of the MacNachton secrets and Efrica's safety were far more important. He could always pay Malcolm handsomely to continue the work for him, knowing the man would protect the MacNachton secrets as well as he protected those of his own clan. After all, people descended from some pagan priestess rumored to be a shape-shifter could be marked as demons and the devil's minions as easily as any MacNachton.

Once back at the castle, Jankyn hurried to his chambers to secure his work and wash the ink from his hands. He then went in search of Efrica, needing to see with his own eyes that she was safe and was well aware of the danger stalking her little heels. An odd noise echoed through the hallway, and Jankyn halted, hoping the noise would come again so that he could determine exactly where it was coming from and whether or not he should trail it to its source.

"Cursed cats," muttered a man who hurried past Jankyn. "Hate the sly beasts, but they keep the vermin under control, aye?"

Jankyn murmured a polite agreement and the man disappeared into a room. Now Jankyn knew why the sound had so firmly caught his interest. It was similar to the one a cat made when caught in a fight. This cat, however, was probably facing two-legged vermin she would not be able to control. He listened intently, thankful for the empty silence of the hallway he stood in, and was rewarded with a soft sound that unmistakably was a hiss. Clinging to the shadows, moving swiftly and silently, Jankyn headed in the direction the sound had come from, a sound that told him a Callan was in danger. Instinct told him that it was Efrica, and he felt his blood heat with fury and the thrill of the hunt.

With her back against the cold, stone wall and the two men in front of her, Efrica could see no clear route of escape. She had thought she had been cautious enough to be safe but had obviously not been as careful as she could have been, for she had given these men the chance they had clearly been waiting for. It had never occurred to her that she might need a bodyguard to make a quick trip to the privy. The fact that both men were bleeding from wounds she had inflicted did please her, but she knew those wounds were going to cost her dearly if she did not get away.

They lunged at her and she did her best to keep both men from getting a firm grip on her at the same time. This time they were not deceived by her small size or her sex into thinking it would be easy to capture and hold her. Once Lachlan slammed her against the wall so hard she was surprised she did not feel or hear a bone crack. She decided they were definitely planning to make her suffer for the injuries she had given them. When they finally got her pinned against the wall, she hissed at them. The looks upon their faces told her that, during the battle, she may have revealed her ancestry a little too clearly. Their brief confusion faded, turning into looks of hard determination. Efrica knew she could not fight them anymore, that she was too bruised and exhausted.

Suddenly Jankyn appeared behind the men. Efrica decided that that wolf-eyed, teeth-baring look he wore held its own wild beauty at times. By the looks upon the faces of her attackers as they were suddenly lifted off their feet and flung aside, she knew they had not seen or heard Jankyn's approach, either. Thomas sprawled on the floor several feet away and did not move, but Lachlan began to stand up. Efrica saw Jankyn start to turn toward that man, fury still marking his features in a way no one could see and forget. She hurled herself into his arms with the last of her strength, wrapping her arms around his neck.

"Shield the teeth, Jankyn," she whispered, fighting to remain conscious until all danger had passed.

It was not easy, but Jankyn reined in his fury and bloodlust. He pressed his lips together before turning to face Lachlan. The scent of their blood, still flowing from the slashes Efrica's nails had inflicted, made that control even more difficult. As he stood there holding a trembling Efrica, Jankyn ached to make the men pay dearly for touching her, hurting her, and making her taste such fear.

"When I look again, ye and that other piece of offal had best be gone," Jankyn said to Lachlan, then turned his attention back to an increasingly limp Efrica. "They have hurt you."

Hearing the snarl in his voice, Efrica struggled to speak. "Nay so badly. A bit dazed and bruised is all. Ye dinnae need to be ripping any throats out. Could cause talk, ye ken."

Jankyn sighed loudly. "Ye do ken how to take all the joy out of a mon's life, lass."

Efrica attempted to smile, even though she was not sure he was jesting, at least not completely. "Are they gone?"

"Aye, scurried away like rats, they did. Weel, a wee bit more slowly as one rat had to carry the other." He picked her up in his arms when he realized that her grip upon his neck was probably all that kept her standing. "Are ye going to swoon?"

"Callan women ne'er swoon."

She had barely finished saying the words when she went

completely limp in his arms and he rolled his eyes over her false bravado. He did not know where her chambers were, had made it a point not to know. That left his chambers and he was reluctant to take her there. Having Efrica in his room, upon his bed, could offer up more temptation than he could resist. Jankyn started toward the garden to find a bench where he could sit and hold her until she came out of her swoon. If anyone chanced to see them there, they would think it was two lovers trysting.

Once in the garden, Jankyn sought out a bench set between two small rowan trees, hard up against a high wall, and sat down. He settled Efrica comfortably upon his lap and studied her face in the soft light of the full moon. Even though he still ached to kill the men who had attacked her, he was glad she had stopped him again. He did not want her to see him commit such violence. The fact that she knew what he *could* do to a man was unsettling enough.

For a moment he wondered if he had become ashamed of what he was, then shook his head. He held none of the hard arrogance of his ancestors, that blind pride that had allowed them to see Outsiders as little more than dumb beasts to feed upon, but he *was* proud to be a MacNachton. The MacNachtons were more civilized now, had more respect for all life. It was fear that kept them all so secretive about their nature, fear of the dire fate awaiting anyone who was decried as a witch, a sorcerer, or a demon. And it was fear that allowed Lachlan and Thomas to escape his fury, fear of the look of horror and revulsion upon Efrica's sweet face as he rose from the bodies of the two men, their blood staining his mouth. She understood he was merely of a different breed, as she was, and that he was not some soulless, undead creature from an unblessed grave who fed upon the living. However, knowing of his nature and seeing it displayed were two different things. Jankyn knew it would pain him far more than he cared to think about if she turned from him in fear and loathing. What he felt for her had obviously far surpassed lust and liking.

He pressed his lips to her forehead and inhaled deeply of her sweet scent. Even David's mother, a woman he had wanted to marry and claim as his mate, had never moved him as deeply as this delicate woman did. Efrica truly was his mate, and yet even as he held her in his arms, he did not think he had ever felt so alone, for he could never claim her. It made his past sense of loneliness seem like no more than a bad mood. Although he felt certain she cared for him in many ways, and desired him, he was going to have to resist the temptation to try to win her heart. She was a woman who loved the garden, the sun, and children. He could give her only shadows, windowless rooms, and quite possibly, an empty womb. He could not do that to her.

She stirred in his arms and slowly opened her eyes. Jankyn stared into those warm, soft amber eyes and felt such a confusing wealth of emotion he was tempted to toss her to the ground and run for the hills. Instead, he kissed her, even as a mocking voice in his head called him an idiot.

Efrica was startled when Jankyn's lips met hers. For a very brief moment, she resisted the temptation of welcoming and returning his kiss. As she slipped her arms around his neck, she told herself the occasional lapse in good judgment would not hurt her. When she parted her lips to allow the kiss to become more intimate, it took but one stroke of his tongue to banish the last twinge of caution. The heat of desire burned away all thought of anything besides how good he tasted and how alive he made her feel. His hands stroked her body and soon had her trembling with need, aching for him to touch those places he was so carefully avoiding. She was just thinking of how much she wanted to feel his skin beneath her hands when he burrowed his long fingers into her hair and pain shot through her head.

Jankyn heard her moan, and she jerked slightly in his

arms. Since he felt a little dazed himself, it took him a moment to understand that it was not passion that caused her to do so. He quickly turned her around on his lap to examine the back of her head. He was relieved to discover that the swelling there was not too great, but there was a cut that needed to be cleaned.

"I thought we werenae going to do that anymore," Efrica said when she felt she could speak calmly.

"We werenae and we arenae," responded Jankyn as he set her on her feet and stood up. He quickly wrapped a steadying arm around her slim shoulders when she swayed slightly. "'Tis unwise, especially since we will be spending time together. Where are your chambers?"

Efrica asked him as he escorted her back into the castle, "Why are we to spend time together?"

"Aside from the fact that ye have two men hunting ye?" He nodded when she frowned and then quickly told her what Malcolm had said. "In some ways, I need your protection as much as ye need mine. Ye cannae denounce or accuse those two bastards for what they have done, for unfair though it is, ye could easily be blamed for their actions or forced to marry one of them. I must needs play the courtier more than I have. My retirement from all gatherings has given the rumors and dangerous whispers fertile ground to grow in." Stopping before the door to her chamber, he opened it and gently but firmly pushed her inside. "I will see ye on the morrow. Be sure to clean the cut upon your head."

He shut the door, not surprised to see that she looked startled. It had been an abrupt leave-taking. Although he knew she was bruised and battered, the temptation to follow her into that room and continue what they had begun in the garden had almost been too strong to resist. He needed to cool the fire in his blood before he approached her again.

As he started toward his own bedchamber, he caught sight of Lady Eleanor at his door. Keeping to the shadows, he changed direction and returned to the garden. Jankyn looked up at the full moon and thought of the royal hunting grounds not far from the castle walls. A hunt would ease the bloodlust that still hummed in his veins after having to let Lachlan and Thomas yet again slip free. It might also ease the tight knot of unsatisfied desire that gripped his innards. Despite knowing that is was risky, he left the garden and headed for the royal hunting grounds. Tonight he would feed.

Seven

Efrica tensed as Lady Eleanor approached her. Jankyn had only been playing her guard, and she his, for one day, but Efrica was sure Lady Eleanor was coming to speak to her about him. The few times she had caught sight of Lady Eleanor yester eve, the way the woman had been watching her and Jankyn had given Efrica chills. Jankyn neither trusted the woman nor wished to be with her, but Efrica did not think he saw her as any real threat.

"Where is your champion?" asked Lady Eleanor as she stopped only a few inches away from Efrica, her smile of greeting cold.

"My what?" asked Efrica, determined not to let this woman intimidate her.

"Jankyn, of course. I suppose he clings to your skirts to keep Armstrong and Oliphant at a distance."

"As my kinsmon, he would naturally wish those two to stay far away from me. They have been a trouble to me."

"Jankyn is your kinsmon? I didnae ken that there was a kinship between MacNachtons and Callans."

"My sister is married to Jankyn's laird, who is also his cousin."

"That hardly makes him a kinsmon," Lady Eleanor snapped, then swiftly controlled her irritation. "Ye cannae be quite so naive, can ye? Do ye nay ken the mon's reputation? He is insatiable."

The tone of gentle advisor, which Eleanor had adopted, made Efrica clench her teeth. "That may be, m'lady, but I doubt Jankyn would e'er consider dishonoring the sister of his laird's wife." The way Lady Eleanor stared at her made Efrica uneasy, for the woman's pale blue eyes seemed to see right into her heart, a heart Efrica constantly lied to. "Jankyn feels it his duty to protect me from further insult."

"Ye consider young Lachlan's and Thomas's wishes to make ye wife to one of them an insult?"

"Their manner of wooing isnae much to my liking."

"I think ye may prefer your *kinsmon's* manner of wooing. Ah, but what woman wouldnae, aye? He is the sort of mon who easily makes a woman lose all good sense and caution. Many have fallen victim to his beauty and his charm. I should hate to see ye, young and innocent as ye are, be deceived by the sweet lies he tells so weel. As I was," she added on a mournful sigh.

If the woman expected Efrica to offer her any sympathy, she would rot where she stood. It was bad enough that the woman spoke to her as if she were a child, and a rather witless one at that. That Lady Eleanor would play the part of an innocent seduced and abandoned by her heartless lover was infuriating. Did she really think Efrica was fool enough to believe that?

Efrica was forced to admit to herself that some of her fury was bred from pain. Lady Eleanor's character might be as ugly as sin, but she was physically beautiful, very beautiful. To look at this woman and know that Jankyn had held her, kissed and caressed her, and made love to her made Efrica feel as if she were bleeding inside. Efrica was not sure whom she hated more at that precise moment, Eleanor for reminding her of Jankyn's lecherous nature and all the lovers he had had, or Jankyn for being so free with his favors.

It was a poor time to have a revelation, she mused. The woman facing her was hunting for a weak spot, and Efrica realized she had a big one. Her heart had not listened to any of her lectures nor believed any of the lies she had told herself. It had gone on its merry way. Efrica knew that, if she was not already in love with Jankyn, she was but one kiss away from it.

"I am sorry if ye feel ye were ill treated, m'lady," Efrica murmured, silently wishing the woman would leave, would in fact go very far away. France would be a good start.

"Such things happen. One must learn from them. Aye, and try to pass that knowledge on to others, to try to save the heartbreak such men can cause. Oh, but despite my pain, I have few regrets. If one must slip from the path of virtue and good sense, one couldnae ask for a finer lover to lead one astray. So fierce in his passion, so skilled. But I shouldnae speak so plainly to such an innocent."

Given a little encouragement, Efrica suspected Lady Eleanor would quickly begin to speak even more plainly, but she would not offer the woman the chance. The very last thing she wished to hear was any intimate detail about the affair. Her own imagination conjured up more than she could stomach as it was.

"Nay, mayhap ye shouldnae." Efrica could tell by the slight widening of Lady Eleanor's pale blue eyes that she had not managed to keep all signs of her rising fury out of her voice.

"Now, child, ye must nay think ill of Jankyn. He is but a mon and they have e'er sought their pleasures where they can. Tis the nature of the beast. I should have been wiser. As a widow, and a few years older than ye, I am excused a few errors in judgment, as weel." Eleanor smiled and shook her head. "Twas a verra sweet error, I confess. My late husband was many years older than I, and thus, I had no idea passion could be so wondrous, that a mon could banish all a woman's senses with but a stroke of his hand or a kiss."

One more such confidence and Efrica feared she would have to walk away or she would scratch the woman's much-praised eyes out. Jealousy tore at her insides. It was madness. Despite the feelings she had just acknowledged, she still felt Jankyn was all wrong for her, so she had no right to resent his finding pleasure elsewhere. This particular pleasure had also been sought before she had even arrived at court. That bit of good sense did little to ease the pain she felt, however.

"How odd that he hasnae yet arrived to stand guard o'er ye," Lady Eleanor murmured. "I hope he isnae unweel, or hurt."

There was something in Lady Eleanor's expression that caused Efrica to feel a growing sense of alarm start to cut through her misery and pain. "Jankyn has often been absent from these gatherings."

"True, yet I thought his need to protect ye had caused him to put an end to his self-imposed exile."

"He had work to do."

"Of course. That must be what he tends to now—his work. Ah, there is my good friend Lady Beatrice. I must speak with her. It has been a pleasure speaking with ye, Mistress Callan."

About as much pleasure as having a tooth drawn, Efrica thought, even as she mumbled a polite farewell. By the look that fleetingly passed over Lady Beatrice's round face as Lady Eleanor approached her, Efrica was sure that Lady Beatrice did not consider the redhead a friend. Efrica would not be surprised to discover that poor Lady Beatrice had a faithless husband or was about to be made to think she did.

Efrica glanced toward the entrance to the great hall and

frowned. Lady Eleanor's words concerning Jankyn's absence troubled her. The woman was well aware that Jankyn had been avoiding the many gatherings at the court, that he had been avoiding her. That touch of concern in the woman's voice had been feigned; of that she had no doubt. Was it a warning, or was the mention of Jankyn taking ill or being hurt meant to make Efrica do exactly what she was doing—worry?

Deciding she would drive herself daft if she did nothing, Efrica looked for David. When she espied him, he was looking toward the entrance to the great hall and frowning. The possibility that he expected Jankyn, knew the man intended to be there, only added to Efrica's unease. She slowly made her way over to where David stood beside a faintly blushing Fiona. To her relief, Fiona moved away to speak to her mother just as Efrica reached David's side.

"David, did your father say he would be here tonight?" she asked.

"Aye," he replied. "I was just wondering what might be keeping him."

After a moment of thought, Efrica told him what Lady Eleanor had said and explained why it bothered her. "All things considered, it was probably just said to make me worry, and yet—"

"Exactly. And yet. Just let me tell Fiona that I must leave but will return soon, and I will go with ye to find him."

A moment later, David was escorting her out of the great hall. The fact that he felt the need to reassure himself concerning his father's well-being made Efrica feel better about her own sense of unease. At least she would not look so foolish if Jankyn's absence proved to have a simple explanation.

"Mayhap he became caught up in his work," she said, slipping her arm through David's as they started down a dimly lit corridor.

"Nay. He was just about to bathe when I was prepared to leave. He told me to keep an eye on ye until he could get there. E'en though I kenned Lady Eleanor wouldnae be pleasant to ye, I didnae see her as any threat." He blushed. "After my father turned away from her, she tried to crawl into my bed. Thought to hurt my father, or insult him, I suspect."

"Och, David! Ye didnae!"

"Nay! Twas a sore temptation, I admit, but I had already met Fiona and suspected she was the lass I have been searching for. I didnae want that adder slinking up to Fiona and whispering poison in her ear. I suspicion that is what Lady Eleanor was doing to ye, aye?"

"Weel, aye, but I ken that your father is bound to no one. Tis his business what he does and no one else's." She scowled at him when he snorted.

"Lie to yourself if ye wish, Efrica Callan, but dinnae expect anyone to believe it. Ye and my father fair stink of wanting whene'er ye come within sight of each other." He grinned briefly when she gasped in shock. "Dinnae get all outraged. I wasnae speaking of lusting alone, but that greater sort of wanting, lust being only a wee part of it. I dinnae ken why the two of ye dinnae stop all this dancing about and just settle down to it."

"Your father doesnae need another woman. He has had far more than his share already."

"Ach, Effie, ye ken as weel as I that those women meant naught to him. If one did, he would still be with her, wouldnae he. Ye also ken that the MacNachtons are free with their favors until they find their mates." He shrugged. "Nature of the beast, I suppose."

"Ye werenae."

"I was, though nay as free as some. But I came here to find a wife, aye? My father didnae, and trust me in this, he didnae do any wooing, or seducing, either. Nay, 'twas offered up to him from the first time he walked into the great hall. Coyly or boldly, but most decidedly freely. Being a mon with no ties, he accepted. If the two of ye would cease playing whate'er strange game ye are playing, there would be no more offers accepted."

"I love the sun," she whispered, unable to deny David's insights.

David stopped and looked at her, his hands on his hips. "So does Bridget and her bairns. Whene'er the sun deigns to shine, they go outside. I thought ye accepted what we are."

"Dinnae be an idiot. Of course I—" She tensed and grasped him by the arm. "Did ye hear that?" she asked, but could sense by the tension in his body that he did. "Steel on steel."

"Your ears are sharper than mine, I think. From what direction does it come?"

After listening carefully for a moment, Efrica gasped. "From the direction of Jankyn's chambers."

David disappeared into the shadows and began to move with a silent speed that deeply impressed Efrica, who was hard-pressed to keep up with him. It was definitely a MacNachton trait one could envy. She nearly ran into him when he stopped abruptly. Peering around him, she almost cried out and ran past him. Jankyn was fighting with three men. Another man was already sprawled upon the floor and it looked as if he was dead, or would be soon. They all had the look of hired swords, and Efrica had little doubt in her mind as to who had hired them. When she realized that Jankyn was fighting them in the manner any man would do, using few of the skills the MacNachton blood gifted him with, she nearly cursed. Even his expression, though feral in many ways, was controlled. He obviously feared being caught doing what MacNachtons did so well—putting the fear of God into their enemies. And that, she suddenly understood, was why David had halted, and still hesitated.

"Go," she hissed. "Do what ye do best and free your father to do the same. I will warn ye if anyone approaches."

"Can ye do that?"

"Aye. If I but set my mind to it, I can tell ye who just belched in the great hall. Go."

Efrica nearly missed David's attack, so swiftly did he move. Although that ever-curious part of her wanted to watch the battle, she turned her mind to protecting the MacNachtons' backs. Better than anyone in her family, she was able to ignore sounds she recognized as no threat to her, and listen for the others. Her boast to David had been an exaggeration, but not by very much. She did not expect the battle to last much longer anyway. Once David and his father turned the full MacNachton ferocity upon their foes, those men who did not die would run screaming into the night.

Silence alerted her to the end of the battle. Since she stood at the only way out of this corridor and no one had run past her, Efrica decided that two MacNachtons in their full glory were more than enough to defeat four mercenaries. When she turned to join the victors, she saw David crouched by Jankyn, who sat upon the floor with his back against the wall. She suddenly recalled her sister telling her that the MacNachtons were not actually immortal, that they just lived so long it was easy to think they were. Bridget had also told her that the MacNachtons were very hard to kill, but that it could be done, and had told her how. The loss of too much blood, too rapidly, was one, Efrica recalled and ran to Jankyn's side.

"Curse it, Father, when did ye become so particular?" snapped David as she knelt next to Jankyn.

Efrica was appalled by the number of wounds Jankyn had suffered. David had bared Jankyn's chest and she counted three wounds there. There was blood upon his leggings as well, and the slow drip of blood sounding from behind him indicated there was at least one wound upon his back. What truly alarmed her, however, was that the wounds showed no sign of closing. His Pureblood body should have already been starting to heal itself. Efrica could even recall Bridget telling her of how she had once badly scored Jankyn's face with her nails when he had startled her and had watched those wounds close right before her eyes. Efrica saw no hint of this miracle.

Then, suddenly, she understood what the problem was. Jankyn had lost too much blood to heal himself. He needed blood, and by the looks of the bodies strewn around them, neither he nor David had taken any from the men. Except for the man who had been felled by Jankyn's sword and barely clung to life, the other three men had been killed very cleanly. Efrica suspected it was done that way to avoid any chance someone might see the bodies and talk. As she stood up, she wondered why she felt no qualms about what she was going to suggest, then realized that it was because these mercenaries had intended to murder Jankyn. The least the barely surviving mercenary could do before he died was give Jankyn back the life he had been so eager to take away.

"That one still lives," she said calmly, pointing to the man Jankyn had defeated with his sword and ignoring the wary looks both father and son gave her. "I can hear the death rattle building in his throat so I wouldnae dither about for too long."

"I thought he might already be dead," murmured Jankyn.

"Nay, there is yet life in him, but 'tis fading fast. I will wait for ye in your chambers."

She hurried the few feet to his door and entered his room. As she shut the door behind her, she caught a fleeting glimpse of David nearly dragging his father toward the dying man. For a moment she feared she had done or said something to make Jankyn so reluctant to do what he needed to save his own life, but quickly shook off that guilt. She was certain she had not, but Jankyn was probably well aware of how unsettling Outsiders found such needs. She hoped he would soon realize she was not one of those. It was now very important to her that Jankyn knew she accepted him for *all* that he was.

Eight

Jankyn grimaced with distaste as he and David quietly let the last mercenary's body slip into the water. It had not been easy to get all four bodies out of the castle, but luck had been on their side. Not only had no one seen them within the castle, but the foul night weather had hidden the moon, giving them all the shadows they needed to hide in as they took the bodies to the burn not far from the castle walls. The bodies would be quickly discovered as the burn was not deep, but only the one who had hired the men would be able to guess what had happened to them.

"I cannae believe ye were just going to let yourself die," muttered David as they hurried back to the castle.

"Weel, I dinnae think I would have died," Jankyn said. "We could have tended the wounds to slow the bleeding, and with a lot of my wine, I—"

"Would have died. E'en now ye arenae at your full strength. If ye were, toting two bodies to the burn would-nae have made ye sweat. Why? Because Effie was there?"

Jankyn sighed. "Aye and nay. Think, David. Think on how the rumors would fly if four men were found with their throats savaged. Such things stir up fear and superstition. Once the whispers begin, so does the search for anyone who is different. This time that could weel include Efrica and her cousin. There are two men at court who have seen up close how a Callan can behave when attacked. Aye, and the same two men might begin to wonder how I could toss them about with such ease. S'truth, according to Malcolm, there are already whispers seeping through the court."

David cursed, then frowned. "So, it wasnae because Efrica might have seen ye feed?"

For a moment, Jankyn considered lying to his son, then inwardly shook his head. "Tis a difficult thing for Outsiders to watch. It marks us too strongly as predators, and marks them as prey. Trust me in this, there is naught that frightens a person more than the thought that *they* are the meal. E'en I have felt that fear chill my blood when a wolf howls in the night. Tis one that is bred in the bone, one that probably goes back into the dark mists of time when people were undoubtedly more the prey than the predator. I suppose I didnae want to see that fear in Efrica's eyes or have her look at me as if I were more beast than mon. Howbeit, as that chill began to seep into my emptying veins, the one that too often foreshadows death, I was beginning to think myself a great fool for hesitating."

"And then she told ye to get on with it."

As they stepped inside the castle, out of the rain, Jankyn paused to squeeze some of the water from his clothes and hair while David did the same. "Aye, she did. Yet she left, didnae stay with me."

"I think she did that for your sake. She is a clever lass and she kens a lot about us. I suspicion she quickly guessed what ye needed and then why ye were nay taking it. She let ye ken she was aware of what ye needed to do to heal yourself, then gave ye the privacy ye seemed to want."

"Weel, aye, I suppose she did. That was kind of her." He looked at his son in surprise when David cursed.

"The two of ye are enough to make a person daft. She is your mate, isnae she."

"David—"

"Aye, she is. So why do ye nay woo her and claim her?"

"Because I believe it would be unkind and curse us both in the end. Aye, there could be compromises made, as Cathal has made for Bridget, but there is one thing Efrica wants and needs that I may ne'er be able to give her."

"What?"

"Children. Ye are the only child I have bred, David, and I have been indulging myself with women for thirty years or so. E'en Cathal, who is a mon of both worlds, feared he might not be able to breed a child. Despite the many Pureblood women Efrica's brothers have bedded down with when they come to visit, only two bairns have been born."

David sighed and dragged his hand through his hair when they paused just outside the door of Jankyn's room. "Weel, then, why not become lovers? At least ye could have that."

"And then who would take her to wife? Men prefer their wives to be untouched when they come to the marriage bed."

"Unless that wife has a verra fine dowry, one sweetened with a bonnie piece of land. Mayhap I am a selfish bastard, but if I stood in your place, I would take all I could. I would glut myself with sweet memories to hold in my heart, ones to be brought forth later, when I am again alone. Weel, I best go and clean myself up and then hie myself back to the great hall ere my Fiona thinks I have deserted her."

Jankyn watched his son walk away, then turned to frown at his door. *Why not become lovers?* The very thought of being Efrica's lover made his knees weak, as if he were some untried boy facing the loss of his virginity. Cursing his son for putting that idea into his head, Jankyn entered his chambers. When Efrica turned from staring into the fire and smiled at him, he felt as if he had come home and he silently groaned. *Why not become lovers?* As Jankyn walked to his bed and flung himself down on it, he knew that one small hint of welcome from Efrica and he would give in to the temptation to start making some of those sweet memories.

Efrica moved to stand beside the bed. "Are ye still weak? Do ye want some of your wine?" She frowned at him as she suddenly noticed the state of his clothes. "How did ye get so wet?"

"Nay. Aye. Tis raining." He had to bite back a grin when she rolled her lovely eyes.

"Why did ye go out in the rain?"

"Ah, weel, we couldnae leave four dead men lying about the corridor, could we? David and I took them outside the walls and tossed them into the burn. Luck was with us the whole way. No one stumbled upon us as we left the castle, and the foul weather hid us as we went to the burn. So the only one who will ken what happened to those men when the bodies are found is the one who hired them. He willnae be talking, will he."

"She," Efrica said as she grimaced at the muddy state of his boots. "Here, let me get these off ere ye ruin the bedclothes."

"She?" Jankyn asked, absently shifting around enough to allow Efrica to remove his boots.

"Aye. I believe your lover Lady Eleanor hired them."

There was a definite bite to her words, Jankyn noticed. "My former lover. My former lover of but a verra brief time many weeks ago. I should be surprised that a woman would hire mercenaries to murder a mon, but I am not. Cold and vicious is Lady Eleanor. Vanity dressed in a rich gown. How do ye ken she is the one?"

As she grabbed a drying cloth and began to rub his hair dry, Efrica explained. When she looked at Jankyn, he was grinning at her, and she thought that an odd reaction. Then she realized what she was doing and cursed softly.

"What am I thinking of?" she muttered, glaring at the drying cloth.

"That I am wet?"

"Tis habit, ye ken. Someone comes in wet, then ye hurry to get them dry and warm so they dinnae take a fever, but that isnae a problem with ye, is it?"

"Nay, but feel free to continue."

There was an odd glint in his eyes, as if he challenged her. Efrica also sensed some change in him, as if he was no longer so intent upon keeping a distance between them. Perhaps, she mused, he had been as affected by his brush with death as she had. As she had seen his wounds, had realized that he could possibly die if he did not feed soon, she had decided she would stop lying to herself, would stop trying to run away from what she felt for him. Efrica was not sure what he felt for her, save for lust and some liking, but she could accept that for now. She herself was still uncertain if there could be any future for them, but there was definitely the here and now and she would grasp it. If nothing else, she could gather up a lot of lovely memories to warm her heart whenever she felt alone.

When Efrica began to unlace his doublet, Jankyn tensed. The soft smile she wore and the way she kept glancing up at him from beneath her long lashes was taking the chill from his skin more rapidly than any fire could. He was not sure if she was so innocent she could not understand how this was affecting him or if she played some game. When she had him bared to the waist, she placed her hands upon his chest and he had to clench his hands into tight fists to keep from grabbing her and tossing her to the bed. If she were a woman of experience, he would know exactly what she was after, but he dared not guess wrong with Efrica.

Efrica felt the heat of his skin beneath her hands and shivered slightly. His chest was broad, the strength beneath his smooth, lovely skin clear to see and feel. That tiny flicker of hesitation she had felt a moment ago faded away. Perhaps they were not destined to be together forever, but her heart and body were not concerned with the future at this time, anyway. It was going to hurt when their time together ended and they each went back to their normal lives, but at least there would be fewer regrets mixed with that pain. She would be able to close her eyes and remember passion shared, instead of just wondering how it might have been. She leaned forward and kissed his chest, feeling him tremble beneath her lips.

That was an invitation if ever there was one, but Jankyn felt compelled to give her one last chance to escape with her virtue intact. "Dangerous, lass. Verra dangerous indeed."

"Is it?" She placed her hands on his broad shoulders and felt the heat of his gaze flow through her veins. "What is this then?" She kissed him.

"Madness," he whispered against her mouth and yanked her into his arms.

Jankyn had no more willpower to refuse the gift she offered. As they kissed, Efrica revealing that she learned the intricacies of kissing very quickly, he hurried to unlace her gown. He needed to see her, needed to feel her soft skin against his. When he felt her small hands tugging at the laces on his hose, he realized she felt the same need. There would be no turning back now.

When her gown fell to the floor, Jankyn stood up and tugged her chemise off over her head. Despite the fact that he was trembling with need, he almost smiled when he saw that she wore braies. He quickly removed those, then her shoes and stockings, before nearly tossing her down on his bed. As he threw off the rest of his clothes, he wondered fleetingly where all of his well-practiced seductive skills had gone.

Efrica got one good look at a naked Jankyn before he was sprawled on top of her, kissing her. His kiss swiftly banished that brief moment of alarm she had suffered upon seeing the size of that part he would soon be trying to fit inside her. She ran her hands over his strong back as she tilted her head to allow him to spread his warm kisses over her throat with more ease. A soft cry of pleasure escaped her when he caressed her breasts with his elegant hands.

"Ah, Efrica, ye are so cursed beautiful. So soft and sweet to the taste," he murmured against her skin as he kissed the spot between her full breasts.

He closed his mouth over the hard aching tip of her breast and gently suckled. Efrica gave herself over completely to the pleasure flowing through her. It was not until he slid his hand between her legs that she regained any of her senses, but his clever fingers soon banished all hesitation and shock over such an intimate touch. Efrica was aware of nothing save how he felt beneath her hands, his scent, and his touch. By the time he settled himself squarely between her thighs and she felt him nudge himself inside her, she was shaking with the strength of her desire.

"This may hurt ye a wee bit, love," he said, the sweat beading on his body as he fought the strong urge to just thrust himself into her heat and keep thrusting until the nearly painful need possessing him was satisfied.

"Get it over with."

Jankyn almost laughed. If not for all the signs of a passion burning as hot and wild as his own, he could easily take those curt words amiss. Then he decided she was probably right, that quick was best. He grasped her by her slim hips and drove himself deep inside her. Pressing his face into the cool linen cover on the pillow under her head, he fought to remain still, to allow her to grow used to him. He had heard her gasp of pain and did not wish to add to it by moving too quickly. Then he felt her hands stroke his back, her small feet stroke his legs, and most telling of all, heard a soft rumbling noise that could not be called anything other than a purr. He pushed himself up on his forearms and looked at her.

"I dinnae think we are done yet, Jankyn," she murmured, caressing his chest with her hands as she wrapped her legs around his lean body.

"Nay," he whispered. "Not yet."

He slowly moved within her, savoring her heat. The look of pure delight upon her face severed his control, however. To his relief, Efrica did not quail beneath the increasing ferocity of his lovemaking. He felt her nails score his back as she met his every thrust with a greed that matched his own. When she cried out his name as her release rippled through her slim body and he felt her body drink from his, Jankyn had to cling to what few tattered bits of control he could gather up even as he joined her in that blind fall. He buried his face in the pillow, fighting the urge to make her his true mate.

Even as the sweetest satisfaction he had ever tasted washed over him, a hunger lingered. Jankyn turned his head and softly kissed the life-giving pulse in her neck. He would hold her in his bed for as long as she and fate allowed, but it was going to be hard not to take that final step. There was not a part of him that did not crave that ritual mixing of her blood with his, of tasting that sweet elixir that gave her life and leaving his mark upon her lovely neck. It had to be offered, however, and despite the desire she shared with him so willingly, he was not at all sure that she wished to be his true mate.

Feeling certain that his hunger no longer revealed itself upon his face, he slowly pulled free of her body. The murmur of regret she made brought a smile to his lips as he turned onto his side. He propped himself up on one elbow, rested his chin in his hand, and idly stroked her stomach as he gazed at her. She was looking beautifully sated, even a little debauched.

When she smiled at him and languidly pushed her tousled hair from her face, Jankyn felt his heart break. He was pleased she revealed no misgivings, but he suffered a sudden strong regret that he was not a normal man. A man who could woo her with walks in the garden, could make love to her in a sun-bathed meadow. A man who could offer her a house filled with windows and then fill it with children. A man she could fret over when he came home cold and wet, in need of her help to get warm and dry to stave off the threat of a fever. A man who could grow old with her. A man who did not have to worry that, no matter how long-lived Callans were, there would come the day when he would stand over her grave knowing he faced many, many empty years ahead.

Jankyn suddenly understood why so many Purebloods reached a time in their very long lives when they suddenly began to spit in the eye of the reaper, to boldly risk suffering one of the few ways a Pureblood could die. It could be that they had grown too arrogant, too sure of their own immortality, but Jankyn suspected that, in some strange way, they had simply become bored with their lives. Or as with the old laird, Cathal's father, who had married an Outsider, they could not bear the thought of life without their mate, a life so long that they could find themselves standing over the grave of their child, their grandchild, and on and on. Aging as an Outsider did was a frightening thing, but Jankyn began to think that living so long you saw your own blood-line die out one by one could be more so.

"Ye look troubled, Jankyn," Efrica said, smothering the hurt she felt over his lack of love words.

"I was wondering what happens now, love." He kissed her and asked softly, "Are ye my lover now? Aye or nay?"

"Aye," she replied without hesitation.

Nine

"Weel, ye obviously dinnae have to worry that your lover cannae give ye children."

Deciding it was safe to leave the bucket she had been draped over for far too long, Efrica ignored her cousin and crawled back to her bed. As she buried her face in the pillow, she heard Barbara set a few things down on the table beside her bed. It was obvious that Barbara wished to discuss matters. For a moment, Efrica considered feigning a swoon, but then carefully urged her body into a seated position, collapsing against the pillows Barbara hastily plumped up behind her. She frowned at the bread and what smelled like hot cider set on the table.

"I dinnae think I can eat anything," she mumbled.

"Aye, ye can. Sip the drink and nibble at the bread. Twill settle ye." Barbara sat at the end of the bed, crossed her arms over her chest, and stared at Efrica until she began to do as commanded. "Time to decide, Cousin. I didnae fully agree with what ye were doing, but I understood. Just because ye love and desire a mon doesnae mean he will make ye a good husband. Howbeit, there is now love, desire, *and* a bairn."

"Mayhap 'tis just the fish I ate last eve."

"Dinnae play the fool. I have suspected this for a few days now, and I am sure ye have kenned it for just as long, if nay longer. Callan women always ken early when they are with child. Wheesht, if some of us put our minds to it, I wouldnae be surprised if we could tell exactly when the seed took root. Why the frown? Why the hesitation? Does this nay answer one of the doubts ye had when ye thought ye and Jankyn couldnae wed?"

"It does."

"And so?"

"Curse it, Barbara, he hasnae said he wants me as his wife, his mate."

"Ye mean he hasnae said that he loves ye."

The bread and hot cider having revived her, Efrica sat up straighter. "Nay, he hasnae. We have been lovers for a month, and weel, wouldnae he have said so by now if he felt that way?"

"Have ye told him how ye feel?"

"Nay, but I believe my actions should tell him a great deal, dinnae ye? I was a virgin, a weel-bred, richly dowered virgin sent here to find a husband. I have put that at risk. Aye, *and* my good name."

"True, but men dinnae always see it that way. As my husband says, a mon thinks desire all the reason one needs, doesnae always look beyond that." Barbara blushed faintly. "He reminded me that he thought desire was all that drew me to him, although he hoped for and needed more. He was waiting for me to tell him there was more for he dared not trust his own judgment in the matter."

Efrica slowly ate a piece of bread. The royal court had moved a fortnight ago, courtiers and all traveling along with it, and Barbara's husband and children had joined her. That had allowed Efrica to have not only her own bedchamber, small though it was, but regular insights into the male mind provided by Sir Matheson through Barbara. Her brothers had provided some understanding of men over the years, but little concerning matters of the heart. Yet Sir Matheson was not Jankyn. That left Efrica wondering if she could fully trust the man's opinions.

"Effie, I ken ye had reasons to think Jankyn a poor choice for a husband. Aye, and they were good ones. Yet when ye became his lover, I thought ye had changed your mind, that ye had finally kenned what ye wanted."

"Oh, aye, I did. I do. I kenned it the night Jankyn was attacked. I kenned it as I listened to Lady Eleanor speak of what a great lover Jankyn was and I stood there wondering how she would look bald." Efrica smiled faintly when Barbara laughed. "I also kenned it when I thought he might die and calmly told him to take what he needed to heal himself. That was when I was certain I accepted *all* that he was." She lightly patted her stomach. "Only the chance that I might ne'er carry his child still troubled me, but that is no longer a concern. As for that fretting I did o'er the fact that I love the sun and he is a mon of the shadows? Weel, David showed that to be foolish by saying that, when the sun deigns to shine, go outside. And as for the fact that he willnae age in step with me, weel, Callan women age weel, and lovers rarely die hand in hand. There is some comfort in the knowledge that *he* will always be there for this bairn and any others we may be blessed with. Howbeit, *he* hasnae spoken of a future or of love."

"Mayhap not, but I think that, if ye dinnae hold his heart now, ye could if ye wished to. The mon cannae keep his eyes or his hands off ye. He shows no interest in any other women though they still pursue him. And, Effie, he followed when the court packed up and moved, ye and I trotting along as weel. That was no small thing, was it? He couldnae just mount a horse and travel with us. Such a journey for him was one of constant risk." She nodded when Efrica stared at her in shock.

"Now that I think on it, e'en David was, briefly, surprised by Jankyn's decision to follow us. I did worry o'er it, but Jankyn simply said that, if he could travel from Cambrun to the court, he could travel from the old court to the new."

"Yet since David was officially betrothed by then, he didnae need to keep an eye on that, did he?"

"Nay, he didnae." Efrica got out of bed.

"What are ye planning to do?"

"See Jankyn and hope that I can find the courage to say something, anything, that might give him the prod or the courage to speak."

"Ye need to do that now?"

"I need to start sometime. I dinnae think it will be a problem easily solved, or quickly." Efrica sighed and shook her head. "I wish it was, not only for this bairn's sake, not e'en because Duncan will be looking for someone to kill if he discovers I am with child but without husband, but so that we can leave this place and these foolish gossips."

"Oh, dear, ye have heard all the rumors, havenae ye. They are worrisome."

"More than worrisome, Cousin. Dangerous. For all his strength, speed, and cunning, e'en his ability to heal in the blink of an eye, Jankyn has his weaknesses. He *can* be killed. Tisnae easy to do, but it can be done. He can certainly be shown to be, weel, different. Verra, verra different. All Jankyn will say is that such rumors have always dogged the heels of the MacNachtons. Then he kisses me and I forget what we were talking about," she muttered. "Weel, 'tis past time to do something about it."

"Such as what?"

"We both ken who spreads these tales—Lady Eleanor, Lachlan, and Thomas. Why anyone should heed what they say, I dinnae ken, but mayhap people need to be reminded of that." Noticing the startled look upon Barbara's face, Efrica asked, "What is it?"

"What ye just said—that people need to be reminded of exactly *who* is spreading the rumors. *I* should have thought of that. I have dealt with these people far more and far longer than ye have. All I can think of to excuse my stupidity is that I was too aware of the fact that a lot of what they were saying is true. Nay the foolish puzzling o'er if he is a demon, a devil, or some undead thing, but all the rest of it. He *is* different. He *does* shun the light. He *does* have eyes like a wolf. All of that." She shook her head. "I certainly have some skill at scorning such talk. We Callans arenae so obviously different, but we do have a few odd things about us, and I have always managed to ridicule away any whispers about us. I am pleased no one has mentioned his teeth, though. They would be difficult to explain away, although we did have an uncle who filed all of his into points."

"Aye, I remember him. Tis also good no one has thought too long on when or if they have e'er seen him eat."

"Doesnae he eat anything?"

"Some. He loves sweet things. But I dinnae think the food we eat provides sustenance for him. Nay enough, leastwise. Tis blood a MacNachton needs, but it has been a verra long time since they looked to people to provide it. Innocent people, anyway. Men like the ones who tried to murder Jankyn deserve whate'er they get," she added in a hard voice.

"Ye really do love him, dinnae ye."

Efrica smiled. "Aye, and I think I have since I first met him. All those reasons I had for why he could ne'er be my choice were born of a fear that, weel, the choice had already been made. I realized that I would rather live in Jankyn's shadowed world, than live in the bright sun without him. S'truth, without him, e'en the sun would probably ne'er ease the chill in my heart." She shrugged. "I just hope he feels the same for me, or nearly so."

"Oh, I truly think he does." Barbara stood up and walked to the door. "Mayhap he kens all those doubts ye had and but needs to be shown that they are gone. Ye set to work on that and I will start to mute these dangerous whispers."

Still planning various conversations that might work to nudge a few love words out of Jankyn, Efrica knocked on his door in the distinct pattern they had devised. Not only did Jankyn want to be sure he did not open the door to Lady Eleanor, who still hunted him down now and then, but he liked to be prepared for guests who did not know his secrets. If nothing else, he had to put away his personal supply of wine so that no one inadvertently discovered what *enriched* it.

When Jankyn opened the door, every thought in Efrica's head blew away. He stood there wearing nothing but a wide, slightly lecherous grin. He grabbed her by the hand, pulled her into the room, and shut and barred the door. Before Efrica could gather the wit to speak, he was kissing her, his clever fingers rapidly divesting her of her clothes. When he tumbled them down onto his bed, she decided they could have that serious talk later.

There was an intensity to his lovemaking that soon infected her. She quickly began to return his every kiss and caress with the same fervor with which he gave them. Then, suddenly, shock broke through the passionate daze he had put her in as he placed a kiss against the soft curls between her thighs. The protest she began to make swiftly died, banished by the pleasure of his intimate kiss. Again and again, he pushed her to the very edge with his tongue and his fingers, only to retreat until she was shaking with need, demanding he cease his tormenting. He did, but not in the way she had expected him to, using his mouth to give her the release she needed. Efrica was still gasping from the strength of it when Jankyn almost roughly joined their bodies and took her to the heights a second time.

It took several minutes after Jankyn had collapsed on top of her, before Efrica had the strength to turn her head and look at him. As always, he had his face buried in the pillow. "Weel, greetings to ye, too." She smiled faintly when he laughed. Then he turned his head to meet her gaze and she blushed. "Ah, weel, um, was that a sin?"

He brushed a kiss over her mouth. "Nay. Oh, I suspicion some priest would say so, but that priest would also decry me as Satan's own and gleefully light the kindling piled about my feet." He kissed her again and then rose from the bed to get a cloth to clean them off with.

"I thought the MacNachtons believed in the church and all. Father James is a MacNachton." She was so caught up in the thought that some of the MacNachtons might be nonbelievers, she barely twitched when Jankyn gently cleaned her off and then crawled back into bed.

Jankyn pulled her into his arms, enjoying the way she sprawled on top of him, and he settled his back against the pillows. "Oh, we believe in God, love. Tis the church and the men who rule it we have some doubt in. We both ken that some of them are more steeped in sin than ye and I e'er could be. Aye, some have a true calling, a deep belief, as James does. Howbeit, too many are simply younger sons sent to a life in the church because there was little choice or they hope to gain the power and riches denied them by birth. Until that changes, I take leave to question them. Nay God. Just them."

Efrica nodded, for she and a great many of her kin held similar views. When one belonged to a group the church would quickly condemn, no matter how deep one's belief was, it was inevitable that cynicism would result. The fact that Callan women had suffered because of their tendency to bear twins, something that stirred a few dark suspicions, had certainly made her doubt the men of the church.

Feeling a need to escape such dark, serious thoughts, she kissed Jankyn's chest. "So, if it isnae a sin for ye to do that to me, then it cannae be a sin for me to do whate'er I may wish with ye."

Jankyn tensed with anticipation as she began to kiss and caress her way down his body. He had planned to spend the day making love to her, and he felt both pleased and guilty that she was falling in with his plan so easily. Then he shuddered with pleasure as she brushed a kiss against his erection, and he decided he could wallow in guilt later.

Staring down at a sleeping Efrica, Jankyn fought the urge to crawl back into that bed, take her into his arms, and never let her go. He had struggled over the past few days to think of some way to tell her he was leaving, but had turned craven each time he had looked into her eyes. He could not lie to her, or push her away with cruelty, so he was just going to slip away like some thief. It was for the best, he told himself yet again. The whispers about him had not faded but grown louder, and more people were heeding them. If he stayed, there could be trouble and Efrica could easily be at risk as well. It was time to return to Cambrun and leave her to find a man who could walk in the sun at her side. Resisting the urge to steal one last kiss, he walked away, slipping into the shadows.

"Efrica!"

Opening one eye, Efrica wondered what David and Fiona were doing in her bedchamber. Then she remembered that she was in Jankyn's bed and blushed. Hastily wrapping the bedcovers around herself, she sat up.

"Has something happened to Jankyn?" she asked, suddenly finding David's presence ominous.

"Aye. He has left," replied David.

"Left? To go where?"

"Back to Cambrun."

Efrica knew that once shock released its tight grip upon her, there was going to be a lot of pain flooding in. "Why?"

"Because of the talk swirling about amongst the courtiers and their ladies. I thought I had convinced him that we could fight it, but I should have understood how concerned he was about my safety and yours." When David saw Efrica glance at Fiona, he took his betrothed's hand in his. "She kens all about the MacNachtons, Effie, so ye dinnae need to guard your words."

"Except for the ones I feel inclined to direct at your father," she muttered. "He didnae e'en say farewell."

"Mayhap because he didnae want to say that word to ye. He left because he felt he was a danger to ye, Effie, nay because he wanted to leave ye. I ken I will have trouble making ye believe me, but ye are his mate."

"And so he leaves me?"

"Aye, to keep ye safe and because he feels he isnae right for ye, would only make ye unhappy."

Fighting to think clearly, Efrica recalled the intensity of Jankyn's lovemaking over the last few days. There had been a hint of desperate greed at times. Barbara felt sure Jankyn cared for her, and now David said so. Her own instincts told her he did. She just prayed she was not fooling herself, believing he cared simply because she could not endure the pain if he did not.

"So, he left because he felt those rumors about him had grown to be a real threat?"

"Aye. I swear to ye, he would ne'er have walked away from ye if he didnae think it was for your own good."

"Weel, then, first we must silence the talk." She explained what her plan was, the one Barbara was already acting upon, and David smiled.

"Clever, lass. Then what?"

"Then I go to Cambrun, sniff out whatever cave your father has crawled into, and beat some sense into him."

"Another good plan," David said and then laughed.

Ten

"Where is he?"

Efrica marched up to her sister and her husband, ignoring their startled looks and in no mood to apologize for her abrupt entrance into their great hall. It had taken her a fortnight to get to Cambrun. She did not care to think too much on what Jankyn may have been up to during that time. As one complication after another had slowed her down, delaying her arrival at Cambrun, David's assurances about how Jankyn felt about her had lost some of their power to calm her. She wanted to trust Jankyn, to believe he would not go from her arms straight into the embrace of another woman, but she had no vows from him to cling to.

"Where is who?" asked Bridget.

Despite the look of sweet confusion and innocence upon Bridget's face, Efrica knew her sister was fully aware of *who*. Efrica suspected Barbara had written a letter. There was also the chance that David had written to his mother. She doubted Jankyn had said anything.

"Jankyn," she snapped.

"I hope ye didnae travel here alone, lass," said Cathal.

"Nay. I left the men who brought me here in the village," she replied. "Jankyn has gone to ground, hasnae he."

"He must have angered ye more than usual for ye to chase him all the way here," said Bridget.

"Sister, I truly hate to deprive ye of your sport, but I have had one wretched week of dealing with idiots at court. That was followed by a wretched week of rain, washed-out roads, broken wheels, limping horses, and men muttering about wee lasses who dinnae have the sense God gave a flea. Since I didnae start that journey in the most cheerful of moods, I am now teetering on the edge of a glorious tantrum."

"Ah, thank ye for the warning."

"My pleasure. Jankyn?"

"In the caves. He has been hiding in his room, buried in work, since he returned."

"Weel, he is about to discover that ye can run from a determined Callan lass, but ye cannae hide."

She ignored Cathal's hearty laughter and headed out to corner Jankyn in his lair. Fury carried her down into the depths of Cambrun. She faltered only briefly when she stepped into the large cavern that served as the great hall of the Purebloods, drawing every eye her way. The eldest of them, a handsome white-haired woman named Agnes, grinned and pointed to a thick iron-studded door set in the wall near the far end of the cavern.

When Efrica reached the door, she lifted her hand to knock, then changed her mind. She would not give Jankyn the chance to turn her away or lock her out. Efrica pushed aside the traitorous, weakening thought that he had left her because he did not want her, did not care for her at all, and that he was in there with another woman. As she reached for the door latch, she heard several encouraging whispers coming from the shadows behind her. They gave her the strength to open the door, step into the room, and slam the door shut behind her. The way Jankyn jumped in surprise, nearly tumbling from his perch upon the back of a stone bench, gave her a brief moment of satisfaction.

Jankyn stared at Efrica and felt his pulse leap with delight, even as shock had him gaping at her. He had not expected her to follow him, if only because of her pride. The fact that she had pleased him beyond words, until he all too clearly recalled his reasons for leaving her. Those remained unchanged. Even the truth he had uncovered about his heritage did not really change much.

"So, this is where ye came to cower and hide," she said as she walked closer to face him.

"Cower? I am nay cowering!" He scowled when she rolled her eyes and crossed her arms over her chest. "Ye heard the whispers, lass, the talk of the devil, sorcery, and demons. That brings the sort of danger that can reach out to all who stand too close to me. Aye, and sharpens the eyes of all who look at my companions. Ye cannae risk that."

"Words spit out by a jealous whore and two penniless swine who think rape is a sort of wooing."

"Nay matter who says the words, they stir fear and superstition. When such feelings are stirred up, wisdom doesnae often rear its head until they are sweeping up the ashes from the foot of your stake."

A chilling image, but not one that needed to become fact, she told herself firmly. "Ye didnae e'en try to fight the lies."

"How? By standing beneath the noonday sun?"

She ignored that. "First, one starts with the ones who dinnae like the people doing the whispering. Few of the women at court have any fondness for Lady Eleanor. Lachlan and Thomas have few friends as weel. Then, of course, one reminds certain women of just how alive and warm ye are." She was pleased by the look of horrified embarrassment that crossed his beautiful face. "The fact that said demon's son was often seen strolling about in the full light of day with his adoring betrothed, his verra red hair clear to see, was also helpful. And, of course, the crowd which saw Lachlan laid out flat by a wee lass was easily convinced that he and Thomas were naught but spineless weaklings who undoubtedly tried to hide their cowardice and ignominious defeat at your hands behind lies."

"Ye laid Lachlan out flat?"

She nodded. "His sneer annoyed me."

Jankyn stared at her in amazement. Slowly, he climbed down from his perch and walked toward her, stopping about a foot away. Any closer and he knew he would reach for her. There did not seem to be a part of him that did not ache to feel her in his arms again. That would, however, put an end to what he suspected would be an intriguing and revealing conversation.

"So, ye came here to tell me I dinnae need fear returning to court?" he asked.

"Mayhap," she replied. "Although why anyone would wish to return to that wretched place, I dinnae ken."

"Efrica, why have ye come?"

"Why did ye leave?"

"To protect you."

"Oh, aye? What if I tell ye I had the passing thought that ye nay only fled the whispers, ye fled from *me,* from *us,* and what was happening between us?"

"There may be some truth in that." He stepped close enough to reach out and briefly place a finger against her lips when she started to speak, silencing her. "I am wrong for ye, love." He waved a hand to draw her gaze to the dark, windowless cave they stood in. "This is where I live. E'en when I go aboveground, 'tis only to places as dark as these. Ye are a creature of the light, the sun. I can ne'er join ye there."

"That is sad, but it doesnae mean *I* cannae walk about in the sun whene'er the mood strikes me."

An all-too-familiar glint entered his eyes, and as he

stepped forward, she stepped back. Despite how badly she ached to be held in his arms again, she felt talking was more important now. It did appear that what David, her cousin, and her own instincts had told her was true, that Jankyn loved her, but she needed to hear the words. She also felt it was important that Jankyn hear and believe that all of her earlier doubts and fears were gone.

"I am a great many years older than ye," he said, almost smiling when, each time he stepped forward, she stepped back, for she was backing up toward his bed.

"True, and I *do* worry o'er how *ye* will feel if ye wake up one morn and see that I have aged and ye havenae."

"It willnae matter."

No words of love and no sweet flatteries, yet she believed him. "Weel, we Callans tend to be long-lived, for Outsiders."

"Good, for the day your life ends, so will mine in all the ways that matter."

Efrica felt the edge of something hit the back of her legs, but was so stunned by his words, she did not even attempt to stop herself from falling. Relieved to find a soft bed beneath her to break her fall, she propped herself up on her forearms, only to find Jankyn leaning over her, one hand on the bed on either side of her hips. She felt the heat only he could stir within her begin to flow through her veins and rushed into speech.

"And, I *do* want bairns, but if God decides we will have none, I can accept that. I have nieces and nephews to love and help care for." They were words he needed to hear, and she was determined to lay that ghost to rest before she told him the truth.

"Are ye asking me to marry ye, love?" He held her gaze with his. "Are ye truly ready to be my mate?"

"Aye, Jankyn. I love ye. I love ye more than the sun, more than anything," she replied softly.

A soft gasp of surprise escaped her as he pulled her up

into his arms and kissed her as if he was starved for the taste of her. Soon she was working as feverishly to rid him of his clothes as he was to rid her of hers. He settled her on the bed with a tenderness that only enflamed her more, and she purred with welcome and pleasure when he entered her embrace. The feel of his flesh against hers, the warmth of his lips upon her skin, and the touch of his hands soon had her trembling with need. He kept her balanced on the precipice of delight until she was nearly begging him for relief. Then, suddenly, he was there, deep inside her. Efrica felt herself shatter. As she began the tumble into the sweet abyss of desire, she felt a sharp pain on her neck, and then her release intensified tenfold.

"Efrica," Jankyn whispered when he finally regained the strength to speak. He kissed the tip of her nose and grinned over how dazed she looked. "Efrica, my heart, my mate." He kissed the hollow at the base of her throat.

"Am I your heart?" she asked, shaking free of her sated lethargy just enough to wrap her arms around him.

Jankyn smiled at her and brushed his lips over hers. "Aye, ye are. Did ye doubt it, lass?"

"A wee bit," she murmured. "Ye left me."

"Aye, to keep ye safe, to let ye find a mon who could walk in the sun with ye and fill your home with bairns. I left heart and soul behind in your wee hands, love, but I thought it was for the best."

"Weel, ye were wrong."

Before he could respond, there was a pounding on his door, and Cathal's voice cut through the thick wood. "I have the priest here. I am nay sure if our Father James will be performing a wedding or muttering last rites o'er Jankyn, but ye have five minutes ere I come in to see for myself which will be required."

Efrica echoed Jankyn's curse as they scrambled out of the bed and hurried to get dressed. Even if they stepped out of the chamber fully dressed, Efrica was certain everyone would easily guess what she and Jankyn had just been doing. Five minutes was not enough time to hide kiss-swollen lips, tidy her badly tousled hair, or find something to hide the telltale mark upon her neck.

When Jankyn opened the door, took her by the hand, and stepped out into the cavern, Efrica felt a blush heat her cheeks. Cathal, Bridget, Father James, and every Pureblood in the place stared at her and Jankyn, then stared at her neck. There was a brief moment of utter silence, then cheers and congratulations. Efrica was still reeling in surprise when Agnes and Bridget dragged her off to Agnes's chambers to try to make her look less debauched and more like a bride.

It was not until she was being escorted back to Jankyn, her hair brushed and decorated with ribbons, that Efrica realized she had been given no warnings, no words of advice, and asked no questions. "Are ye nay going to say anything, Bridget?" she asked her sister.

"Nay, ye have made your decision verra clear." She met Efrica's frown with a little smile. "The mark, Efrica. I ken, mayhap better than any other, that ye would ne'er have allowed him to mark ye as his mate unless ye were fully committed—heart, soul, and mind. Aye, and Jankyn would ne'er have marked ye his mate unless he felt the same."

Agnes patted her arm. "I ken 'tis difficult for ye who arenae born MacNachtons to understand, but when Jankyn took from ye e'en as he gave to ye, the bond was made and it cannae be broken."

Efrica blushed, realizing that everyone knew exactly *when* she had been given her mark. Then Jankyn was at her side, taking her hand in his and tugging her before the priest. He looked so proud, so pleased, she lost the last of her embarrassment. Smiling at him as she knelt by his side, she repeated her vows in a clear, steady voice. As Jankyn spoke his vows, she knew he meant each and every word.

* * *

The soft light from many candles gave Jankyn's skin an intriguing glow, Efrica decided as she ran her fingers up and down his strong arm. The celebration of their marriage had been all any bride could hope for, and Efrica felt truly welcomed into the clan. There was little of the anger and resentment that Bridget's marriage to Cathal had caused. She suspected each child born to the clan had thrown a little more water on the lingering fires of rebellion within the clan.

Jankyn moved to lie beside her, propping himself up on one elbow. "What are ye thinking of, love?'

"That the Purebloods are finally seeing that your laird is right, that the MacNachtons cannae remain alone, a breed apart, and survive."

Idly caressing her stomach, Jankyn nodded then sighed. "Love, I dinnae say this to give ye hope as it might prove a false one, but I am nay as pure of blood as I thought. There is more Outsider blood in me than the wee drop or two I thought I had. In the days when the Nightriders rode, spreading fear and death, some of my direct ancestors also spread their seed. The bairns born of those unions were usually cast out to die, considered demons and the devil's evil spawn, but my kinsmen saved a few. The ones saved were my ancestors. They married Purebloods, of course, so I cannae say how much Outsider blood I have, but 'tis more than I was led to believe. It doesnae, however, mean that I can give ye a bairn. I—" He frowned beneath the silencing finger she placed against his lips.

"It was obviously enough."

Jankyn inhaled so swiftly, he coughed. "What do ye mean?"

"I mean that I already carry your child." She grinned at his look of shock.

"But ye spoke earlier as if ye still feared there would be no bairns."

"I spoke thus because I needed *ye* to ken that it didnae matter to me, needed ye to believe it. This may be the only bairn we e'er have, and I needed ye to understand that it *truly* doesnae matter."

He held his hand flat against her stomach and whispered, "Are ye certain?"

"That, my bonnie husband, is one thing a Callan always kens for certain." She felt tears sting her eyes when he tenderly kissed her stomach. "Ye are pleased?"

"Och, daft lass. I was pleased beyond words that ye came after me, that ye wished to be my true mate. This? This is a miracle, a gift from God that leaves me truly humble." He pulled her into his arms and kissed her. "I love ye, my wee cat. I dinnae deserve such happiness, but I will accept and hold fast to it. I will spend my life making sure ye ne'er regret becoming my wife, my mate."

"Just love me, Jankyn. Tis all I need. Weel, that and, mayhap, ye making me purr now and then."

Jankyn laughed. "How about now?"

"Twill do for a start."

His Eternal
Bride

Adrienne Basso

One

Scottish Highlands
Late summer, 1321

A clash of swords, anguished cries, and the coppery scent of fresh blood shattered the peaceful calm of the night. Anaxandra's legs tightened instinctively around her mount as she halted her horse, which was ambling through the forest at a slow gait. Stiffening, she raised her head, her ears alert to every sound.

Her companion pulled beside her, negotiating the densely wooded path with difficulty. "The sounds of battle are near," he said, his brow knitting together with concern. "These Highlanders are said to be a fierce and combative race, and they enjoy pursuing their enemies at night."

Anaxandra smiled. "I know. Tis why I wanted to come, so I could see it for myself."

A high-pitched scream wretched through the air, causing the horses to jump and paw the ground nervously. It took effort to calm the jittery beasts.

"We should come away," Anaxandra's companion, Randulf, urged, tugging on the sleeve of her gown. But

Anaxandra ignored the summons, and turned her mount toward the sounds of the fighting. Under her command, the animal increased its stride, bringing her deeper into the low-hanging forest, ever closer to danger.

She did not bother to check if Randulf followed, confident he would obey her directive. Perhaps it was reckless to venture so near a battle, but danger of any sort was always appealing to Anaxandra.

She was a female who did as she pleased, who followed her whims and allowed her passionate and volatile nature to rule her actions. She was a creature of power and influence among her kind, and though many had tried, there was no male who dominated her life or made demands upon her person.

The long-suffering Randulf was her self-appointed guardian, and she tolerated his presence because he amused her. He, in turn, worshipped Anaxandra, defending her against all criticism and tolerating without complaint her uneven moods and streaks of temper.

The noise of the fighting grew louder as they followed a rocky outcropping up a hill until they reached the crest. The pair tried to remain as quiet as possible, fearing detection, but they soon discovered this precaution was unnecessary.

In the small clearing below, two groups of men fought with fierce determination, unaware of anything but the struggle that consumed them. The sides were composed of uneven numbers, but it soon became apparent that the smaller force possessed the greater fighting skills.

"English," Randulf whispered in her ear. "They have more men, yet they appear to be losing this fight."

Anaxandra nodded in agreement. The English knights were mounted on destriers protected by armor and carried both sword and shield. Battle-axes, billhooks, and iron ball-and-chains hung from their belts. Their faces were obscured by helmets, but even at this distance Anaxandra could see their eyes were filled with hatred.

Ignoring Randulf's pleas to stay hidden, Anaxandra urged her horse closer, craving a better view. The Highlanders were mounted on smaller horses, and neither man nor beast wore armor. The Scots carried no shields, only large, long-bladed swords they lifted with both hands as they attacked.

The initial impact of those heavy swords upon ironclad flesh was horrendous. One by one the English knights were gradually unseated, and they dropped like stones upon the hard ground.

Those who were not dead or unconscious soon rose to their feet, swords drawn. A few of the Highlanders also dismounted, ready to engage their enemy in final combat. The melee that followed was horrific, but one Highland warrior quickly caught Anaxandra's eye, for he fought not only with strength and skill but with absolute confidence.

He hacked his way through the center of the English, and when he lost his sword, he flipped his opponent's helmet off and elbowed the man in the face, snapping his head back. The knight staggered for a moment, then came back for more.

The Highlander was ready. He punched him in the face, striking his nose. Blood spurted in a high arch as the bigger man reeled and fell, clutching his face in agony.

"Callum!"

The Highlander turned at the call, easily catching the claymore that was tossed his way. He wiped the blood off his palm down the front of his shirt, then transferred the weapon to his dry hand.

Sword held high above his head, the Highlander charged toward three knights, letting out the most terrifying, barbaric snarl Anaxandra had ever heard uttered from human lips.

The sound made every hair on her body stand up as if in response.

"He is magnificent," she whispered in awe.

Her gaze remained riveted on his face. It was strong, arrogant, fearless. In the moonlight his eyes were a silvery blue. Cold, piercing, and deadly, they were filled with a mad glint of bloodlust. Anaxandra shivered with delight.

Soon, only one English knight remained, cornered against a large tree trunk. A ring of Scots encircled him.

"What do ye say, lads?" a Highlander on horseback called out. "Should we show him mercy?"

"English swine. They killed innocent women and children and tortured an old man for amusement." The Scottish warrior turned his head and spat. "Skewer the bastard."

The deed was accomplished swiftly and with far too much mercy for Anaxandra's taste.

The tension of the night eased, and the mood of the soldiers turned jovial. Laughing and joking, the Highlanders quickly stripped their vanquished enemies of armor, weapons, and clothing.

"Shall we bury the dead?" one man asked.

"No," the man called Callum replied. "Leave them for the wolves and vultures. Tis what they deserve."

Weighed down with their spoils, the Highlanders departed the glen, leaving behind a tangle of naked bodies, the ground on which they lay steeped in blood.

There was deadly silence once they had departed. Anaxandra slid from her horse and walked among the carnage, her mind replaying the intense battle and the skill of one Scottish warrior in particular. She had to see him again!

How long Anaxandra stood there, she could not say. A restless stirring beside her roused her from her near catatonic state.

"The bodies are still warm," Randulf announced. "Tis foolish to waste such bounty."

Anaxandra's stomach lurched. She usually enjoyed the hunt as much as the kill, but on occasion was not averse to have others do the work. Yet for some reason the notion held little appeal.

"I have no need of sustenance," she said. "If you wish to feast, be quick."

With a cry of glee, Randulf fell upon the bodies and the sounds of his suckling cut through the silence. Anaxandra mounted her horse and waited impatiently for him to finish. Finally sated, he returned, and Anaxandra led the way through the dense forest.

They came through the woods on the fringe of the keep and tied their horses to a fallen tree trunk. Through the darkness, a noisy celebration could be heard from behind the stone walls that encircled the castle.

"We walk from here," Anaxandra announced.

"What?" Randulf exclaimed. "You cannot enter that dwelling. These Highlanders are a close, tight-knit group that do not take kindly to strangers. You saw what they did to the English."

"But I am not their enemy," Anaxandra retorted. "They will have no cause to harm me."

"Lucifer's horns!" Randulf cursed loudly and hurried to keep stride with Anaxandra. "Unescorted females do not suddenly appear on the doorstep in the middle of the night. Your arrival will cause great suspicion and raise questions you cannot answer."

"I can hardly arrive in the daytime with a proper escort and chaperon," Anaxandra snapped.

"You should not go at all!" Randulf insisted, and when Anaxandra did not stop walking, he hissed, "Your stubborn defiance will get you killed."

"It will take more than a broad Scottish sword to end my existence," Anaxandra retorted.

Her step did not falter even when she realized that

Randulf did not follow. Perhaps it was best—it should be easier for one, rather than two, to slip in unobserved. Though her heart pumped in a nervous beat, Anaxandra did not slow as she drew closer to the castle.

The keep was a large, two-story structure with a square tower on each of the four corners. A walkway connected the corners, and there were sentries posted at equal intervals across its entire length. Obviously, the clan had made good use of the abundant amount of stone in the area, having constructed the majority of the dwelling from it.

For further protection, there was an outer wall of stone. A sturdy log bridge provided the only entrance through this formidable barrier. The bridge was lowered and crowded with people intent on entering the castle to join in the celebration.

Anaxandra quietly joined their ranks and passed through the great curtained wall of stone without incident. With hood drawn and head bowed, she entered the great hall. As she had predicted, there was so much jovial excitement that no one initially questioned her presence or challenged her attendance.

Still, Anaxandra tried to keep to the shadows. But the lime-whited walls of the great hall reflected the light from the many torches positioned throughout the room, giving it a brightness she found disconcerting. There was such a crush of people she was hardly noticed, yet as she strayed too far into the center of the room, a group of young women gathered together in a circle tossed her curious looks.

Anaxandra pulled back to the edges of the wall, trying to lose their gaze. Though she had spouted words of bravado in front of Randulf, she was not a fool. There would be no way to protect or defend herself if anyone decided to question her.

She also knew her greatest threat would come from the

women, not the men. Anaxandra's erotic beauty had always been cause for great jealousy among females. It was part of the reason she had always roamed so freely in the mortal world—it helped to avoid the malice of the other females of her kind.

She lifted a flagon of ale from a servant hurrying by with a full tray, then drank and watched, searching for her warrior. She expected him to be seated in a place of honor, but there was no high table on a raised dais in this hall, only rows of wooden tables set at equal heights.

The tables were filled with boisterous men and women, eating, drinking, laughing, and singing. A few were even dancing. Servants scurried along with a hurried purpose, attempting to keep the trenchers full of food and the drinking vessels topped with ale and wine.

Anaxandra continued to cling to the edges of the hall, the rushes beneath her feet giving off the fresh sweet scent of mint with each step she took. Her eyes continued to search among the many male faces in the hall, and just when she began to wonder if she would ever find her warrior again, he appeared.

He was garbed in a clean white shirt, with a blue and black plaid worn casually over his left shoulder. His dark hair waved back from the broad plane of his brow and shoulders, and the hard line of his granite jaw softened as he laughed and joked with the men who surrounded him.

Fascinated, Anaxandra moved closer. In the light of the hall she could now see an expression of inner fire in his eyes, a fire so intense it threatened to consume all who dared to venture too close. It was that fire that had first captivated her, that she now craved.

She knew in that instant that fate had at long last bestowed upon her what she had always desired—a worthy mate. Never before had she beheld anyone who inspired such longing within her, who drew her close and held her fast. Surely he was more than a mere mortal man, for he'd cast a spell on her that she was powerless to break.

Anaxandra's heart raced with excitement. She had to get him alone! But how? He was surrounded by companions, clearly the center of attention. Her foot tapped impatiently on the hard stone floor until she realized he was drinking far more than he was eating. Eventually, he would have to leave the hall to answer nature's call.

Her observation proved true. Within the hour, the warrior left the circle of soldiers. She followed his progress doggedly with her eyes, then positioned herself in the archway where he exited.

The moment he returned from the garderobe, Anaxandra pushed herself directly in his path. Their eyes locked and Anaxandra's breath caught. She found herself lost, floating in the deep passion of his eyes, and for an instant she was speechless with wonder.

His brow lifted. "What are ye looking for, lass?"

"You," she whispered, feeling a flash of heat at the sound of his deep voice.

He smiled, revealing a row of strong, even white teeth. "Now, how can that be? We have no acquaintance with each other."

"Are you certain?" A slow, seductive smile spread across her face as she placed her hand against the center of his chest. His heart beat fiercely under her palm. Unable to resist, her fingers began to slip over the hard muscles. Anaxandra heard him suck in a sharp breath. "I know you well enough to give you great pleasure. And to take pleasure from you in return."

His brow furrowed, as though he was trying to remember if he did indeed have an acquaintance with her.

Catching him in a mesmerizing stare, Anaxandra summoned forth all the feminine wiles she had learned through the ages. "I am a bold woman, mighty warrior. Bolder than any you have ever known."

Passion running high, she traced the tips of her fingers over the hard rippled muscles of his stomach, then lower, until her fingers brushed against the front of his kilt. He groaned deep in his throat. Anaxandra smiled, then repeated the motion, this time touching his rigid penis. Impatience made her rough, but the warrior did not seem to mind.

Triumphant, she pressed him against the stone wall and leaned all her weight into him.

"Who are ye?" he whispered.

"Your destiny," she answered.

Callum McGinnis's head could not seem to stop spinning. He knew he had drunk far too much ale, but this victory celebration over the English had been hard fought. The rogue band of knights that had been terrorizing the people of his clan for months was now destroyed, and it was a relief to finally rid them all of the tyranny.

Since arriving at the great hall, he had joined his men in toast after toast, and clearly the alcohol he had consumed was making him hallucinate. For surely at any moment he would wake from this erotic, outrageous dream and find himself alone, his rod stiff with wanting, his balls heavy and tight.

This strange, unknown female could not be real. A mysterious raven-haired woman dressed in an unusual-looking gown of scarlet, with eyes as dark as midnight, skin as pale as snow, and hands as bold as a courtesan.

"Why fight it? What is there to keep us from taking our pleasure together?" she breathed raggedly in his ear as she took his hand and placed it on her breast.

For an instant, Callum could not breathe. The air felt weighted, too thick to drag into his lungs. Though his mind insisted she must be a vision, at this moment she felt very solid and real. Nearly every part of his body ached, taut and ready, urgent with desire.

He reached out with his other hand and traced her winged eyebrow with one finger, fighting to understand the impossible allure of this dark, wicked beauty. The passion he felt gathered power and beat through his body in a thundering rush.

"You need not be so gentle, my warrior. I am not in search of tender wooing."

As if to prove her point, she lifted her chin and caught his finger in her mouth. She tongued it playfully, then bit down hard, drawing blood.

"Och!" Callum yelped and tried to extract his wounded digit, but she began to suck on it, holding it deep within the cavity of her warm, wet mouth.

He closed his eyes and hissed in pleasure, fantasizing it was his penis so snugly engulfed. Somehow he knew that all he need do was voice his request and the woman would drop to her knees. It was tempting, ahh, so tempting.

"We need more ale and meat pies and another barrel of wine," a calm voice announced. "And ask Rowen to fetch more wood for the kitchen fires. There are several haunches of venison that are only half-roasted."

Maev! The sound of her familiar voice startled Callum back to reality. Mustering every bit of his considerable will, he dropped the hand clutching the woman's bosom to his side and pulled his finger out of her mouth.

The female whimpered in distress and tried to recapture her prize, but he held her off and swallowed his desire. This was wrong. He knew it in his head, but more importantly, he knew it in his heart.

"Maev, lass, I heard ye calling for help." Callum removed himself from the shadowed archway and brought himself into the light. "Is there anything I can do for ye?"

Maev McClosky placed one delicate hand on her hip and

shot her betrothed a withering stare. "Nay, I can manage. Besides, it looks like ye already have yer hands full."

Callum felt a wave of guilty heat rush over his cheeks. He turned toward the archway, but the mysterious woman had disappeared.

"I was returning from the garderobe," he said slowly, raking his hand over his face, trying to piece together in his mind exactly what had happened. "Suddenly a woman appeared, wanting to speak with me. I dinna know who she was—I'm sure I've never seen her before."

"Hmmm." Maev gave him her back and continued issuing orders to the serving lad as if nothing unusual had occurred. Her dismissive gesture increased Callum's guilt tenfold.

He waited until she was finished, then grabbed her hand to prevent her from running away. She turned to him and Callum's heart jolted at the sight of her proud, beautiful face. Her features were refined, her skin fair and smooth, her almond-shaped eyes bright green and intelligent.

He had known her since they were children, but it was only in the past year he had discovered that he loved her. Fiercely, passionately, and with such determined single-mindness that the mere thought of any man so much as looking at her for too long drove his thoughts to murder.

"I put my hand on her breast," he blurted out sheepishly. The priest was always telling him that confession was good for the soul, yet at this moment it did not feel very good.

"Did ye now?" Maev tilted her head to one side and appeared to be considering the matter most carefully. "I suppose I canna blame ye, Callum. Though I caught only a fleeting glimpse of her, she certainly had a magnificent bosom."

Callum did not know what to make of Maev's casual attitude. If the positions had been reversed, he would have already dispatched the man who dared to lay a hand on his future wife to hell. "Ye're supposed to be jealous, Maev."

"Och, I am?"

"Yes, ye are." Callum lifted his lips into his most charming smile. "As nephew of the laird, I am considered a prized matrimonial catch. Yet ye are the woman I have chosen."

"We chose each other." Her eyes sparkled like green fire. "Though when you start acting too full of yerself, I wonder at the sanity of my decision. And dinna be expecting to hear any words of flattery or praise falling from my lips. There are more than enough folks clamoring to fill that role. I swear to the Almighty, if ye hear much more of that kind of talk, yer head will swell so big it willna fit through the door."

Her sharp words were spoken in a teasing manner, and for a moment Callum believed Maev had dismissed the incident. Yet she stood there in thought for several heartbeats, and he watched her face gradually turn troubled. He focused on that lovely face, feeling the pain he had caused her with his thoughtless actions.

"It meant nothing," Callum said, feeling a sudden rush of sobriety. He waited anxiously while Maev considered his words.

"I have to know that I can trust ye," she said solemnly. "Even when the women are practically throwing themselves at ye, questing for yer attention and regard."

He felt his face flush. "Ye can trust me, lass. Tis you I love, Maev. Now and always."

Callum stepped forward and ran his hand possessively over her back. Maev was small and delicate; her bones felt fragile beneath his fingers. But within her delicate body was a strong spirit. It was one of the things he admired most about her. She would not be a wife who submitted docilely to his commands, but would question and speak her mind regardless of the consequences.

Once given, her loyalty was unshakable, her support

rock solid. With Maev by his side, Callum knew he would be a better leader and, more importantly, a better man.

Using his knuckles, he gently traced a path along her cheekbone up to her temple. He repeated the motion over and over until Maev closed her eyes and swayed toward him.

This simple act of forgiveness unleashed all the desperate love bursting from Callum's heart. He cupped Maev's cheek and slowly bent his head down until their lips met.

She made a mewing sound, and for an instant he feared she protested. But then Callum felt the tremor that ran the length of her body as Maev turned her head to catch his mouth more fully. Unleashing his restraint, Callum parted his lips and slid his tongue into her mouth, tasting her sweetness.

Her arms lifted and tightened around his neck as she surrendered blissfully, raking her fingers through his hair, arching her body against his. His knees nearly weakened at the need that flowed from her body to his, and he groaned loudly as her eager movement roused the full length of his penis.

Reaching out, he traced a finger along the outer roundness of her breast. Maev gasped with delight and he grew bolder, dragging his thumb back and forth across her nipple. Each delicate caress brought forth a shiver of passion in her, and each of those shivers drove his own passion higher and higher.

Even through the layers of clothing, the heat of Maev's flesh seared him. He positioned their bodies so they were pressed hip to hip, with his hardness intimately touching her feminine softness. One hand roamed boldly down the swell of her buttocks, and the blood began to thunder in his head.

"Must we stop, my love?" he groaned, tearing his mouth

away from hers, kissing a path along the slender line of her jaw.

"I fear so," she squawked as she sprang back from him.

Holding tightly to his control, Callum sighed heavily. He knew this was coming, though it was always a physical disappointment to hear the verdict. Their heated embraces always ended well before consummation because Maev had decided she needed to remain a virgin until they were wed, and no matter how passionate their lovemaking got, she never strayed from the course.

Maev took another step away from him, then cast him a strange, sideline glance. He sensed her sudden anxiety. Perhaps seeing him intimately engaged with the mysterious stranger was causing her to rethink her decision about their physical relationship.

Yet as much as he longed to posses her completely, he did not want to win her under those circumstances. Maev deserved better.

Her absence from his embrace left Callum with an ache of emptiness, as if an essential part of his being was gone. Knowing he could at least alleviate that discomfort, he slid his arm around Maev's shoulders and drew her to nestle against his chest. She trembled, and he ran his hand beneath her hair to gently caress the nape of her neck.

"I'm sure ye think me daft for insisting that we wait until we are wed," Maev whispered. She let out a shuddering breath. "'Tis just that it means so much to me."

Her words faltered. Callum sighed again, tipped his head, and planted feather-like kisses on her eyebrows, cheeks, and chin. This enforced celibacy was one of the most difficult things he ever had to endure, but it was so important to Maev and therefore important to him.

"I think ye are determined to test my warrior's strength, Maev McClosky," Callum said in a light teasing tone. "And though I might be suffering, lass, I'll not be broken."

"Aye," she answered with a sudden smile. "There's no one in all of Scotland that can best ye."

"Flattery, Maev? Do ye dare risk it?" Callum wiggled his brows in an exaggerated motion. "Willna my head be swelling too big for the doorway?"

"Yer head is the least of the swelling parts that concern me at the moment, Callum McGinnis," Maev replied with a saucy wink. "Now stop yer teasing and come help me carry up a fresh barrel of ale."

With a good-natured groan, he followed her out of the hall, hardly believing he took no offense at having to perform such a menial task. When feeling bold, his men dared to tease him about his devotion to his future wife, but Callum turned a deaf ear to their jests.

Respect. It was not an emotion he ever expected to feel in connection to any woman, but Maev inspired it in him. She was everything he wanted, and more, and he ached with the truth of knowing he would never love another living creature as much as he loved Maev.

The sky was dark, with the clouds hanging low and leaden, but Anaxandra knew dawn was fast approaching.

"We must seek shelter," Randulf urged, and though she longed to disagree, Anaxandra knew she had no choice.

They were creatures of the night, part of a race of immortals that could not tolerate even the slightest kiss of sunlight. To do so would cause great pain and threaten their survival.

"I remember a section of caves located on the far side of the mountain," Anaxandra said. "If we hurry, we should reach them before the light appears."

Randulf nodded. They drove the horses to a full gallop, then abandoned the animals when the climb became too steep. With the waning moon as their guide, they trudged through the mist that enveloped their feet and legs, searching with increasing desperation for a cave deep enough to shut out the sunlight.

"Here, I've found one," Randulf declared with relief. "The opening is not very large, but the cavern is deep."

"We will have to make do," Anaxandra replied. "There is no time to find another."

As they pushed themselves inside, fighting to find the depths of darkness, Anaxandra replayed the events of the night in her mind. The warrior had been perfect, the essence of all that she needed and desired. Yet she had failed to dazzle and capture him.

Bile rose in her throat as she remembered the melodic sound of the Scottish woman's voice. It was that sound that had caused the warrior to turn away from her. Though she had not lingered overlong, Anaxandra had seen that the other female was small and delicate, clearly an unworthy mate for such a skilled warrior.

A crushing sense of loss struck Anaxandra, but she pushed it from her mind. This was not over. When the time was right, she would return.

And when she left, she would not be alone.

Two

Three months later

The late morning sun shone with a bright, clear brilliance, yet it could not obliterate the gusts of a cool breeze that hinted of winter's close arrival. There were some members of the clan who had fretted over the day's weather, but Maev was not one of them. She cared not if it rained or snowed or rained *and* snowed. There was no force of nature strong enough to dampen her spirits on this magical day—her wedding day.

"Hold still, Maev, or else I'll never get this wreath of flowers to lay straight on yer head."

Maev took a deep breath and tried to obey her mother's orders, but it was difficult. Her nerves were a tangled mass, and the only bit of relief she could find was in constant movement.

"All done?" Maev asked in a restless tone, straining to see her reflection in the thin sliver of mirror that was one of her mother's most prized possessions.

"Goodness, lass, ye'd try the patience of a saint!" the older woman exclaimed, but after a final adjustment, she stepped aside to let Maev view the results of their morning's work.

"Is that really me?" Maev asked in a quiet voice.

"Aye," her mother replied, tears gathering in the corners of her eyes. "And a more beautiful bride the McGinnis Clan has never seen."

A broad smile crept across Maev's face at her mother's words. With a sigh of delight, Maev ran her fingers over the delicate material of her emerald green kirtle. The fabric had been a gift from Callum, and she and her mother had spent hours enhancing its natural beauty with carefully stitched gold embroidery around the neck and sleeves.

At her mother's suggestion, they had paired the dress with a red chemise undergown and the result was colorful and vibrant. Maev's golden blond hair hung down to the center of her back. It had been dressed with red ribbons and pearls, then a wreath of fresh flowers had been positioned on the top of her head like a crown.

"I feel like a princess," Maev said as she took an unsteady breath. "I hope Callum recognizes me when I arrive at the church."

"I imagine he'll have eyes for no one else," her mother replied.

Swallowing her emotions of joy, Maev turned and gave her mother a heartfelt hug. Though Brenda McClosky had not given birth to her, she was the only mother Maev had ever known. Brought to the village as the sole survivor of a brutal attack on a poorly guarded group of pilgrims by a rogue band of outlaws, the infant girl, whom no one else wanted, had been taken in by the kindhearted, recently widowed Brenda.

The bodies of the pilgrims had been stripped bare, leaving no clue as to the babe's heritage. Many of the clan feared she was tainted with foul English blood and would have naught to do with her, but Brenda dismissed such claims as superstitious nonsense.

As Maev grew older, her new mother demanded acceptance for her adopted daughter that was eventually, if grudgingly, given. Maev, in turn, adored her mother, appreciating all her care and sacrifice, and they shared a close, loving bond.

A rap at the door to their small cottage interrupted the bridal preparations. With an eager smile, Brenda opened the door, admitting a young soldier.

"'Tis time," he said. "Callum has sent me to escort the bride and her mother to the church."

Though polite, the lad did not seem eager for the task, no doubt believing that it was an unmanly request to make of a warrior.

"I am ready," Maev declared, stepping forward into the sunshine.

When he caught sight of her, the young soldier was so startled that his eyes widened. Feeling a rush of feminine power, Maev preened for him. "Is anything wrong?" she asked.

"Ye're a vision." The lad's cheeks flamed scarlet when he realized he had spoken his thoughts aloud.

A glowing smile crept across Maev's face. "I thank ye for yer pretty compliment. Now we must make haste, or else I shall be late."

The trio stepped outside into the bright sunlight. Maev broke into a smile when she caught sight of the magnificent horse Callum had sent for her. Pure white from head to hoof, the large stallion's freshly washed and brushed coat gleamed like starlight. A garland of wild flowers had been wound through the horse's mane, and beneath the saddle was an elaborately embroidered cloth that trailed to the ground.

Once Maev was atop the great beast, Brenda fussed with her gown, trying to ensure it would not crease overmuch. When Brenda was finally satisfied, they set off. Strutting importantly, the young soldier led the horse, and Brenda walked proudly beside her daughter. Maev did indeed feel like royalty when she entered the main section of the castle courtyard perched upon the impressive white stallion.

There were smiles and compliments from the waiting crowd as she rode past, though Maev could not fail to notice that many of the comments were restrained. A subtle yet strong reminder that most members of the clan thought she was marrying far above her station and would have preferred Callum to have selected one of their daughters or sisters or nieces as his bride. Though she had lived among them all her life, Maev knew that many would always view her as an outsider.

Yet nothing could dampen her joy on this magical day. The emotions shivered in her chest and weakened her knees when she first caught sight of her groom. Their eyes met and Callum smiled broadly, a smile so genuine and happy that Maev felt as if someone had gripped her lungs and squeezed.

He was such a handsome man—and he was all hers! His dark thick hair had been combed to some measure of order, though it was worn far longer than any other and his clean-shaven jaw was square and determined. There was a large silver broach studded with precious jewels pinned to the plaid on his shoulder, and the bare legs beneath his kilt were lean and strong.

She dipped her chin, feeling a sudden burst of shyness, and when she raised her head, Callum's eyes sparkled back at her, filled with love. The last of her nuptial nerves vanished in an instant, and Maev knew that more than anything else in the world, she wanted to see that expression every day of her life.

In keeping with the old tradition, the bridal couple stood outside the church, so all could witness the exchange of vows. The gentle breeze set the women's brightly colored veils to fluttering, the cool air providing a welcome relief among the tightly packed crowd.

"Is there anyone here who can give reason why these vows should not be taken?" the priest demanded.

Maev held her breath and listened to the rustling of the people clustered behind her as the clan members shifted on their feet and looked toward one another. She was painfully aware of the small jealousies among some of the women toward her, especially since she was marrying the future laird.

Maev let out her breath when the priest gave a nod of satisfaction, relieved that no one would publicly voice any objection. She turned her head and kept her gaze steadily on Callum, drawing strength from his strong and steady demeanor.

"Join hands," the priest commanded.

Maev willingly complied, marveling anew at how the hands of a man who wielded a broadsword with such deadly ease possessed such a gentle touch. She repeated her vows in a loud voice, wanting everyone to hear. The ring of gold Callum placed on her finger felt warm and comforting, tangible proof of the bond they now shared.

"What God has united in holy matrimony, let no man dissolve. You may seal yer pledge with the kiss of peace."

Maev raised her face expectantly. Callum, it appeared, needed no further encouragement. He swept her into his arms and captured her lips in a searing kiss that sent her heart fluttering.

At his action, a mighty roar of approval went up from the men, echoing through the courtyard. A few of the women let out small sighs. Now that all had borne witness to the couple exchanging vows in the open courtyard, the crowd pressed forward into the church to celebrate mass.

When that ended, the couple received a final blessing and then the real celebration started. The great hall was soon filled to near bursting as everyone indulged in the elaborate wedding feast.

The best hunters of the clan had set out for three days in search of the choicest animals, and the most skilled cooks had turned the meat into countless mouthwatering delights. No expense had been spared in food or drink or decoration for the laird's nephew.

Maev and Callum sat together on a raised dais in the center of the hall, holding hands beneath the table and smiling with unconcealed joy. Course after course of sumptuous food was served, and both the wine and ale flowed freely. When the guests were sated with food and drink, the dancing began.

The bride and groom joined in, and Maev was soon breathless as she was passed from one eager partner to the next. The sound of so many footsteps on the stone floor thundered up into the hall's wooden rafters and mingled with the music and laughter.

As the tune became livelier, Callum tightened his grip on Maev's hand and pulled her from the dance. She stumbled, staggering for several steps until Callum caught her by the upper arms to steady her. Laughing, she braced her hands on his chest and then realized he had maneuvered her into a small room.

She noted briefly that it was the chamber where the castle steward did the accounts, but her interest in her surroundings ended the moment Callum reached up and framed her face with his hands.

"Finally, a moment alone," he declared, bending his head. His mouth teased hers open, and he eagerly thrust his tongue inside. Maev sucked upon it hungrily. He tasted marvelous, like spiced wine and excited male.

Caught in the passion of his kisses, Maev leaned into

Callum's hard strength. His lips and tongue stroked and explored her mouth, then he was kissing her neck and biting her earlobe and nipping a path down her sensitive neck to her shoulder.

"Sweet Maev," he whispered. With the back of his hand he stroked possessively across the peak of one breast.

Maev quivered helplessly as her nipples tightened and ached, sensitive even through the layers of fabric. Need for him flooded her, pulsing and demanding.

"Ye are too beautiful," he whispered. "And I love ye too much."

Then he lowered his head and gently bit her nipple through her garments. She gasped and he nibbled at it again, while tweaking the other with his fingers.

"Callum," she cried, arching her back, hugging his dark head against her, her fingers slipping through the thick, silky waves of his hair.

His throat vibrated with deep sounds, and Maev realized she, too, was moaning. The room around them blurred, and all the thoughts in her head were pushed aside by passion and need. Roughly, he lifted her and set her on the edge of the wooden table where the accounts were done. Her senses forgot everything but Callum as he spread her legs and pressed himself against her, ignoring the garments bunched between them.

Maev cried out at the feeling of sinful excitement. Did he intend to take her now, while their bridal feast continued just beyond the open door?

Willingly, her arms circled his neck, fitting her even more intimately against him. She felt his hand sliding up her inner thigh, then brushing lightly against her curls. Widening the angle between her thighs, he parted her swollen flesh, exploring until he found the silken pearl that throbbed at his touch.

Maev gasped against his mouth. Every portion of her

body came alive. Her blood ran faster, her skin burned hotter. Callum's mouth continued to torment her with deep kisses, his hands inflamed her with slow, sweeping caresses. She tottered on the edge of pure abandon, her will crumbling in ruins about her. It was not the ideal place to lose her virginity, but logic had no place where passion reigned so strongly.

Callum slid his other hand down to pull her skirt up higher, baring the skin of her hips and thighs. The rush of cold air on her heated flesh startled her, and suddenly Maev froze as she felt a cold sense of horror invade her soul. She imagined the raised brows and snide whispers if she could not produce a wedding sheet tomorrow morning stained with her virgin's blood, proof of her honor and worthiness to wed the future laird.

With a cry of regret, Maev pulled away. Pangs of apprehension went through her stomach. She looked into her beloved's eyes, their faces so close that their noses were nearly touching.

"Can we not wait until we have more time to pleasure each other? Please, Callum, I dinna want this first encounter to be so hasty."

"I burn for ye, Maev," Callum declared. His breathing was harsh, his face looked pained. "I fear our first time together will be over very quickly, at least for me." He let out a grim smirk. "But I shall not force ye."

Maev groaned. "Och, Callum, 'tis as much a sacrifice for me as it is for ye." She kissed him hard, trying to convey her own sense of passion and physical need. "I burn for ye as well."

He took her hand and placed it at the junction of his thighs. "This is what ye do to me," he said in a husky voice as he rubbed her fingers against the hard length of his fully aroused penis.

Turning her hand, Maev let her fingertips graze along the

length, lingering at the velvety tip. A few drops of moisture escaped and she gently massaged them into his skin. Then she reached lower and toyed briefly with his heavy balls. "Do ye want me to . . . to bring ye some relief?" Maev whispered, remembering the night she had closed her fingers around his warm, pulsing flesh and had stroked and pulled, quickening the pace until his jaw clenched and his entire body tightened and his warm seed had spurted.

Her fingers moved faster as she recalled the intimate act and the pleasure it had brought both of them.

Callum audibly sucked in air. He groaned loudly as his penis flexed inside the sheath of her fingers. Then he gritted his teeth and pushed her hand away. "No." He took a deep breath. "Yer hand willna satisfy me today. I want to thrust myself deep inside ye, where it's hot and tight. I want to take my time teasing and tasting every inch of yer lovely body." His voice was a little slurred, as if he was drunk on passion.

Maev's lips curved in a wobbly smile. Never had she loved him more than in that moment. She reached up and smoothed the hair back from his forehead. "If we rush the rest of the toasts and cut off the speeches before they get too long, we can be alone in our bedchamber within the hour."

Callum's handsome face broke into a wide, mischievous grin. "I always knew ye were a clever lass, Maev McGinnis." He pulled her close and kissed her, then gripped her hips between his hands and set her on her feet. They fussed with each other for a few moments, making sure their garments were back in place.

Then laughing like a pair of naughty children, they entered the hall and rejoined the celebration.

Callum sighed with satisfaction as his gaze raked over the naked body of his bride. She was extraordinary. Illuminated in the candlelight, her body was a thing of great and rare beauty. Every inch of it. The nape of her neck, the hollow of her throat, the line of her shoulders.

Her breasts were small but perfectly formed, the nipples a dark rose. Her waist was narrow, her hips curved with womanly roundness, and the golden curls between her thighs looked soft and delicate.

No woman should ever be so tempting. He had waited nearly a year to claim her, and now, aroused by the sight of her pale, pink flesh, his heart pounded in anticipation of finally achieving what he had craved for so long.

She was staring at him with an intensity he had only dreamed of, eliciting a powerful need in him to satisfy her in every possible way.

"Are ye frightened?" Callum asked. "I've heard it can be painful for a lass her first time."

"I'm not afraid. Mother told me the pain is sharp, yet brief." Her face broke into a shy smile. "I love ye, Callum. There is nothing I would not do to please ye."

She took a few steps closer. He could feel the warmth of her body, smell the flowery scent of her lovely skin. Her glorious hair surrounded her body like a silken veil of spun gold, and he could barely contain his need to run his hands through it.

Nothing could spoil this incredible moment.

Yet as he approached his bride, a shiver of unease passed through Callum's body. Something was wrong. Battle instincts honed through years of rough warfare made him turn in alarm.

The door was barred shut from the inside, just as he had left it, but there was a movement in the far corner of the room, a shadowy figure of evil. The hair on Callum's nape started to prickle. Naked and defenseless, he lunged toward his sword, which had been left near the bedchamber's doorway.

As he rushed toward it, he heard Maev's scream of fright and agony. *God Almighty!* Heart pounding with fear, he grabbed his sword with both hands, turned, raised it high above his head, and charged straight ahead, a mighty battle cry upon his lips. He could not clearly see his enemy, but he knew the enemy was there, threatening all that he valued, all that he loved.

Callum's feet came off the ground as he connected with the unseen warrior. Dimly he could hear Maev's screams continue. Callum felt numb. He fought with courage and strength, striking out fiercely, yet this time his efforts yielded no victory. As he struggled to get closer to Maev, Callum felt a crushing blow at the back of his head. A light of sharp pain exploded in his brain, then total darkness descended upon him.

"They have been shut up in that bedchamber for nearly two days," Brenda said, her brow furrowing as she glanced at the strong wooden door. "I dinna care how loving a couple they might be, 'tis unnatural to go so long without food or drink. Ye must demand that they open the door. At once. I want to see my daughter."

The laird of the McGinnises raised his brow and gave her a masculine snicker. "Maybe she disna want to see ye."

"Then she can tell me to go away," Brenda retorted. Drawing herself to her full height, which was little more than five feet, she signaled to the female servants waiting in the hallway.

The pair hurried forward, and after a quelling glance from Brenda, the laird moved aside and allowed them to pass. Arms ladened with trays of food and drink, they stood at a respectful distance behind Brenda.

The older woman raised her arm and knocked, and when there was no response, she called out, "Maev, 'tis yer mother. I've brought ye and Callum some lovely refreshments. Open the door so we can deliver yer meal before it gets cold."

The silence continued. Brenda tried again, this time offering to have the tub fetched so the couple could have a nice warm bath.

"They might be sleeping," one of the servants volunteered.

"Or just plain exhausted," the other chimed in, and both women giggled.

"Aye," the laird agreed. "Just leave the trays in the hall. When they have a need, they'll come looking for the food."

It was a logical suggestion, but a nagging sense of unease began to grip Brenda. Perhaps it was the worry of a protective mother, but it suddenly became vitally important to see and speak with Maev.

She lifted the door latch, but was unable to budge the heavy wooden door. "Tis barred from the other side," Brenda said. Her pulse raced and her heart started pounding with fear. Turning toward the laird, she asked, "Can ye open it?"

Irritation flashed through the laird's eyes, then he expelled a resigned sigh. "Dinna expect me to protect you from my nephew's wrath," he warned as he braced his shoulder and rammed it against the wood. "Most men want to be alone with their brides, and Callum is no exception."

It took several attempts before the door broke free. It slammed open noisily, assuring that if the couple had been asleep, they would certainly be awake now.

The moment the way was clear, Brenda pushed past the laird and entered the bedchamber. But she could scarcely credit her eyes with the sight that greeted her.

"Mother of God!"

Callum lay sprawled on the floor, his left cheek pressed

against the cold stone. Maev was on her back on the bed, her head twisted at an odd angle. Both were naked, their flesh an unhealthy, pasty white color. Beneath each of them was a large, dark pool of dried liquid.

Blood. Oh, dear God, she had never seen so much blood. The scent of it seemed to surround her. A horrible, coppery taste coated Brenda's tongue. Sobbing and crying Maev's name, Brenda ran to her daughter's side. She lifted her limp body into her arms, trying to ignore the smears of deep crimson on the white bed linens.

Behind her, Brenda could hear the laird's shouts of surprise and grief. There were footsteps and yelling, screams of anguish and horror.

"He's dead."

"My God, who could have done this?"

"We must search the castle grounds at once. Whoever is responsible for this carnage will be caught and punished."

Brenda cradled Maev's head in her lap. She smoothed back a few strands of her daughter's hair, revealing a pale cheek streaked with dry blood. Maev's body was cold, yet still pliable. Brenda continued to stroke her face and hair, a gesture that had always comforted Maev as a child.

Suddenly, she felt the faint pulse of life at Maev's neck. Tears streamed down her face as Brenda's heart soared with hope. Pressing her ear close to the spot, she waited and listened. The beat was so weak she could barely hear it. But it was there. Feeble and sporadic, with long moments of somber silence between each thump.

"She lives!" Brenda hugged Maev's limp shoulders as her lips moved in an anxious prayer of thanks.

In all the commotion, no one heard Brenda's exclamation. Except for Maev. Miraculously, her eyes opened. She gazed in solemn confusion at her mother for several long moments.

"Callum?" she whispered weakly.

Brenda slowly shook her head. "He's with the Lord."

Maev's face contorted with pain. Her eyes seemed to lose focus and then her lashes fluttered closed.

It was a tragic day for the Clan McGinnis. Those who had so recently gathered to celebrate Callum's nuptial joy now huddled together at his grave and offered prayers for his soul. Maev, her body and spirit broken, her mind unhinged, did not attend the funeral mass or the burial. Brenda remained by her daughter's bedside, trying to offer healing and comfort.

"Please, love, ye must try and swallow a wee bit of the broth I made for ye," Brenda pleaded. "Nothing has past yer lips for days."

Maev turned and gave Brenda a blank stare. Her sunken cheeks were nearly the same white color as the linen on the pillowcase where her head lay. Callum, God rest his soul, was dead, but the life had been taken from Maev also, and the mystery surrounding the fatal attack was a heavy burden for all of them.

The castle grounds and village had been thoroughly searched, but no intruders had been found. The door had been barred from the inside; the height of the bedchamber and sheer drop to the ground outside the chamber's window made it difficult to believe someone had escaped so easily.

So how had the killer gotten out of the room?

There were no large stab wounds on either Maev or Callum, which made the presence of so much blood another mystery. The laird had questioned Maev endlessly, yet she had no answers, repeating constantly that she had seen nothing, remembered nothing.

As the mood of the clan grew restless and edgy, the initial sympathy toward Maev began to wane. It worried Brenda, for she knew there were many who now viewed her daughter with great suspicion and believed she was somehow part of this heinous event.

Suddenly, the bedchamber door burst open and the laird came charging through it. He was encircled by a ring of his most loyal warriors, and from the thunderous expression on his face, she knew there had been more trouble.

Brenda's stomach clenched at the sight of them. "What is it? What has happened?" she asked worriedly.

The laird ignored Brenda's question and looked beyond her, firing a glance of hatred at Maev so strong it pierced Brenda's soul. She knew he blamed Maev for Callum's death, but it seemed ludicrous to think her helpless, grief-stricken daughter had had anything to do with his nephew's demise.

"Callum's grave has been desecrated, his body taken," the laird announced. "I want to hear what Maev has to say about it."

Brenda caught her breath at the accusation. "Maev is weaker than a kitten, flat on her back and wallowing in grief and misery. She hasna the strength to walk to the garderobe, let alone dig up a grave."

"Tis sorcery," one of the men declared hotly. "The work of the devil and the devil's handmaiden."

"Aye," another agreed. "We should bury her in the grave she has robbed and leave her there till her flesh rots from her bones."

Brenda gasped. She glanced wildly from side to side, but the men were blocking the doorway, cutting off the only avenue of escape. Besides, she could not leave without Maev, and her poor daughter was in no condition to flee.

The thought resonated with frightening clarity in Brenda's mind, and she squeezed her eyes tightly shut. Her lips began to move in quiet prayer as the men argued over Maev's fate.

"If we kill her, the magic could get stronger. It might be wiser to banish her."

"Aye, set her far away from all decent folk."

"No," Brenda shouted with newfound vehemence. She opened her eyes and turned frantically from one man to the next, but their faces all held the same expression of vengeance.

The heir was dead, his body taken, and someone had to pay. Many had always been suspicious of Maev's origins, and now they believed they had proof she possessed evil powers.

"There is an ancient stone tower on the northern border of the McGinnis lands," the laird said. "Bring her there, and tell her if she ever ventures farther than a mile or two from it, she will be put to death."

"She will die if ye leave her alone out there," Brenda cried. Panic tightened her chest. She practically threw herself at the laird, clinging tightly to his plaid as she pleaded for her daughter's life. "Ye must not do this to her. She has done nothing, nothing!"

The laird's expression would have chilled the sun. "My nephew is dead, his body taken. Clearly, sorcery is the cause."

"But how can ye blame Maev?"

The laird's lips twisted with disgust. He spoke tightly. "She is alive."

Silence filled the air around them. "If ye send her away, then I'm going with her," Brenda declared.

"Think hard upon yer decision. If ye go, ye may never return."

"She is my child. And she is innocent."

The laird had no reply. Brenda felt as if the world were spinning crazily around her. Thankfully, her righteous anger kept her moving at a lightning pace. She was given little time to prepare for the journey. Brenda quickly dressed an unresponsive Maev in a warm gown, then insisted that the trunks containing her daughter's dowry be loaded in the cart.

Fearing to leave Maev alone with the men for even a minute left Brenda no time to gather any of her personal belongings from her cottage, but she gave it nary a passing thought. Her main concern was for her daughter, whose head she held in her lap throughout the long journey as the cart bumped and swayed over the uneven terrain.

As they climbed higher in the mountains, the air became cooler, the woods thicker. Finally the men stopped beside a tall, round, stone tower. It stood on a low ledge at the mountain's peak, weathered and abandoned, with thick vines clinging up the sides. The entrance door swung in the desolate wind, its hinges creaking.

Brenda saw no signs of life. It was so quiet, she could hear her breath catching in her throat. After unloading the women's possessions, the escort of men turned and left, saying nothing.

With her arms clasped firmly around Maev's waist, Brenda led her daughter into the dwelling. It was dark and gloomy, with sections of the stone floor and walls missing. They both shivered as the wind whistled through the openings and swirled against their legs.

There were no candles or torches to light, though in truth Brenda was not anxious to illuminate the area. She had already spotted several piles of rat dung and could only imagine what other wild creatures had found sanctuary within the tower.

There was a lone wooden stool pushed near the cold hearth. Brenda set Maev upon it, propping her shoulder against the wall so she would not topple over. She took a deep breath and tried to force her mind to formulate a plan of action, biting her lips when she could not get her thoughts organized.

The place was a hovel. Crumbling, remote, isolated, lacking in even the basic necessities. It was barbaric to be expected to live here for the rest of their lives. As Brenda looked around her, the final vestiges of hope she had been clinging to throughout this ordeal began to fade. She sank to her knees and began weeping.

To what manner of hell had they been condemned?

Three

Three years later

As she stood braving the harsh elements on the rampart of the tall, narrow tower, Maev McGinnis could see the vast forest stretching out for miles in every direction. The land was spacious and intimidating, an untamed wilderness filled with unknown dangers, clearly not a place for the weak or timid.

There was one poorly defined path leading up to her prison tower and that remained empty. As always. Maev spent many hours staring toward that endless horizon, yet she never saw any signs of travelers, either on foot or horseback, no human movement of any kind. She often wondered how she would react, what she would feel, if she saw someone approaching. Fear? Relief? Indifference?

Though it had been days since the last storm, the air still smelled of rain. Plumes of pale pink and violet blazed across the sky with luminous splendor as the sun began setting. It was a rare moment of pure beauty and majesty, yet Maev felt no emotions.

A shudder shook her shoulders when a strong gust of

wind blew, making her lips twitch. She pulled the ends of her threadbare shawl tightly together, but it offered little protection from the cold.

She saw a pair of deer darting through the thick brush, heard a flock of birds rustling and chirping in the trees, then spotted several rabbits racing through the small clearing. She hoped they were heading toward one of her snares. It had been many months since she had eaten meat, and her body hungered for the sustenance she had so blithely taken for granted in the past.

The men of the McGinnis Clan were skilled hunters, taking pride in ensuring that none of their people ever went hungry. But Maev's hunger was no longer something that concerned these men. She was an outcast.

Not that she much cared. Living among the clan in her childhood home would not alleviate the pain in her heart, would not eliminate the despair that clung to her spirit like a dense fog.

It seemed more and more the only thing that ever broke through Maev's constant mist of pain was worry for her mother. It had been a harsh winter, and Brenda had suffered through most of it with fever and chills. As spring arrived, she remained weak, and Maev knew the longer she was ill, the harder it would be for her mother to regain her health, especially without the hearty food needed to build her strength.

Deciding it would be worth the effort to check the snares, Maev carefully descended from the tower. The steep, winding wooden steps were worn and unsteady, despite her weekly attempts to repair them. Since the sun had dipped beyond the high, narrow, stone window slits at the top of the tower, the single room where she and Brenda lived was cast in gloomy shadows.

Maev groped her way carefully toward the glowing embers of the hearth. A crude square table, a low stool, and a rickety three-legged chair with a broken back were the only pieces of furniture in the room, but Maev knew she would make a great deal of noise if she smashed into any of them. And that noise would startle and disturb her mother, who had not risen from her bed for over a week.

"I'm going to check the traps," Maev whispered as she knelt beside the pallet that Brenda rested upon. She casually touched her mother's forehead, distressed to find it warm and feverish.

Brenda heaved a high-pitched sigh. Her lashes fluttered and her eyes slowly opened, as though she were fighting to waken. "I worry for yer safety, Maev. Tis too late for ye to go outside in those woods. Best wait until morning."

"I willna be gone long," Maev assured her mother. "I'm hoping to find a plump rabbit so I can make a hearty stew for our dinner."

A shadow crossed Brenda's brow. Maev was instantly angry with herself for mentioning the possibility of a good meal, not wanting her mother to be disappointed. Since arriving in this desolate place, Maev's appetite had been sparse, but Brenda often spoke of warm, crusty bread; rich, thick stews; and other gastric delicacies that they would never again have the opportunity to eat. For the past few years the women had existed by consuming anything edible they could forage from the surrounding woods and the occasional small animals Maev managed to trap.

It was a meager and miserly existence.

Maev banked the fire, added several pieces of precious wood to the small blaze, tucked the only other thin blanket they owned tightly around her mother, then gathered the crude bow and arrows she had crafted and quickly left. She walked several feet beyond the tower and paused. Shading her eyes against the glare of the setting sun, Maev peered into the horizon, trying to decide which way to go. There was only enough light to check a few of her traps.

Taking a gamble, Maev headed west, hoping the light lasted long enough for her to reach those snares she had set farthest away. As she walked, she stopped to gather some of the tender green shoots that were pushing through the thick, mossy soil, knowing they would in all likelihood be the only food for dinner that night.

As she feared, the traps were empty. Maev closed her eyes in despair. Brenda needed the nourishment that only fresh meat could provide. Each day she seemed weaker, her strength ebbing, her spirit fading. As she watched her mother's suffering, Maev was acutely aware that she was responsible for Brenda's condition.

If not for Maev, Brenda would be home where she belonged, in a comfortable, cozy cottage, her belly filled with warm food. She would have female friendship and male protection and the spiritual guidance of a priest. Instead, she was marooned in the middle of a desolate, harsh forest with a daughter broken in spirit as her only companion.

This woman who had taught her all the important lessons of a good life—how to love and laugh, to be loyal and kind, how to hold her head high—deserved better.

And what of ye? Dinna ye deserve better? Maev pushed the thought away, burying it deep inside her mind. She deserved nothing. Callum was gone and so was her desire to participate in life. The laird and his clan had thought to punish her by making her an outcast, but Maev truly did not care.

Without Callum there was no meaning, no purpose, no joy, no dreams, no future. It was as if she had fallen into a deep black hole. The inner light of her soul had simply drained out of her, and she had neither the strength nor the desire to try to regain it.

If not for her mother, she would have allowed this ultimate despair to claim her mortal flesh long ago, but Brenda had sacrificed everything to save her and Maev would not repay such selfless love with cowardly cruelty.

Knowing Brenda would worry if she was gone too long, Maev turned and started back. As she drew closer, a strange silence enveloped the small clearing where the tower stood amid the thick woods. Maev had become accustomed to the usual sounds of nature that now surrounded her, but something was different. The air had changed. She glanced up at the sky, saw no twinkling stars, and realized that thick clouds had formed, threatening rain.

Hoping to avoid a drenching, she quickened her pace. She was rounding the east end of the tower when she saw it. A cloth sack, tied at the top with a heavy rope, lay propped against the entrance door.

Startled, Maev froze. Her first instinct was to turn and hide. Whoever had left the parcel could still be in the area. Perhaps they were watching her at this very moment.

Suspiciously she cast her eyes about, but saw no one. A clap of thunder struck, and lightning cut a gash through the dark sky. Maev hurried toward the door. The first raindrops struck her cheek as she bent to examine the package. Absently she brushed them away, then continued struggling with the knot. Finally she untied it. With trembling hands, she opened the sack.

"Oh, my God!"

Rain pelted the back of Maev's head, the water falling in droplets from her hair to trickle down her spine. But she noticed neither the cold nor the wet—her eyes were captivated by the contents of the cloth bag.

An entire haunch of venison! Maev was amazed. There was enough meat to feed her mother decent meals for weeks! But delight turned to suspicion and then fear. Who could have left this much-needed food? And what did they want for it?

"Is anyone there?" Maev called out, then once again cast her eyes toward the forest, but the darkness was complete. Whoever had left the meat was not visible and in all probability long gone. At least she hoped they had departed.

Clutching her bounty tightly to her chest, she entered the tower and bolted the door behind her.

He stood in the darkness, watching her lift the heavy cloth sack, hoping she would be pleased when she viewed its contents.

"Oh, my God!"

Her voice was raw and rough, as if she did not use it much, but it still held traces of familiarity. The sound recalled memories of her tenderness and love, her sweetness and affection. It made his heart ache.

"Is anyone there?"

She turned toward his hiding place, and he craned his neck forward, hoping to see her face. He knew the darkness would shield him from her view, while his keen vision would enable him to drink in the sight of her.

She was thinner, her face drawn, her cheeks hollow, yet her delicate, refined features were in evidence. Even at this distance he could feel the pull of her almond-shaped eyes. They beckoned his heart, but he could not answer the call.

He never thought he would see her again, never believed it would be possible to hear her voice, to delight in the delicate sway of her hips as she walked. *Maev*. The past exploded into the present, and pain shot through him. Intense, dark pain that should have lessened with time but seemed more acute than ever. Pain that ripped away the layers of protection he'd carefully built between himself and the nightmare world he now inhabited. Pain that had been buried deep within him for three long years.

Maev. My beautiful bride. I have finally found you.

* * *

Brenda dozed fitfully as Maev cooked their dinner. Her fever had worsened, and Maev hoped waking to the aroma of the roasting meat would bolster her mother's spirits. Eventually the tantalizing smells did rouse Brenda, yet while the older woman praised her daughter's culinary efforts, she was able to swallow but a few bites of the juicy meat.

Even more worrisome to Maev was the realization that her mother lacked the strength to ask how she had procured such bounty. It was yet another indication of Brenda's worsening condition.

Since there was no salt to preserve the venison, Maev made a large pot of stew using whatever meager food supplies they had in the sparsely stocked larder. She left the pot bubbling gently over the dwindling fire, hoping a cup of rich, hot broth would tempt Brenda's appetite in the morning.

Her cooking chores, coupled with her concern for her mother, left Maev little time to dwell on the identity of their unknown benefactor. Yet later that night, as she curled herself into a tight ball and huddled into her lumpy pallet fashioned from dried grass, Maev could not help but wonder if the mysterious stranger would return.

A few hours later, Maev awoke to the sound of her own cries and whimpers as the nightmarish vision of Callum's lifeless face staring up at her filled her being. She jerked upright from her pallet, the taste of fear sour in her mouth. Her breathing hitched. Damp with sweat, she pushed off her blanket and sat listening to the racing of her heart. Brenda snored gently on the pallet beside her, unaware of her daughter's pain.

The shaking slowly subsided. Maev had never before dreamt of him. In fact, during her waking hours she could barely recall her beloved's handsome face, and she preferred it that way. There was only sadness associated with Callum's memory and more pain than she was able to endure.

Restless and edgy, Maev left her bed. She climbed the tower steps into the cool, star-filled night, breathing deeply. She looked up at the moon and shivered, wishing she had brought her blanket. It was peaceful here, and she intended to stay until the dawn broke through the darkness.

A sound drew her attention to the opposite side of the tower. Maev tilted her head and studied the large shape that filled the shadows, waiting for it to disappear.

But it did not. Instead, it moved closer. Oddly, she felt no fear, for a storm of hunger swirled around her as the shadow stepped into the moonlight and revealed itself.

"Callum," she whispered, tears filling her eyes. She believed she could no longer recall his features, but she realized she had been deluding herself. She knew him now, even though he was but an illusion. "First I dreamt of ye and now ye appear to me as a vision. Have I finally lost my wits?"

Lucifer's horns! Callum had not intended for her to see him. He had crept inside the fortress and watched her sleep, and when her restless dreams woke her, he had slipped from the room and climbed the tower, hoping when she fell back to sleep, he would have a chance to gaze upon her beauty once again before the dawn broke.

He had come here full of rage and grief, drawn by a need older than time to be near the woman he had loved and lost. He had planned to watch her from afar, but when she appeared on the tower, less than a few feet from him, the opportunity had been irresistible, even though he knew that nothing but trouble would come of it.

She thought him a ghost. Perhaps that was better than her knowing what an evil, decadent creature he had become. For if she ever learned the truth, she would fear and despise him. As he despised himself.

He glanced over the side of the high stone tower and judged the distance to the ground. It was a long drop, yet he knew he could land without causing himself injury. He lifted his leg, preparing to leap over the side, but then her voice pierced his mind.

"I thought it would be unbearably painful to have ye once again in my heart, to see ye in my mind, but it is not." Her tone was reflective and emotional, the sadness echoing the feelings lingering deeply inside him. "Perhaps I have been wrong in deliberately shutting ye out. Refusing to remember how much I loved ye, how much ye made my life complete."

Though he tried, Callum could not hold back the rush of emotion her words brought to his long-bruised heart. To hear that she still loved him, still felt a bond with him, was a far greater gift than he had dared to hope to discover.

Slowly he lowered his leg. Maev looked at him intently, then swallowed hard. Moving himself closer, Callum reached out and caught her hand. Her gaze, wide and nervous, remained pinned to his. Slowly, gently, he lifted her hand to hold it against the side of his face, craving her touch in a way he could not define.

"Ye're solid," she gasped, pulling her hand away. "And cold. I thought ghosts were spirits who lacked substance and form."

He shook his head, fearing he had frightened her. But the jolt of his reaction to her warm flesh stunned him; the driving need to leap upon her, rip off her thin chemise, and feast upon her naked flesh was a powerful temptation.

But he resisted.

"I am not a ghost," he replied hoarsely.

She choked out a strange, nervous sound and splayed her

hand over her chest as if she were trying to calm her heart. "Now I can hear yer voice. Though it sounds different than I remember. Tis deeper, huskier."

What could he tell her? His vocal cords had been damaged the night he was attacked, the night he was converted to an immortal creature. "Are ye frightened of me?"

"Should I be?"

Callum smiled. His fiesty Maev still existed, despite all that she had suffered. "I will not harm ye," he replied.

She hesitated, then returned his smile. "I know ye're not my enemy."

Her words gave him pause. "Do ye have enemies?" he asked. "Is that why ye and yer mother have chosen to live so far from the rest of the clan?"

Her face crumpled as her eyes closed. "We have not chosen anything," she replied. "I was blamed for yer death and my punishment was to be banished from the clan. Forever. Tis a clever verdict, for it is a slow and unmerciful sentence."

"They believe ye killed me?" Callum was shocked. "How?"

"With sorcery." She opened her eyes, and her lips curved into a mocking grin. "Perhaps they were right. Perhaps I do have black powers. After all, I'm having a conversation with a ghost."

He did not bother to correct her. His mind was still reeling over her revelations. How could the clan be so idiotic as to think that Maev would harm him? How could they be so cruel as to punish her unjustly? "Ye're innocent, Maev. And those who have condemned ye unfairly will suffer for their mistake."

"No!" Her breath came out in a short, desperate gasp. "Please, ye must not seek retribution on my behalf. The suffering of others will not alleviate my pain; it will not recapture all that I have lost. All that we have lost."

He watched as a strange mix of emotions shifted across her face. Maev's selfless concern humbled him. Even in her misery she was willing to defend those who had treated her so unfairly. Though he still thought she was beautiful dressed in her drab, worn nightclothes, it was her inner beauty that called to him, that made him remember why he had loved her so completely.

He needed to get closer to her. Aware of the trace of apprehension in her eyes, Callum slowly edged in her direction. Maev's breathing became shallow and quick, but she did not move away.

Taking care not to crush her with his weight, Callum pressed her against the edge of the tower wall, his hands framing her face, then sliding through her hair, his fingers threading between the long strands. "I always adored yer hair. Almost as much as I adored ye. May I kiss ye?"

"Will it be the same?" A bright sheen of tears glistened in her eyes. "Will I feel that same thrill and excitement when yer lips touch mine?"

"I dinna know," he replied. "Let's find out." Softly Callum pressed his lips over hers. The sensations swirled inside him, strong and true. Relief and joy shot through him. It was the same. Nay, it was even better, for it was such a rare and precious gift, one he thought was forever lost.

He kissed her again and Maev's lips parted, greedily accepting his kiss. Her arms came up and around his neck without hesitation. Callum pulled her hips against his and felt the warm, womanly curves of her body fit against his hardness.

Oh, how he needed her. Needed her to banish the loneliness and heartache he had endured for three long years. Anaxandra had told him she was dead. Enraged, he had prowled the lands of the McGinnis Clan, searching for Maev, yet never finding her. Brokenhearted, he had roamed the mortal world far and wide, a creature of darkness, a being of evil, doing unspeakable things, participating in unspeakable acts.

Yet a small part of his humanity had survived. The part of his soul that Maev inhabited had remained uncorrupted, and by rekindling the love they had shared, he had reconnected with the strongest part of his essence.

The problem was, now that he had found her, how could he possibly leave her again?

Something twisted painfully inside him. Though they kissed slowly and deeply, savoring one another as if they had all the time in the world to be together, Callum knew that was untrue. An inner voice called out to him, warning that prolonging this pleasure would make the parting even more of an agony.

With great reluctance Callum ended the kiss, released her, then stepped away so that she might move. It was one of the hardest things he had ever done, for there might never be another chance to hold her in his arms and show her how much he still loved her.

Her closed eyelashes fluttered open, and her large green eyes looked back at him, searching for answers that he could not provide.

"I must go," he said.

She placed a hand on his chest. "Will I see ye again?"

"I dinna know," he answered honestly.

Then before she could say anything else, Callum vaulted over the side of the tower, scaled down the rough stone with catlike grace, and disappeared into the darkness of the night.

When she awoke the next morning, Maev found herself lying on the pallet next to her mother, tucked snugly beneath her blanket. As usual. The burning embers from last night's fire still glowed, the aroma of simmering meat permeating the small area where she and Brenda lay.

Venison stew. Maev could identify that delicious smell anywhere. There really had been a haunch of venison left for them by an unknown benefactor. That much was true. As for the ghost of Callum McGinnis—Maev was uncertain. It had all seemed very real, and had felt very real, but how could it have happened? And why had it happened now, after all these years? Most likely it was a trick of her weary mind, yet though she tried, it was impossible to forget the vision of Callum's sorrowful eyes.

Maev longed to discuss the incident with Brenda, but she feared her mother would think she had lost her wits if she told her she had seen and spoken with and even dared to kiss Callum's ghost last night.

Needing to clear her mind with some fresh air, Maev left the tower in the late morning on the guise of foraging for food. As she walked the familiar woods, she found herself looking over her shoulder one minute, then gazing off into the shadows of the dense forest the next. Did spirits materialize in daylight hours, or did they roam the earth only at night?

Shaking her head at her foolish notions, Maev concentrated on her chores. She gathered firewood, picked a few mushrooms, then returned home to do the wash. By midday she had convinced herself that the appearance of Callum's ghost had been a dream, yet even as she tried to dismiss it all as an interlude that provided her with an escape from the dreariness of her existence, the incident was never far from her thoughts.

The foul weather returned, and the occasional burst of rain throughout the afternoon gave way to a deluge as night fell. Maev listened to the steady pummeling of raindrops and tried to tell herself it was foolish to feel so disappointed. In her heart she knew if it were not raining so hard, she would be outside on the tower wall, waiting to see if Callum's ghost reappeared.

She slept fitfully through the night, feeling a sense of renewed disappointment each time she awoke and heard the rain. The next day Maev began her chores in a lethargic state. After adding more kindling to the fire to chase away the morning chill, she started preparing food for her mother. Yet when she glanced over at the older woman, a feeling of dread swept over her. Something was wrong.

She approached her mother with some trepidations, fearing what she would discover. Brenda's eyes were opened, but they appeared sightless, gazing off into the distance with a glassy sheen.

Maev knelt beside her and rested her hand on her mother's shoulder. "Mother?"

Brenda's unfocused gaze settled on her face. Slowly, gradually, recognition dawned across her pale features and she moved her thin, white lips. "I'm dying, Maev."

For a moment Maev couldn't catch her breath. "Dinna be daft. Tis just a bit of the fever that's got yer spirits feeling low. Spring will be here before ye know it, and the warm sunshine will lift yer mood. The hawthorn flowers will be in bloom, and I can gather madder root to distill. Ye'll feel better after ye've taken a few doses."

"I need more than herbs and sunshine," Brenda replied with a weary sigh.

The denial leapt to Maev's lips, but the expression of resignation on her mother's face kept the words lodged in her throat. Brenda was right. Her gaunt face was nearly as gray as the coarse wool blanket upon which her head rested, the bones of her body showing prominently through the wasted flesh.

Though Maev longed to convince herself otherwise, there was little hope that her mother would survive for many more weeks. She had been too sick for too long.

"What should we do?" Maev whispered as the helpless

fury she struggled to control stabbed at her heart with a piercing agony. For both their sakes, Maev knew she had to be strong, but deep inside she felt like a frightened little girl.

"We must pray." Brenda closed her eyes. "Ye remember yer prayers, don't ye, lass? My soul will need a lot of help reaching heaven, since I'll be leaving this earth without making a proper confession and having a priest's blessing of the last rites."

Maev threaded her fingers through her mother's and tried to look confident. "My faith in the Lord has been sorely tested these last three years, but if it will bring ye comfort, I shall pray day and night."

Brenda's mouth curved into a slight smile. "Ye always were a good girl, Maev. And ye grew into a fine woman. I am proud to call ye daughter."

Maev willed back the tears that threatened to form. Brenda's devotion to her had always been absolute. She had generously shared her home and her heart; she had given everything to her adopted daughter, including her very life.

The two women began to pray together. Brenda quickly grew tired, but Maev continued. When her voice grew hoarse, she closed her eyes and prayed silently, offering different prayers to every saint she had ever heard of, pleading for mercy for the good woman who deserved a better fate.

As Brenda slipped into a calm sleep, Maev realized that she had to do everything in her power to give her mother the peace she desired, the peace she had more than earned. Her mother wanted a priest to hear her confession and administer last rites, and Maev knew she was the only one who could grant this final wish. Though it was difficult to judge, she believed Brenda would not survive more than a week or two. Time was of the essence.

In her heart, Maev knew this was the right thing to do, the only thing to do, yet the significance of this decision filled her with a rising panic. Brenda had taught her that it took great courage to follow your convictions, and never before had that lesson held more meaning.

Maev prayed she would have the inner strength and fortitude to accomplish this all-important task. For her mother's sake, she must put the bitterness behind her, swallow her pride, tame her fear, and return to the castle.

And truth be told, the thought of going back to face the members of the McGinnis Clan scared Maev half to death.

Four

As night fell, Maev sat on the stool by the hearth, her chin propped pensively on her fist, her ears tuned to her mother's breathing, which at last had deepened into the steady rhythm of sleep. She had decided to leave just as the dawn began to break tomorrow, hoping to return before Brenda's condition worsened, hoping also to bring the one thing that would ease her mother's suffering. A priest.

Maev forced herself to eat, then began making preparations for the journey. If she was lucky, the weather would clear by morning. A steady rain and muddy roads would make walking more difficult and tiring and slow her progress.

After returning the food her mother could not swallow to the stew pot, Maev prepared for bed. But sleep would not come. Suddenly, there was a loud thump, followed by a muffled groan.

Her head whipped around toward the sounds, which came from the base of the staircase that led to the outside tower rampart.

"Callum?"

After a moment of silence, he moved into the soft glow

of the firelight so she could see him. Maev instantly noticed the uncertainty in his eyes.

"Oh, Maev, I tried," he whispered as an expression of distress passed over his face. "Yet I find that I canna stay away."

Maev blinked back her tears. "I am overjoyed that ye are here. Even though I know ye are not real, ye make me feel less alone, less afraid."

He studied her for a moment, then opened his arms. Maev stood and walked into them, wrapping her arms around his shoulders. She pressed herself tightly against his chest and felt him sigh into her hair.

"This is madness—"

She lifted her head and set her lips against his, stopping the words. At the touch of their lips, the pain and loneliness in her heart receded. It was madness, *her* madness, and more and more she was coming to depend upon it to survive.

When the kiss ended, she pulled him toward the fire. They sat close together on the floor, facing each other. He seemed so real, so alive, her heart almost broke.

There were so many questions to ask, but now was not the time. Her focus must remain on her mother and the mission she was about to undertake in the morning.

"Ye seem worried," Callum remarked. "What is wrong?"

Maev ceased toying with the fraying hem on the sleeve of her nightclothes. "My mother is dying. Is there anything ye can do to help her?"

Regret filled Callum's eyes. "I have no powers to ease her suffering."

"I feared as much." Maev cleared her throat. "I am going to the castle tomorrow to fetch the priest. My mother's last wish is to have him hear her confession and grant her absolution of her sins."

Callum bolted up from the floor. "Ye cannot return to the castle. Ye will be killed."

"I am well aware of the danger," Maev replied as a shudder went through her. "But I have no choice."

"Let me do it."

She could not help the gasp that escaped from her lips. "What? How?"

"I move easily and swiftly in the dark. I will snatch the priest from his bed and bring him here just before dawn breaks."

Maev pushed shakily to her feet. "If the priest finds himself in my tower prison with no recollection of how he got here, it will be all the proof he needs to verify my sorcery and demonic powers. Then my life, and my mother's, truly will be forfeited."

Callum's jaw clenched tightly as he came to stand beside her. "Then I shall find another priest. One who disna know any of the McGinnis Clan. I willna allow him to know where he has been brought, so when I return him to his parish, he will be unable to find ye again. Ye will remain safe."

Maev wished with all her heart she could agree. "That could take days, perhaps longer. My mother will not last that long."

Maev could see Callum's frustration mounting, but they both knew she was right. "At least let me accompany ye on the journey."

"No. I need to believe that ye are here, watching over my mother, or else I fear I willna be able to leave her. I will go alone."

"Maev." His eyes softening, he captured her face between his hands, cradling it gently while he kissed her all over, then planted one final kiss on the tip of her nose. "Ye always were the bravest woman I knew. Promise me that ye'll be careful?"

"I shall."

She nestled herself close to his strength, wishing she felt as brave as Callum believed her to be. As weariness and emotion took hold, she yawned. When she did it again, Callum brought her back to her pallet near the fire and tucked her into bed. Holding his hand tightly, Maev finally fell asleep. When she awoke, he was gone. As she had expected.

Maev banked the fire, dressed in her warmest clothes, left food and water within easy reach, and kissed her mother. Brenda was barely conscious. It frightened Maev, yet she reasoned it would be better if Brenda was unaware of how long Maev was away.

Convincing herself that Brenda would be fine on her own, Maev at last stepped outside into the cool, damp morning.

She was quickly brought up short by the sight of a small brown mare with a white mark on its forehead tethered to the lowest branch of a tree that stood next to the tower.

Hardly daring to believe the animal was real, Maev cautiously approached. The horse's ears perked as she drew near, and when she was within reach, the animal nudged Maev's arm in a friendly greeting.

Callum. Maev felt a sudden rush of tenderness that caused her breath to catch. Only he could have left the beast. But Callum was not real. He was merely a fragile illusion of her lonely mind. Yet there was no denying the things she had needed most had definitely materialized—first the venison and now this sturdy little mare.

How was this possible? Maev shook her head in confusion, knowing there was no time to ponder this latest mystery. Now that she had a horse, she should be able to reach the castle and return before dark.

Maev briefly stroked the animal's nose, still finding it difficult to believe the animal was real. After getting acquainted,

Maev led the horse into the forest. She stopped the moment she found what she needed, and climbing the trunk of a fallen log, Maev was able to reach the stirrups and get up and into the saddle.

Using her legs and the reins, Maev guided the pretty mare to the path that led out of the forest, unsure how long it would take to reach the castle. She had no memory of arriving at her tower prison three years ago, but she did recall others in the clan speaking about visiting the mysterious stone tower during her childhood, so she reasoned it was not an impossible distance.

It felt odd to once again be astride a horse, but Maev soon began to relax. For a few miles she was even able to forget the reason she was taking this journey and enjoyed the freedom of riding. After several hours, Maev's stomach rumbled with hunger, but she ignored it, filling her belly with water from the stream that ran near the clearing when she stopped to give the horse a brief rest.

Her pace was a little slower when she resumed her quest, owing to the steepness of the hills. With only the position of the sun to guide her, Maev worried that she had taken a wrong turn until suddenly the curves of the land began to look familiar. Heart thundering in her chest, she moved steadily forward, each stride of the horse bringing her closer to her childhood home.

She crested the final hill, and a tear rose in Maev's eye at the sight of the familiar castle walls. Even at that distance she could make out the distinct shapes of men and women as they hurried about their daily chores. It felt as if it had been a lifetime since she, too, had been a part of this life, this community.

A part of her longed to ride boldly through the open drawbridge, head held high, yet she knew it would be a foolish waste of pride. With certainty she would be stopped long before she reached the chapel steps.

No, she would be unable to get inside without being caught. But the priest knew no such restraints, and Maev was well aware that he visited the homes of the farmers who tended the outlying fields on most afternoons. All she had to do was wait until he was a safe distance from the castle and then she would waylay him.

Maev hid her mare in a small cluster of bushes and left the horse contentedly munching on sweet grass. Then she positioned herself just off the main road, allowing a clear view of all who passed upon it.

Within the hour her patience was rewarded by the sight of the portly priest, his long, dark robes flapping in the wind, walking up the road. She waited until he reached the bend in the path that would shield her from the castle view before stepping from her hiding place.

"Good afternoon," Maev said, meeting the priest's eye with a boldness she was far from feeling.

His round face turned an unusual shade of red. He sputtered a few times, then hastily made the sign of the cross. Maev suppressed a wild urge to hiss at him, but good sense stopped her. She needed his cooperation. Antagonizing him would hardly be wise.

"I was unsure if ye would recognize me," Maev continued. "But I can see that ye know who I am."

"Ye shouldna be here, lass," the priest answered, a thundering frown upon his forehead. "If the laird hears of it, there'll be no protecting ye from certain death."

Maev clenched her hands. "I have no wish to cause trouble. I am here not for myself, but for my mother. She is gravely ill and craves the comfort of confession. Will ye accompany me now to administer the last rites?"

The priest's grim expression deepened, and he gave a weary shake of his head. "I dinna dare disobey the laird's commands. All in the clan know 'tis forbidden to have any contact with ye or yer mother."

"But we have done nothing wrong! It was all wicked lies!" Maev felt herself getting angry. "Blame me if ye must for something I most assuredly didna do, but no one with a reasonable mind and a fair heart can find my mother guilty of anything. Her only crime has been her selfless love of me and her unconditional loyalty."

The priest twisted the prayer beads that hung down from his waist. After a few moments he cleared his throat. "I canna help ye," he replied, casting his gaze downward. "Ye'd best leave before someone sees ye and raises the alarm."

Maev tried to ignore the sad heaviness of failure that invaded her heart. "Please, ye must reconsider, ye must not allow fear and ignorance to keep ye from doing what ye know is right," she implored, willing to humble herself and beg all day if that was what was necessary to gain the priest's cooperation. "How can ye possibly refuse the request of a dying woman who begs for the Lord's comfort? Even ye wouldna be so cruel as to deny her soul a chance to reunite with her savior."

For an instant the priest looked contrite, and Maev dared to hope she had convinced him. "Yer mother's fate was sealed by God," he replied. "If He wanted her to have a priest by her side at her final hour, He wouldna have allowed her to be banished. Tis God's will and I canna interfere with His dictates."

A scream of pure frustration lodged itself in Maev's throat. "How can ye be so cruel and still call yourself a man of God? Where is yer famous Christian forgiveness and mercy when it is needed most sorely?"

The priest dragged in a weary breath, and his face went sickly white. "I leave it to God to be merciful, lass." He reached into his pocket and removed a small wooden cross. "Tis said this humble crucifix was blessed by the Holy Father himself. Take it to yer mother. I shall pray that it brings her comfort in her hour of need."

With an audible swallow, Maev took the cross. A part of her wanted to hurl it in the dirt and crush it under the heel of her foot, but she knew it was the only comfort she would be able to bring to her mother. Unless she could somehow overpower the priest and force him to come with her.

Maev dismissed the notion the moment it came to her, yet it rankled her greatly to return to the tower with so little. "May yer conscience haunt ye for the rest of yer life, Father. And may ye always remember how ye chose to be a coward and turned yer back on an innocent soul when asked to do the Lord's work."

With the taste of failure filling her mouth, Maev pivoted on her heel and walked stiffly toward the small cluster of bushes where her mare was hidden. In truth, she had expected this very reaction from the priest, but she had dared to hope there might be a chance for salvation.

Bitter with disappointment, she began the long ride back to the tower, fearful of what she would find.

Brenda slipped from this world to the next as the dawn approached. Maev arrived in time to cradle her mother in her arms, singing her favorite songs, repeating her favorite stories from Maev's childhood antics. It was a peaceful passing. Maev still felt twinges of guilt that she could not provide the comfort of a priest's blessing, but in her heart she knew that she had done all she could.

Filled with weary sadness, Maev began the solemn burial tasks. She hauled buckets of water from the stream for over an hour until there was enough clean water to properly wash the body. With that chore reverently completed, she carefully dressed her mother in the beautiful crimson and green wedding gown that they had both spent so many hours together sewing.

It was the finest garment that Maev owned, and she clearly remembered how proud Brenda had been the day Maev and Callum had married. In Maev's eyes, that made this garment the most appropriate choice in which to bury this very special woman. When the body was at last ready, she placed the cross the priest had given her gently in her mother's folded hands.

It took Maev a very long time to dig a deep grave. Lacking the appropriate tools, she worked steadily using a flat rock, first loosening the hard soil and then meticulously lifting it away. After she had gently placed her mother's body within the deep cavity, she slowly reversed the process until a high mound of dirt marked the spot.

She covered the entire area with small rocks, then fashioned a wooden cross out of sturdy branches. When the grave was complete, Maev fell to her knees and prayed diligently for her mother's soul, begging for God's understanding and mercy.

Physically and emotionally exhausted, Maev returned to the tower. As if in a trance, she struggled to cleanse the dirt from her body, but the nagging voice reverberating in her head left her nearly paralyzed with fear.

She was now utterly and completely alone.

Callum watched from the shadows as she scrubbed away the dirt and grime, her breath catching in small gasps and sobs while she bathed from a shallow wooden bowl. Her grief tore at his heart; her pain caused a tightness to lodge deep in his chest. He knew he should wait until she slept, so he could gently call to her in her dreams. But her grief was too extreme, her pain too harsh to ignore.

He took a step closer. Maev had finished removing the soil from her body and now rested upon her pallet. She was on her back, naked, with her hands at her sides. Her eyes were shut tight. There were streaks of tears still visible on her face. She looked like a corpse.

Callum knelt beside her and reached for her hand. She gasped when their hands touched. Her fingers were cold.

He rubbed them gently in a reassuring manner. Maev's eyes flickered open.

"Oh, thank God ye have come to me tonight," she sobbed, turning toward him.

"I am here, lass," he assured her huskily.

"She's gone," Maev muttered between sobbing gulps. "She's gone and now there is no one left on this earth that I love. Or who loves or cares about me."

"I am here," Callum replied.

Maev let out a shriek of hysterical laughter. "Aye, I have ye, along with my madness, to bring me comfort. Tis a match made in heaven, is it not?"

Callum did not know how to respond. He knew she thought him a ghost, but would revealing the truth of what he had become bring her comfort or cause her even greater distress?

Her expression of worry and fear tore at his heart. Callum hunched his shoulders around her and tightened his embrace, pressing his face against Maev's hair. She had left it unbound, and Callum could not deny himself the pleasure of lifting a thick section of it to his lips. It ran through his hands like a golden waterfall, smooth and silky with the sweet scent of lavender teasing his nostrils.

Her sobs subsided, and gradually he felt the tension ease from her body. He meant only to give her a kiss of comfort. But one kiss begot two, then three, and somehow his clothes were gone and they were both naked and straining toward each other, caught up in their mutual passion and need.

Everything happened very quickly. Within minutes Callum found himself kneeling between Maev's silken thighs, his throbbing penis poised at her entrance. He looked down at the glistening folds of her femininity, so delicate and sweet, so moist and ready. One thrust forward and she would be his. Finally he would be able to claim what had been stolen from him; finally he would be able to recapture part of his humanity.

He lifted his gaze up to her face. She was staring at him with sightless eyes. There was no fear reflected in their depths, yet no recognition either.

"Say my name," he whispered.

Her lashes fluttered and a look of pure agony crossed her beautiful face. "Callum. Ye are my Callum."

Every muscle in his body tightened and he began to shake. Her pain was almost a living entity. She thought him a ghost, a being of mist and imagination, but that was not true. From deep within the edges of his mind, a small voice urged him to continue, to take what she offered, what he so desperately needed.

But he couldn't. So much had already been taken from her. He rolled away, landing on his back beside her. He angled an arm over his eyes, sick with shame.

How could he corrupt the last decent, pure, beautiful thing from his former life? How could he use her trust and her love to try to escape the living hell his existence had become? Had he truly sunk to such a decadent level?

He felt her move. "Callum?" Her trembling body pressed against his side; her slender arm moved over his chest. She ran her fingers lightly over his muscles, then snuggled her face against the hollow of his shoulder. The hardened tips of her nipples branded his skin like burning embers. "I know ye're not real, yet ye feel solid and warm and alive. I can even hear yer heart beating." She let out a small, startled laugh. "The madness is overtaking me now, but I no longer fear it. Nay, I welcome it, because it brings ye to me."

Callum squeezed his eyes closed. His body screamed with wanting her, her silken softness beckoned him, but he controlled himself. He had to tell her the truth. All of it. There was no other choice. And when she learned what had happened, what he had become, he could only pray that she would turn to him instead of running away.

He dragged in a deep breath, drawing her fully against his chest. Her body continued to tremble, and he realized she had reached the near breaking point of emotional and physical exhaustion. His confession might very well destroy her mind. Though he knew a cowardly part of him was relieved at the excuse for a delay, it would be best to wait until she had slept and recovered a bit from all this turmoil.

"Go to sleep, Maev. I'll keep ye safe."

"I canna sleep. Ye've made me all restless and tingly."

He smiled in the darkness, hardly believing that this time *he* was the one who was refusing to consummate their union.

"Shall I dump ye in the cold stream, lass? Tis exactly what I had to do on far too many a night when ye left *me* feeling all restless and tingly."

He felt her smile against his chest. "A dunk in frigid water is exactly what I deserve, for I realize now that I surely tried yer patience."

"Ye tried far more than my patience," he said with a chuckle.

Then wrapping his hands around her thighs, Callum gently spread Maev's legs. He rolled her onto her back, before settling himself on top of her, letting his erect penis slide across her wetness. She whimpered and squirmed and he repeated the motion, sliding the warm silken head against her cleft, teasing her where she was so moist.

"What are ye doing to me?" she panted.

"Do ye like it?"

"Too much." She moaned and pushed herself forward. "Put yerself inside me. Please. I need to feel that ye are a part of me."

He gritted his teeth, knowing he could not answer her plea. But he could bring her satisfaction. With one hand,

Callum reached between their bodies. Finding the damp nest of curls, he slowly slid one finger inside, searching for the core of her desire. He found it and she gasped.

Then he leaned over and covered her mouth in a desperate kiss. Drawing the tip of her tongue into his mouth, Callum sucked hard until he felt the urgency in her build, felt the sexual rhythm moving through her body.

He touched her more intently, circling her sex with his fingertip until he felt her whole body seize. Her hips came up off the pallet, seeking his touch. Her hands were clenched at her sides, her entire body shuddering.

"That's it, love," he murmured, pressing his lips to the damp flesh of her neck. "Let it happen, let it happen."

Her hands slid around to cradle his buttocks, urging him closer. Then suddenly, Maev cried out, and at the sound of her pleasure, Callum felt his seed explode from his body. It covered her femininity and mingled with the moisture of her own desire.

His lips thinned, then relaxed. He felt like a randy lad, losing control so shamefully, but Maev seemed unaware of his discomfort. She had fallen into a deep, sated, unconscious sleep. Callum rolled to his side, collapsing onto the hard pallet. The fire in the hearth sputtered and went out. Maev whispered something and snuggled closer.

Callum kissed the top of her head. He drew the blanket more snugly around them and tucked himself even closer to Maev. He wondered if he had done the right thing by her, for she now seemed to need him more desperately than ever.

Yet his need for her was as great. He needed her passion and her love. He needed simply to talk with her and to have her listen to him. He needed the comfort only she could bring him. Going back to an existence without Maev no longer seemed possible.

And yet being together presented a challenge he did not fully understand. How would she react once she learned the truth about what he had become? He dared not speculate, knowing the pain would be extreme for both of them if she could not accept it.

Callum sighed heavily. Though he had not slept during the nighttime hours for three years, he nevertheless closed his eyes and waited for the reckoning that would come with the morning light.

Five

As morning drew closer, Callum became restless. He left Maev asleep on her pallet and began to prepare the tower. Rummaging through her trunks, he searched for gowns made from the heaviest material. He was surprised to discover that most of the clothing was in excellent condition—clearly she had not worn these garments at all, choosing instead to don her simplest and oldest outfits.

Callum removed an assortment of Maev's gowns and then carefully positioned the dresses across the small, high windows that ran along the inner circle of the tower, effectively blocking out the possibility of any natural light entering the room.

The fire had died to a few glowing sticks, but he could see well enough. He decided to wait until Maev awoke before lighting any torches. He added some fresh water to the pot Maev had simmering near the fire to prevent it from scorching. The cooked meat smelled foul to his sensitive nose, and he wondered briefly if it would make him sick if he ate it.

He decided it was not worth the risk, even though he had

not eaten since yesterday. Callum knew from experience he could go for days without feasting on a fresh kill. The lack of nourishment would diminish his physical strength, but his mental capacity would remain intact and that was what he would need most—his wits.

Realizing there was nothing more he could do, Callum positioned himself on the bottom rung of the staircase that led to the tower ramparts and waited, with a growing sense of dread, for Maev to wake up.

Maev awoke so suddenly, she thought a noise must have startled her. She sat up, hoping to see Callum, but the room was bathed in darkness. The fire had gone out, giving Maev no clue if it was day or night.

She felt a draft of cool air, and her skin prickled with gooseflesh. Her mind was still muddled with sleep, her body sore and aching. Maev's stomach rumbled and she turned instinctively toward her mother's pallet, wondering if she could tempt the older woman into eating a hearty meal. But the sight of the empty bed was an ugly, brutal reminder that Brenda was gone.

Maev's breath caught in her throat, and she let out a little sob. At least her mother had finally found peace, though the emptiness of her passing left Maev with a hollow ache inside. She was now completely alone. Well, except for Callum's ghost.

Maev laughed out loud at her lunacy. So this was what the rest of her days were going to be like? Depending on the imaginings of her fragile mind for comfort? She closed her eyes and let out a faint, mortified moan. Just thinking about it made Maev's head hurt and her mouth grow dry.

She reached for her gown and quickly scrambled into the garment. She lit the fire and one of the wall torches, then turned swiftly when she heard the tread of a heavy footstep on the tower stairs. Maev froze, holding her breath.

Callum!

He stared at her, his gaze sweeping from her face down her entire body. There was a glint in his eyes that imparted a strange fluttering in her heart. Maev felt herself blush, remembering her wanton behavior last night.

"Ye're still here," she said. "That means it must be nighttime."

"No. The dawn broke hours ago," he replied.

"Then why is it so dark?"

"I covered the window slits." He made a scornful sound. "The sunlight bothers my eyes."

"Oh." Maev scowled at his comment, unsure exactly what he meant.

He had an oddly frozen expression on his face and seemed unusually nervous, as if he'd rather be anywhere else.

"I have something to tell ye." His mouth contorted into a world-weary grimace of disenchantment and Maev felt the pulse at her neck begin to quicken with fear. "I'm not a ghost, Maev."

She almost laughed. "Aye, Callum, ye're not a ghost or a goblin or a faerie prince. Tis my mind playing tricks on me. I know ye're not truly here with me. I know ye're not real."

"Not real? Does this feel like air?" He grabbed her hand and pressed it against his chest.

He was right. His chest was solid, hard, the bone and muscle unyielding. Queasy chills coursed over Maev as she forced herself to hold his gaze. "I know ye feel real to my touch, but it canna be true," she whispered. "Ye're dead."

"I *was* dead. But now I am reborn as a creature of the

night, an immortal who must feed on the blood of the living to survive."

The shock of his words reverberated through her entire being. Maev put her hand on the wall to steady herself and commanded herself to breathe. She blinked her eyes several times, wondering if she had heard him correctly. When she had her emotions contained, she turned and looked directly at Callum, who met her gaze impassively. "How is that possible?"

"I was attacked in our bridal chamber on our wedding night. These creatures possess strengths far beyond those of mortal men. Though I fought hard, I was overpowered. And once subdued, I was converted."

"I remember nothing of what happened in our bridal chamber," Maev muttered. Without thinking, she reached out and touched his arm, feeling the solid strength of him. "Who did this horrible thing to ye? Where did they come from?"

He took a few steps back from her, and Maev let her hand fall to her side.

"These creatures roam the world at will. They live nowhere and everywhere." Callum frowned. "Do ye remember the mysterious woman who appeared in the hall on the night of our victory celebration?" he asked.

"Aye." Maev took a step closer, and Callum turned away from her. His profile looked dark and troubled.

"She is known among her kind as Anaxandra. She saw me fighting the English and decided she wanted me as her mate. If given the opportunity, I believe she would have attacked me that night, but ye interrupted her before she had the chance."

Maev's chest tightened in pain. "Is that what ye have become? Her mate?"

All expression was wiped from Callum's face. "I'll not lie

to ye. I have been with Anaxandra, but that was a long time ago. It meant nothing. I didna even enjoy the sexual release; 'twas more like a stud servicing a mare."

Maev winced at his crude analogy, but hearing the truth still stung. The mystery surrounding Callum was now revealed, yet Maev was unsure if she preferred believing he was a ghostly apparition of her mind. This new reality frightened her.

She looked into his stoic face, his remote eyes, and could almost feel the hatred and frustration boiling inside him. This was not the man she had loved and married. Or was it?

"Why have ye come to me?" she whispered. "Why do ye not stay among yer kind?"

His eyes glistened. "I needed ye, Maev. Yer spirit called to me, and even though I knew I should stay away, I couldna."

She frowned and stared up at him. "And now that ye have found me, what do ye want?"

For a moment, Maev saw bewilderment in Callum's eyes. "I just want to love ye, lass. Though I worry if I let myself, ye'll be in danger."

"Danger? From whom?"

"The immortals." His voice grew hoarse, hesitant. "I couldna bear to bring ye more heartache."

She stared down at her hands, rubbing her thumb over a smudge of dirt on her palm. "What more can an immortal do to cause me pain? Humans have already turned my life into a living hell."

"You have no idea what powers the immortals possess." Callum's face contorted into an ironic smirk. "They are wicked, fiendish, evil creatures who do not understand mercy or show compassion under any circumstances."

Maev shuddered. "And now ye are one of them?"

"Aye." He glanced at her with new alertness. "Does it disgust ye?"

Yes. Maev barely managed to hold back her honest answer. Guilt swept over her, followed quickly by pity and despair for him. It was hardly his fault, and yet she could not easily dismiss his revelations, could not easily accept what he had now become.

"Are ye all right?" Callum asked as he approached her, his hands half-raised as if he feared she might collapse in a heap at his feet.

His words unlocked Maev from her paralysis. She backed away from him, her mind whirling. "No, I am not all right. Would ye please leave?" she asked, with more anger than she had known she felt. "I need to be alone."

Callum narrowed his eyes. "I canna leave the tower. Tis daytime. The light burns my flesh."

"God Almighty!" Maev experienced a sharp stab of pain in her midriff. Unconsciously she put her fingers over the spot just beneath her ribs, but the pain did not ease. With a small sigh of distress, she slipped quickly out the door and walked into the gentle flood of sunlight, hardly believing something so comforting and natural could cause Callum harm.

The surrounding forest was deep and thick, and Maev welcomed the feeling of being encircled in its primeval splendor. She walked swiftly, with no particular direction in mind, needing the fresh air and solitude to digest this news that had left her shaken and speechless.

Maev knew she had no right to judge Callum harshly for what had happened, yet the mixture of jealousy and anger dominated her feelings. If he had not flirted with the female immortal, this never would have occurred. Would it? Or had Callum's fate been sealed the moment the creature had seen him in battle?

Keeping her head down as she walked, Maev repeatedly rubbed her temples with her fingers, but the jumbled thoughts and images racing through her mind kept tripping over each other. The air was lightly scented with heather, the sway of the trees seemed to whisper through the stillness, but there were no answers to be found.

Wandering more slowly, Maev began to meander through the thick trees, hardly caring if she became lost. She stayed outside for hours, resting only for brief intervals before resuming her journey. Yet by midafternoon she was forced to admit that no matter how far she walked, she could not run from the truth.

With a scream of frustration, Maev sat down on a flat rock and cradled her head in her hands. She felt a stinging pressure behind her nose and the threat of unwanted tears in her eyes. She did not understand herself. She did not understand the emotion that moved so strongly beneath the mass of hopelessness that filled her being.

Was it love? Was it possible that deep within her soul she still loved Callum, even though he had become something that terrified her? And most important of all, did she truly wish to be bound in intimacy to such a creature?

Weary and miserable, Maev tucked her legs beneath her and stretched her torso forward into a shaft of sunlight, letting the warmth bathe her face. She closed her eyes and listened to the sounds around her—the drone of bees, the rustle of leaves, the warbling trill of a bird calling to its mate.

Half-drowsing like a cat, Maev gradually succumbed to a light sleep. When she awoke a few hours later, her senses and emotions felt numb and dulled. But she knew there would be no relief from this melancholy until she spoke with Callum.

Squaring her shoulders, she began a determined march toward the tower.

Maev's hand trembled a little as she pushed open the door, but surprisingly the weight from her chest seemed to ease and she suddenly felt a sense of peaceful relief as she entered the room.

"Ye waited for me," she said as the sight of him sitting before the fire sent a blaze of feeling through her entire body.

"There was little choice," Callum declared bitterly. "Even though ye stared at me as if ye were face to face with a venomous snake that was poised to strike, I couldna leave until the sun set."

Maev lowered her head. A growing weight of guilt pressed on her from all sides. Though she had not meant to, she had hurt him. "Ye look and sound and feel the same as ye did when ye walked the earth as a man. Yet ye canna tolerate the warmth of the sun on yer face and must consume the . . . the blood of the living to survive. What else is different?"

"I have the strength of twenty men, my face and body will never age, and if I receive a wound of any type, it heals in a few hours or less." Callum set his back to the fire and stared at her. "The more powerful immortals can summon thunderstorms, enslave a human with a single glance, and transform themselves from a human form to animal and then back to human."

Maev's lashes flew up. "An animal?"

Callum shrugged. "Bats usually, but some become wolves or even rats."

"Have ye ever . . ." Maev's voice trailed off.

"No. I have no interest in learning these things. I can keep the essence of myself the same as it was in my mortal life, and that is what I shall do. I was told that I can even learn to master my craving for blood, though I shall always need it to survive. But it is not necessary for me to kill each time I feed, and the blood of animals provides me with sufficient nourishment. I dinna and willna attack humans."

Maev took a deep breath to stop her knees from shaking. He spoke so casually of these things. "Is there no way to reverse this curse? Perhaps a priest can give ye aid?"

Callum's expression darkened. "I am beyond the help of man or God."

Maev choked back her pity. "Ye will live forever in this state? There is no way to destroy an immortal?"

"A stake of wood or silver through the heart, beheading, or direct exposure to sunlight will kill us." Callum ran a hand through his dark mane of hair until it stood on end. "Are ye thinking ye might have need to defend yerself from me?"

The void that stretched between them had never seemed wider, yet Maev felt the tender love in her heart struggle to narrow it. "I know ye could never harm me, Callum McGinnis, no matter what manner of creature ye have become."

As she spoke the words, Maev knew they were the truth.

Her hand reached out blindly, her fingers curled around his. The touch made Callum tense visibly, as if the contact sent a shock through his body. But Maev remained calm. She knew this was a time when they must give each other strength.

"Oh, Callum," she said softly, drawing herself tightly against him. "I am so sorry for what ye have suffered, my love."

He pressed his lips to her temple. "I'm sorry for what we both have suffered, what we both have lost."

"All I ever wanted was to share my life with ye. I wanted to make ye happy and proud, I wanted to be the mother of yer children. I wanted ye to love me as much as I loved ye." Maev took a deep breath. "Tell me, is that still possible?"

Tenderly he brushed a curl from her cheek. "I'm not certain about the children, but as for the rest, yes, 'tis possible."

"How? Must I, too, become an immortal?"

"No. You can remain as ye are." Callum glanced questioningly at her. "I have already found a place for us to live, where we can be private and undisturbed and shut out the world."

"Is it far from here?"

"Not too far. Tis up in the hills, a true Highland fortress. I canna live permanently more than a hundred miles from the place of my birth unless I bring along at least a pound of the soil. This place can become our sanctuary, yet will allow us to remain in the Highlands."

"What of those who live there now? Will they not be suspicious of us?"

"Suspicious? Why, because I can turn myself into a bat?" Callum's smile was narrow and swift.

Maev joined him in a small chuckle, her cheeks tinted pink with amusement. "Tis hardly a joking matter," she admonished.

Callum's expression dutifully grew solemn. "Those who inhabit these rugged mountains are a different breed. A few are outlaws and brigands, but most are decent folk who have lost their homes through a dispute with a clan member or overlord and seek only peace and refuge. They keep to themselves, and dinna show much interest in the business of others."

"Like us," Maev said, then she laughed, realizing that she and Callum were not at all like any other couple. Yet somehow it did not seem to matter, as long as they were together.

"I've brought horses for us to ride and two extra to carry yer belongings. We can leave the moment the sun begins to set." He cast her a smile that was tense and tight. "Will ye come with me, lass? Will ye share my fate and at long last be my wife?"

"Aye." Maev loosened a shaken sigh. "I have no reason to stay and no regrets at leaving my tower prison. It will take but an hour for me to be ready."

The journey took most of the night. At first it was frightening riding in the dark through an unfamiliar place, but Callum confidently led the way and Maev's nerves eased. With the high mountains looming on the right, they crossed a dozen or more streams until they reached a small, narrow loch shaped like a tree limb. Reed beds lined the shore, and as they came around the bend, Maev spotted a trio of fishermen's huts.

Rugged hillsides rose up like fists on every side of the lock, and the heady scent of heather permeated the air. They followed the shoreline for many miles, then slipped through a small, narrow cavern and emerged on the other side.

In the distance a fox yipped and was answered by another, but Maev paid it no heed. Her eyes were fixed toward the stone structure that was perched on the edge of the hill. It resembled a small fortress, with a wooden stockade wall and battlements protecting it.

Though built on a much smaller scale than the castle that housed the McGinnis Clan, it appeared to have everything necessary to be self-sufficient, including a gristmill, a forge, and even a brewhouse. Maev was surprised to see that the yard within the walls boasted an impressive vegetable garden on one side and stock pens filled with a few sheep and cattle on the other.

A dry moat mined with sharpened sticks encircled the defenses, with an open drawbridge crossing the man-made ravine that defended it. It was eerie and ominous, yet obviously effective, for the one element lacking in this impressive establishment was people.

Strangely, the property did not have an air of abandonment. All the buildings seemed in good repair, rising off stone foundations with neatly whitewashed wooden walls and thatched roofs. The animals bleated noisily and rustled in their pens, cutting through the stillness of the night.

For a moment it felt odd to be in such a large place without anyone else around, but years of living with only her mother for company had taught Maev to appreciate the silence. Once the horses were fed and stabled, Maev and Callum entered the manor house. Inside the keep, Callum led the way to the master tower, climbing the stone steps to the first two rooms.

"These are to be our chambers," he announced. "I hope ye are pleased with the furnishings."

Maev stepped forward and her feet sank into the lush carpet that covered a large section of the floor. She gazed in wonderment at the luxurious appointments of the room. There were rich tapestries covering the walls, cushioned furnishings, several string lutes hanging near the tapestries, and a game table with elegantly carved chess figures of ivory set out on the board.

After the years of living in her stark, tower prison, Maev wondered if she would ever become accustomed to such spacious luxury. Callum lit several of the large wall torches, and Maev went through the archway into the second chamber.

She stopped instantly, her eyes riveted to the enormous bed that took up an entire wall. It was wide enough for six people and set so high off the floor there were wooden steps beside it. Green velvet curtains hung from the corner posts, and there were rings attached so that the curtains could be drawn about the bed to envelop those inside in total privacy.

Maev realized it would also provide protection from drafts. And keep out even the tiniest hint of sunlight.

"Where did ye get all these beautiful things?" Maev asked with awe as Callum set down her baggage.

He bent toward her and murmured into her ear, "There are few benefits of my situation, but this is one of them. We will never want for material comforts in the human world."

"Ye did all this yerself? Without the aid of servants?"

"I have an arrangement with several of the villagers. They work here on occasion in exchange for goods, mostly food and ale. But at night they return to their homes."

Maev's eyes widened in surprised. "If they are working in the daytime, how can ye communicate with them and give them instructions?"

"The rain." Callum made a satisfied sound. "The other beauty of this Highland retreat is that there are far more wet days than sunny ones. I have found that if I am careful, I can be out-of-doors for short periods of time when the clouds are thick and the rain falls steadily."

Callum lit the large square candle that rested in a brass stand, further illuminating the bedchamber. A massive wardrobe stood across from the great bed. Maev began unpacking her clothes, making use of nearly all the hooks inside the wardrobe. She had been reluctant to take the many lovely gowns she had sewn with her mother in happier times, but now Maev was glad that Callum had insisted she bring them. They fit in well with her new, lovely surroundings.

Just as she was putting away the last of her garments, Callum returned to the chamber, carrying a matching basin and jug filled with warm water and a tray holding ale, goblets, a thick, dark bread, and cheese. After a quick wash, Maev set out to do justice to the simple fare, consuming every last morsel.

Callum watched her with amusement twinkling in his eyes, and she noted he ate nothing and drank sparingly. When the meal had ended, she became acutely aware of the man seated across from her.

His masculine presence seemed to fill the room, dominating the very air Maev breathed. Her pulses raced, her heart began to pound, and it seemed as if the strength of his body reached out to embrace her.

He held out his hand. "Come to me."

It was a lover's request, and the look he gave her made her feel as if her bones were melting. He opened his thighs, and she stepped willingly between them. Then his arms slowly tightened until every inch of their bodies touched.

Their gazes held for a long moment. "I can scarcely believe I am here with ye," Maev whispered.

"Aye. There were times I thought I'd eat myself alive with wanting for ye, Maev McGinnis. Are ye finally ready to become my wife?"

"More than ready," she replied.

Callum's mouth came down on hers with an aching tenderness. Maev pressed herself closer as his hot, hungry lips sent tiny tremors through her. Callum parted her lips with the tip of his tongue and thrust inside with slow, insistent strokes.

He tasted her, devoured her, and she responded in kind.

"Ye canna know how much I need ye, Maev." His voice was a raw plea that spoke of years of need and years of denial.

Maev's hands came up to glide over his chest, and he lifted her in one strong movement, settling her in his lap. She felt the hot, teasing lick of his tongue against her neck, and her nipples peaked of their own volition. The feeling of excitement that rose up inside her was so strong it felt as if she were being carried along on a tidal wave.

His hand worked quickly at the laces of her gown, and Maev soon felt a draft of air across her chest as Callum pulled the garment free of her upper torso.

"My beautiful Maev," he whispered, stroking the lush roundness.

Maev cried out when Callum lowered his mouth to suckle at her breast, his tongue tormenting her with slow, steady strokes. At the same time, his hand reached down to touch the softness between her thighs. A great shudder ran through Maev as the heat from his hand seeped into her body.

Maev shifted restlessly on his lap, briefly shutting her eyes. It was almost too much. Callum's lips worshipped her; his hands drove the longing inside her to a fever pitch.

"Straddle me," Callum whispered before nipping at the sensitive flesh of her exposed neck.

Maev licked her lips in anticipation, then opened her thighs and slid her knees on either side of his hips.

"Like this?" she purred wantonly.

Callum growled his response, positioning the tip of his erect penis on her slick opening. Slowly he surged up inside her. Maev felt full to bursting, but there was no pain, only a deep, lovely fullness. She suppressed the urge to scream with excitement, fearing her cries would startle Callum and he would cease what he was doing to her.

"Yer sheath is so tight, my love, I fear I'm hurting ye," Callum groaned.

"I dinna feel any pain," Maev panted. "Tis glorious. I want more."

Callum's eyes closed briefly and he moaned. Then his hands slid down from her waist to grasp her hips. Maev pushed herself down swiftly while at the same time Callum thrust upward. She felt a sharp stab of pain but it was gone in an instant, replaced by a shimmering taste of joy.

With her maidenhead finally breached, she was stretched fully and was able to meet Callum's next thrust. The heat within her soared higher and higher with each shift of their bodies. The pleasure soon reached a frantic pitch, and Maev's arms tightened around him, her heart aching with joy as she held her beloved against her.

Callum's breathing grew ragged and hoarse, then he cried out and stiffened. Maev could feel his seed enter her body, and it triggered a spasm of release deep within her. Her body shook, and tears of joy fell from her eyes.

One. At last, they were one.

They clung to each other for several long minutes. Then, Callum swung her off his lap and into his arms and strode across the chamber. He lowered her onto the bed and came down over her, his breathing still unsteady.

"I would never have believed it, but Maev, my love, 'twas more than worth the wait."

Maev laughed with embarrassment and buried her face in his chest, breathing in his wonderful, potent male scent, feeling the dampness of his flesh against her burning cheeks. He was all hard muscle and brute strength, and yet beneath it all she felt the tender caress of his love, the essence of his caring and regard for her. Only her.

What they had just shared was a mating so physically intense, so emotionally charged, it went beyond description. It was as if he had been inside her spirit as well as her body.

Maev shifted her face to gaze at her lover. Their eyes met with unspoken thoughts, and she knew he felt the same about their lovemaking. It made her shiver. The realities of the world seemed to fade in that moment. Maev wrapped her arms around Callum's shoulders, hugging him closer.

Her eyelids grew heavy as exhaustion overtook her body

and mind. Cuddled against Callum's strong chest, Maev began to drift off to sleep. Yet in her heart and mind she took great delight in knowing that no matter what happened in the future, this perfect, tender, loving moment could never be taken from either of them.

Six

The weeks and months passed swiftly, and they were the happiest of Maev's life. During the daylight hours, she often lay in Callum's arms, experiencing his passion and generous lovemaking. At night, they roamed their castle fortress, making repairs, sharing chores, delighting in being together.

A few days each week, several of the people inhabiting the scattered cottages in the area would arrive at the castle, looking for work. Once the word spread that there was a female in residence, women began to appear. They offered cooking and cleaning help, and with an eye toward their future needs, the ever-practical Maev set up a weaving hut. In exchange for their labors, each woman was paid with a bolt of fine wool cloth.

Though they kept a slightly suspicious distance, Maev enjoyed the company of these women. They were respectful, and curious about her and Callum, but they kept their questions to themselves. It seemed that everyone in the area had something they wished to keep hidden, and it created a strange, unspoken bond between them all.

It was Callum, however, who provided the true joy in Maev's life. With each passing day, she knew she was falling more and more in love with him. Thanks to the healing power of this love, it no longer hurt so much to remember the past. They shared memories of their childhood, her mother, and the life they had left behind. Though it took time, Maev was even able to find forgiveness for the members of the Clan McGinnis who had cast her out.

The abundance and variety of fresh food made a marked improvement on Maev's health. The hollows in her cheeks disappeared; the color returned to her complexion. She was grateful for this second chance at sharing a life with her beloved, yet deep down there was a slight nagging sense of incompleteness.

Though Callum seemed the same in every way, Maev was all too aware that he was not the man she had known. He never took nourishment in front of her, but she was very aware of his need for fresh blood. While it did not precisely repulse her—after all, she, too, had killed animals to survive—it did set her on edge because it was a stark reminder of the vast difference between them.

A difference that would separate them for eternity.

"Callum, I have thought long and hard and have at last made my decision. I want ye to make me as ye are—I want to become an immortal."

At the sound of her voice, Callum lifted his head. They lay side by side in their massive bed, sated and content after a vigorous bout of making love. He had been drifting off into a peaceful dreamless sleep until Maev's words had startled him fully awake.

She wanted to become like him?

He blinked and turned away from her, scanning their bedchamber with dead eyes. "Ye're talking nonsense, Maev," Callum said in a flat tone. "I'll hear no more of it."

She tugged on his arm until he was forced to turn his head and face her.

"Tis not a whim, nor a passing fancy. I knew it's serious.

I know once it happens, there will be no going back." Maev's mouth twisted, and her grip on his arm tightened. "I also know 'tis the only way for us to be together. Forever."

Callum held his breath. Her voice was slightly roughened, and he sensed a tension in her he had never seen before. "Maev, 'tis impossible."

Her eyes brightened with tears. "Ye canna deny me, Callum. Ye canna deny yerself. Deep inside ye must know 'tis the right thing to do."

He felt her trembling and it amazed him. She was serious! She was willing to sacrifice everything, even her humanity, just to be with him. Never had Callum felt so humbled.

He leaned over and dropped a kiss on her bare shoulder. "I thank ye from the bottom of my heart for yer selfless gesture of love. But I willna do it, Maev. I canna do it!"

"Why? Dinna ye know how?"

"Of course I do."

"Then prove it."

Callum looked at her in frustration, almost laughing at the irony. "I'm not a green lad to be taunted into proving his skills."

Something gleamed in her eyes, and she reached out to take Callum's hands in hers. "And I'm not a foolish lass with a head full of wool. I'm a woman. Yer woman. And I never want to be parted from ye."

The determined set of her jaw let him know how serious she was about the matter. "I canna believe that anyone would willingly embrace this fate," Callum muttered.

"Believe it, for it is the truth."

There was a long silence, broken only by the sound of their breathing. Finally Callum slipped a possessive arm about her and drew her close to his side, loving the feel of her against his bare flesh. "Ye have given me the most precious gift of all, Maev."

"My love?"

"Nay, yer trust."

Her arms tightened around his neck and they kissed. After a moment, Maev lifted her head and gazed at him. "I'm ready. Will ye do it now?"

"Soon," he replied reassuringly, trying to bury any of his lingering doubts. "But there is one mystery we will need to solve. We dinna knew where ye were born. If I convert ye to an immortal, ye must live within a hundred miles of the soil of yer birth or else take along at least a pound of it to keep in yer sleeping area."

"But I dinna know where that soil lies," Maev cried in distress. "What will happen to me if I dinna follow this dictate?"

"Ye will grow very weak and sick."

Maev let out a great sigh of frustration. "It seems that my true origins will continue to rule the direction of my life," she said in a bitter tone. "Is there nothing we can do?"

Callum frowned thoughtfully. "We could discover where ye were born."

"After all these years?" Maev ran a hand through her tangled blond hair. "How?"

"Once ye are converted, yer weakness will come on gradually. The moment it happens, we will begin traveling to the location where ye were found as a babe. From there, we will plot our course carefully, going south. Yer strength will return as we get closer to the place of yer birth, so if ye do not improve, we will return to where we started and head east. If that yields no results, we will head west. Eventually we will discover where ye were born."

Maev's expression turned uncertain. "Then what?"

"We dig up a pound of dirt. Or better, two pounds." Callum began to smile as he realized the plan could work. "We can store the soil in the corner of our bedchamber. It's close presence will keep ye from falling ill."

Maev looked stunned. "I'll have to keep dirt in our lovely bedchamber?"

Callum laughed and shook his head. "I canna believe that is what worries ye most about taking this step and giving up yer human life." He laughed again and hugged her close. "I'll find a beautiful chest, inlaid with gold and precious gems, to store the soil, so yer senses will not be offended."

Her eyes opened wide. "I have no need of such rich excess. A plain wooden chest will be fine. But I dinna understand how we can enact this plan? I fear if we leave our home unprotected for more than a night or two, we will return to find our larders emptied and everything of value within these walls taken from us."

"No one will enter the castle when we are gone. The locals all believe it to be cursed."

"Because of ye?" Maev asked.

"Nay. The property was abandoned and in a state of great disrepair when I stumbled upon it last year. When I asked one of the fishermen why no one lived there, he told me that all the former inhabitants had died from a pox and any others who attempted to take up residence within these walls suffered the same fate."

"Will they not become suspicious because ye and I have not fallen ill?" Maev asked.

"Perhaps." Callum shrugged. "Or they might believe the spell has been broken, but they are too frightened to test the theory just yet. And that serves our purposes very well."

Maev cast him a satisfied look. "Then we can proceed."

A chill of foreboding ran down his spine. She spoke so casually, but he could tell she was apprehensive. A niggling sense of guilt held fast to his conscience, but the truth was that he wanted to keep Maev with him as long as possible. She was the only female in the world who would never ask more of him than he could give. An unselfish woman who would never betray his love.

How could he possibly refuse her most precious gift to him?

Callum slid his hands beneath Maev's hips, pressing her tighter against him. The heat from her body caused an instant tightening of his groin, but he tamped down his desire. He did not want to associate this moment with physical pleasure, though in a strange, twisted way it was an act of love. A pure demonstration of Maev's love for him.

"Are ye certain?" he asked.

"Yes." Her smile was bright, luminescent.

He nodded. Then with slow deliberation, he caressed the sensitive flesh along her neck, making certain he knew the exact spot to strike that would cause her the least amount of pain. Maev whimpered for an instant, and he lightened his touch.

At that moment she was more beautiful to him than she had ever been before, facing her fears, sacrificing everything for their love. As he continued his caress, Maev clutched his shoulders and arched against him, her head tipped back, pink lips parting, eyes closed.

Sinking his teeth sharply into her neck, Callum gave himself up to the moment that seemed to devour them both. Maev let out a short, startled cry, and he felt her warm breath against his ear as she murmured his name over and over again.

He held her in his arms until she quieted, then he eased away from her and slipped out of their bed. She looked small and fragile lying alone on the large mattress, her knees curling in toward her stomach. Callum tucked the furs around her, then brushed a kiss across her brow.

"Rest easy, my love," he whispered.

As he straightened, Callum's head felt light. He placed his hand on one of the wooden bedposts to steady himself. When his balance returned, he reached for his robe. Shrugging into the garment, he retreated to a shadowy corner of the bedchamber. Sighing heavily, he dropped to his haunches, his eyes pinned to the bed as he waited for Maev to die.

When she awoke, Maev felt no difference in her body or her mind, but the weakness Callum had warned her about quickly appeared. When she told an anxious Callum, he immediately made preparations for their journey. After securing the castle and making arrangements for the care of their livestock, they left as darkness fell.

They traveled by moonlight, wending their way down the mountainside, through a valley, then into a dense woods that rustled with the sounds of autumn leaves. Maev remained tired and lethargic, at times almost falling asleep while seated on her horse. Callum took great care to ensure she never lagged too far behind and he even tied her reins to his saddle.

They made camp well before dawn rose each morning. If no cave or abandoned shelter could be found, Callum erected a small tent of thick, heavy fabric that effectively blocked the rays of the sun. After taking nourishment, they slept, wrapped in each other's arm.

Late one evening, a full week after their journey began, they came upon a long wall snaking across the landscape.

"What is it?" Maev asked.

"Hadrian's Wall," Callum replied. "Twas built by the Romans over a thousand years ago to separate the civilized from the barbaric."

Maev frowned and Callum laughed. "The Scots and the English," he clarified.

"I suppose we were considered the barbarians," Maev said with an indignant huff.

"We still are an uncivilized lot, especially in the Highlands, where a man wields a double-edged claymore as though it were an extension of his arm," Callum said, his eyes brimming with amusement. "We march into the Lowland farms to raid for crops and animals and the chieftains in the southwest attack the Anglo-Norman strongholds across the border.

"Robert Bruce longs to unite us and be our king, yet I doubt he will ever tame us completely. A true Scot follows his clan leaders, fighting when and where they chose, accepting orders from no one else."

"There's nothing wrong with a little spirit and courage," Maev insisted.

"Aye, it keeps the blood pumping."

"And flowing freely." Maev laughed, but her joy faded as her eyes lingered on the wall of stone. "How do we get to the other side?"

"Tis easy to scale." Callum led their horses to a cluster of trees and secured the reins to a low branch. With a fleeting glance at the stone structure, Maev lifted her chin and dismounted.

As she drew closer to the unusual wall, butterflies began fluttering in her stomach. The dark cloud of uncertainty that had shadowed her entire life loomed largely before her. Was she at last about to learn the truth of her origins?

Maev felt a wave of apprehension as she held her hand out to Callum. He must have sensed it, for he gave her a smile of encouragement as he helped her climb over the wall. The moment she dropped to the other side, Maev felt a rush of energy enter her body.

She doubled over, hugging her waist. The shock hit her full force, the truth pounding in her brain.

"What's wrong, lass? Are ye in pain?"

Callum's strong arms wrapped around her, and Maev leaned into his strength. She began to shake. "I'm English . . ." The words melted into tears. She turned her head and sobbed against his neck, her body shivering with emotion.

Callum's brows shot up. "For shame, Maev McGinnis.

After all the trials we have survived, and the obstacles we have struggled to overcome, ye fall to pieces over learning that ye were born an Englishwoman?"

Maev let out a final sob, then wiped away her tears with the back of her hand. "Well, when ye put it like that, it does seem rather ridiculous," she sniffed. "Though I'd be lying if I said I wasna disappointed."

Callum lifted her hand and kissed each fingertip. "If ye can love what I have become, then I can surely find it in my heart to overlook the taint of yer heritage."

Maev sniffed. Callum continued to speak, but Maev was no longer paying close attention. Even though she agreed with him, it stung to have Callum cast aspersions on her character. One could hardly fault a baby for the circumstances of its birth. And she had, in truth, been raised a Scot, learning and loving the heritage of her adopted land.

The longer she thought about Callum's words, the more her indignation grew, until finally she sputtered, "I'm as much a Scot as ye are, Callum McGinnis, despite where I was born."

Her words silenced Callum. He narrowed his gaze and stared at her for so long Maev felt her cheeks growing warm. Yet she lifted her chin stubbornly, arched a brow, and practically dared him to disagree.

"It seems as though the English soil has helped ye find yer tongue as well as yer strength," Callum teased. "'Tis good to hear ye finally speaking some sense, lass. Ye know, I've never knowingly kissed an English wench before." His smile grew seductive. "It has an air of the forbidden about it that I find very exciting."

His lighthearted attitude soothed Maev's jagged emotions. She stepped closer and lifted her mouth to his. "Ye always were one to enjoy the forbidden," she agreed as her mouth met his. "And never have I been more thankful for that than at this moment."

They shared a long, deep, satisfying kiss, skimming their hands over each other's bodies, savoring the joy of being together. It seemed as though they were the only two creatures in the universe, and there was nothing that could separate what they were sharing.

Dizzy and on fire for each other, they made love on a lush bed of heath grass, surrounded by heather, with Hadrian's Wall stretching out behind them. They gave themselves over to their feelings and dreams, glorying in how the reality was far better than anything they could have imagined.

Maev let out a cry of joy as Callum's hard body slowly filled her, all silky heat and strength. He rode her hard and fast, and it was natural and erotic, endless pleasure, endless sensation.

They moved as one, anticipating each other's touch, their bodies rising to meet and then demanding more. It was sharp and sweet, molten and primal. They climaxed together, their cries of ecstasy echoing through the stillness of the dark night.

Sated and exhausted, Maev stretched out on Callum's chest, loving the feel of his comforting arms around her as his breath stirred her hair. She touched her fingertips to the springy chest hair peaking through his open shirt. It felt wonderful. He felt wonderful. Everything felt wonderful.

Callum cracked open one eye. "We need to find shelter. Twill be dawn soon."

"In a minute," Maev muttered, feeling too relaxed to move.

She snuggled closer, trying to will herself into alertness. Within moments, however, Maev knew she was losing the battle. Yet just before her eyes began to close, she saw the shadow of a female form fall across Callum's face.

The sight startled all traces of exhaustion from her body. She rolled to her side and scrambled to her feet, standing upright at the exact moment the woman struck Callum. His lack of reaction told Maev he never saw the blow coming.

Maev felt her legs go weak with fear. She rushed forward, but the mysterious woman blocked her path.

"What have ye done to him?" Maev cried.

"He is only stunned," the female replied. "I would never harm something so precious to me, yet I will not tolerate his interference in this matter."

Maev's worried eyes met her adversary's smoldering ones. There was something disturbingly familiar about the beautiful woman who held herself as regally as a queen. Her flowing dark hair complemented her pale skin, and her strange eyes glowered with a fierceness that could terrify a demon.

"Ye're Anaxandra," Maev whispered as recognition dawned.

"I am." The woman turned a hostile eye to Maev. "And you are a great annoyance. I thought I had killed you the night Callum became my mate. It seems the job was left unfinished and must now be completed."

Maev's hands began to tremble uncontrollably. Ever since she had learned the truth, she had longed to confront this temptress, but now that the moment was at hand, she found herself lacking in courage. How could she possibly hope to defeat this evil creature?

Yet how could she not? Her future with Callum, and her very existence, depended upon it. "Be gone from here. Callum is not a piece of goods to be bought or sold or owned on a whim. He is a man of free will, and though ye have repeatedly thrown yerself at him, he has clearly chosen me to be his woman."

The mocking smile faded from Anaxandra's lips, and her face flushed with color. "You are not worthy of him," she said accusingly as rage descended into her eyes.

"I have earned his love," Maev insisted. "While ye have gained his scorn."

Every muscle in Anaxandra's body stood taut with anger at the insult. "He does not love you."

"Aye, he does." Maev squeezed her eyes shut as a surge of confidence and courage rose like a wave inside her. She and Callum had suffered years of agony because of this woman, and now she threatened their newly found contentment. It was simply not to be tolerated. "Callum loves me as I love him. Tis a love born of goodness, of recognition of his nobility. Tis a love ye will never understand and could never achieve even if ye tried for a million years."

"Goodness and nobility," Anaxandra said in a mocking tone. "What a sickening notion."

Her upper lip curled in a murderous sneer as Anaxandra unsheathed an elegant sword. Fearful, Maev backed away, searching frantically for a weapon to defend herself. She glanced fleetingly at Callum's still body, yet worried that even if she could reach him, it would be nearly impossible to wield his heavy claymore.

Anaxandra raised the sword in both hands and swung towards Maev's chest. She jumped back just in time, putting her opponent off balance. Anaxandra stumbled forward, but she turned quickly and aimed again.

Maev managed to deflect the next few blows, but then the side of Anaxandra's sword struck her in the temple. Maev saw an explosion of lights and heard a dull roaring in her head as she staggered to one side and fell. Anaxandra instantly pressed her advantage and attacked. Maev managed to avoid being hurt by rolling away from the wild swings. It was then she realized that Anaxandra had little skill with the weapon.

When she made her next charge, Maev struck back, kicking the sword and knocking it from Anaxandra's hands. With a roar of astonished outrage, Anaxandra fell upon

Maev, her fingers curled liked talons as she sought to scratch and wound.

Using both hands, Maev held off her opponent, but she soon felt her arms begin to tremble with fatigue. Maev knew her strength was failing, yet she was determined to fight to the bitter end. Gathering the last of her reserves, she heaved her attacker forward, thrusting Anaxandra into the open meadow.

At the very instant Anaxandra's body landed in the rolling expanse of grass, the dark fog that had shrouded them all lifted. The sky turned to a smoky blue, and strong yellow rays of sunlight streaked through the fading darkness.

Dawn had broken. And the sun was beginning to shine. The exposed meadow was quickly bathed in a golden light, and it echoed with Anaxandra's screams of agony as a bright ray struck her full force. She fell to her knees, flailing her arms and writhing in pain, trying, and failing, to protect herself from the light. The air sizzled as her flesh burned, the foul stench permeating the very earth itself.

Maev pulled herself into the protective shade of Hadrian's Wall, curling herself into a tight ball as she lay over Callum's prone form. Her heart pounded with emotion as she waited for it to finally end. Though it felt like hours, within minutes all grew quiet and still.

Turning her attention to her beloved, Maev was finally able to rouse Callum from his stupor. After she told him what had happened, he wrapped his arms around her so tightly she feared he would break her ribs.

"Thank the heavens," Callum murmured repeatedly in her ear as he held her close. "I couldna bare to have lost ye again, my love."

Tears gathered in Maev's eyes as she wound her arms around his waist. She felt like shouting with joy, and yet she worried over the repercussions of what she had done. Now that Anaxandra had been destroyed, would her brethren seek retribution?

"The immortals do not live together like a clan and seem to care little about each other," Callum explained when Maev expressed this fear to him.

"Will there be no one who will question Anaxandra's disappearance?" Maev asked.

Callum's face contorted into a frown. "Randulf was often her companion, though she scorned him mercilessly once she made me one of their kind. Still, it would probably be wise to leave no trace of her remains. Without any clues, Randulf will be hard pressed to solve the mystery of her disappearance, if he is so inclined to investigate."

It was difficult to wait until darkness, but they had no choice. Fortunately, while daylight remained, no one appeared in the meadow and discovered the odd rumpled pile of clothing.

Maev and Callum retrieved the garments by the light of the full moon and burned them. Then they buried the ashes, along with the ash of Anaxandra's bones, in a deep hole in the thickest section of the forest.

When they were done, all that remained was the gold talisman studded with precious stones that had hung about Anaxandra's neck.

"What should we do with it?" Maev asked as she lifted the unusual piece of jewelry toward the moonlight. It sparkled with luminous glory. "It must be worth a king's ransom."

"The jewels are rare and valuable, but we have no need of coin. I dinna believe the piece holds any special power, but if it does, the power could be released if we try to destroy it." Callum paused a moment. "We will bury it also, but in a different location, far away from Anaxandra's remains."

Intent on completing their mission while the cover of

darkness continued, they wrapped their cloaks about themselves and untethered their horses. With Callum in the lead, they rode south for several hours. Maev felt her strength increasing with each mile, further proof that she was in truth an English-born woman.

When they found an appropriate spot, Callum dug a very deep hole, dropped the talisman inside, then covered it completely with dark, rich soil, tamping down the earth with his booted foot until it was packed tight. Then he scooped up a fresh section of soil and filled the two leather bags that hung from his saddle.

When he was done, he looked over and smiled, and a great calm settled over Maev. The fear she had felt at the possibility of losing Callum would always be branded in her memory. Yet it made the joy they shared all the more sweet.

Maev coiled her arms around his neck and felt the heat of his passion as she tightened her grip on the solid muscles of his shoulders. But more than anything else, she felt his love.

"Take me home, Callum McGinnis. I might have been born on English soil, but I'm a Scottish lass through and though."

He pulled away, and a delighted smile spread over his handsome face. Everything he felt for her was clearly reflected in his eyes.

"Aye, and I'm proud to say ye are *my* lass. Mine and no other's."

Callum boosted Maev onto her horse, then swung himself up onto his own mount. They made an odd sight, traveling through the moonlit land, a lone warrior and his lady. Although they were bound to a destiny they had not chosen, they had learned to embrace it, because it was the only way they could be together.

Forever.

TO TAME THE
BEAST

Deborah Raleigh

One

The shadows near the castle darkened as a chill settled in the air. Within the thick walls the boisterous celebrations continued unabated, but those servants scurrying about the courtyard abruptly halted with a sense of dread.

"The Beast walks . . ." muttered a grizzled guard, gripping his broadsword in fear.

The Beast walks, echoed on whispers in the still night air.

With a rush of fear, servants hurried toward safety, crossing themselves and mouthing prayers of protection. All knew that to catch sight of the scourge of MacDonnell was certain death.

Standing just outside the open gate, Bane watched the frantic chaos with a cold amusement.

He rarely allowed his presence to be felt. He took scant pleasure in leaving the isolation of his lair and preferred to hunt with stealth.

On this night, however, he desired all to feel his dark force.

Twas, after all, a most special evening.

Within the great hall the Foster laird was celebrating the saint's day for his eldest daughter. The clan was gathered as the maid was toasted and led to the dais as an honored guest.

And a proper sacrifice for the Beast of MacDonnell.

Tonight the lassie turned one and twenty. A thin smile touched his lips. The age he would mark her as his own and lead her to his mist-shrouded lair.

She would come eagerly, of course. The curse would hold her in ruthless enchantment, and she would overcome any obstacle or kill any in her path to make her way to Bane's side.

Not that any would stand in her path, he acknowledged wryly. All knew the ancient legend. And the price demanded to keep the Foster clan from certain death.

Aye. For all their lavish displays of sympathy for the poor lassie, they would truss her up like a fatted pig and toss her into the glen if need be.

He well knew such cowardice. Although two centuries had passed, he could recall with perfect clarity the clansmen who had led him to his own doom. Nary one had been willing to risk the wrath of the chief to offer a warning or lift a sword in his defense.

Honor and loyalty had been sold for no more than a bid to gain favor.

The pale, elegant features hardened. That, of course, had only been the beginning of the treachery.

In the distance Bane could hear the heavy thud of tankards banging against the wooden tables, and he thrust aside his brooding. The celebration would soon be coming to an end. Twas time to claim his sacrifice.

Indifferent to the warriors who lined the battlements, he moved silently toward the gate. What need he fear? His death at the swing of a broadsword now ensured that he was impervious to mortal threat.

An ironic twist of fate that the ancient laird who had

commanded his death would ensure his future heirs would be incapable of halting Bane's revenge.

Almost upon the gate Bane stilled as the sound of approaching footsteps caught his attention. With ease he melted into the shadows, sharply curious to discover who would be daring enough to ignore the thick menace surrounding the castle. Surely they must be daft.

Or desperate . . .

The cold smile once again touched his lips as he tilted back his head to sniff the air. Aye. A Foster lassie. The stench of her blood was unmistakable.

Twas not surprising. This would not be the first occasion his sacrifice attempted to flee, he acknowledged with a flare of disdain. There was little courage or dignity flowing through the veins of his enemy. More than one of the maids would have condemned their entire clan to death if they could slip away and save their own skin.

Content to wait for the lassie to walk toward her doom, Bane absently stroked the delicate golden torc hung about his neck. It would be a simple matter to enchant her as she passed, although not quite so satisfying as luring her away in view of her father and kin.

As the footsteps neared, however, a faint frown marred his smooth countenance.

He once again sniffed the air. There were two females approaching. One an elderly servant. And the other . . .

A Foster lassie, without doubt. But not the one he was seeking.

Stepping deeper into the shadows, he watched them pass through the gate with a narrowed gaze. What would lead the wench out at such an hour? Any woman of sense would be locked in her quarters on such an eve.

Intrigued in spite of himself, Bane studied the slender waif shrouded in silver moonlight.

Although she was wrapped in a heavy cloak, he could tell she was constructed on delicate lines. Far more delicate than most of the raw-boned Foster clan, with a restless spirit that smoldered in the odd, gold-flecked hazel eyes. And unlike the rest of her kin, her hair was not the golden red of a sunrise, but rather a deep simmering fire that tumbled about her ivory skin like licks of flame.

There was little to remind him of the deceitful lassie who had betrayed him near two hundred years before.

Nothing but the smell of her blood.

Lingering despite his urge to complete his revenge and return to his lair, Bane watched as the heavyset servant with a square countenance and braid of course gray hair reached out to grasp the female's cloak.

"Isobella, this is daft. Ye must return to the castle."

With obvious impatience the lassie twitched the cloak from the clinging fingers. "Och, let me be."

"Nay. I cannae let ye," the servant moaned. "There be something terrible foul in the air tonight."

Isobella gave a loud sniff, but Bane did not miss the faint shiver that raced through the slender form.

"Ye would have me cower behind these walls? To await the Beast to come steal my sister as do those pathetic wretches who claim to be noblemen and warriors?"

Her tone was fierce, and Bane lifted a raven brow in surprise. So, 'twas not only her appearance that was at odds with her clan.

"'Tis naught that can be done, mistress. The curse cannae be broken. If Katherine doesnae offer herself to the Beast, every man, woman, and child will be slain. Is that what ye would have?"

"Of course not. But neither do I intend to do no more than wail and bemoan Katherine's fate. There must be some means to halt the curse." The lassie wrapped her cloak even tighter about herself as she glanced toward the nearby trees. "There must be."

"There is none. All who have tried are in their graves," the servant retorted. "If nay worse."

"So we have been told. For too long we have been held in the clutches of fear to even attempt an end to the plague that besieges us."

"Nay, mistress." The older woman hastily crossed herself, perhaps sensing the danger that lurked in the shadows. "Many have entered the cursed glen never to return."

Isobella gave a toss of her head. "Foolish lads and drunken warriors out to seek glory. They blunder forward where stealth is needed. None have attempted to discover the weakness of the Beast so that it might be slain."

"That is what ye intend to do?"

"What else can I do?" The delicate features hardened in the moonlight. "I cannae hide here and do nothing."

Bane stilled, caught in an odd sense of fascination.

"Tis sorely hard, but consider, lassie, there is nay saying the Beast will come for Katherine on this night. It is said in the past he has ofttimes waited days and even weeks afore he claimed his prize."

"But he will come," she said in flat tones.

The servant sighed. "Aye, he will come."

"I will put off my duty no longer. I had hoped that Father would gather his courage and do what is necessary . . . och." Isobella squared her shoulders. "I hoped in vain. Now 'tis upon my shoulders."

"Nay."

"Aye. Go back to the great hall. Stay with Katherine."

Although the command was said in a gentle manner, there was no mistaking the authority in the wench's voice. This was a maid who was accustomed to having her orders obeyed.

Lifting her shawl to dab at her eyes, the servant scurried back through the gate. Left on her own, Isobella paused for a moment, glancing about the darkness with obvious unease. Then, with a tilt of her chin, she briskly moved toward the nearby trees.

Bane found himself hesitating. He had one purpose when he had approached the castle. To capture his prize and return to his lair. Simple and uncomplicated. Just as he preferred his existence to be.

Now, however, he could not deny a strange compulsion gathering within him. The lassie had done something to him that no one had managed in near two centuries.

She had stirred his interest.

Flowing through the darkness behind the slender form, Bane did not bother to ponder his distraction. Aye, what did it matter? Twas enough he must discover more of the wench.

With unnatural ease, he managed to pass through the thickening woods. Not so much as a leaf rustled or twig snapped. His presence, however, remained thick in the air, quickening the maid's step as she glanced over her shoulder with mounting apprehension. She could feel him closing in. Still she continued forward, perhaps attempting to convince herself that the prickles on her skin were mere fancy.

They traveled ever closer to the misty glen that protected his lair. Bane faintly smiled at her courage. Or perhaps madness. Few had ever conjured the nerve to wander so close.

Altering her path, the lassie stepped into a small opening. Then, spinning about, she pressed her back to a tree and pulled a small dirk from beneath her cloak.

"Who is there?" she demanded. "Show yerself."

Bane studied the frantic pulse beating at the base of her throat. God's teeth but she stirred his instincts. Bloodlust. But . . . more. Some sensation that seemed a distant echo of a forgotten memory.

Remaining in the gloom of the circling trees, Bane folded his arms over his chest.

"Do ye think to command me, lassie?"

The pulse fluttered with even more force, but astonishingly she remained poised to fight rather than flee.

"As is my right." Her voice rang through the clearing. "This is Foster land, and I am the laird's daughter."

His lips curled. "How proudly spoken."

"Not proudly, 'tis merely the truth."

"I know who ye are," he said with a cool disdain. "I can smell the taint of yer father's blood in the air."

The hazel eyes widened with startled anger. "Ye seek to insult me while hiding behind the trees? Why do ye lurk in the shadows? Are ye shamed to show yer face?"

"I have no need for shame, my honor is above reproach." He allowed a faint pause. "Can ye say the same, daughter of Foster?"

A dull blush marred her ivory skin. Bane narrowed his gaze. So, the wench felt the sting of her family disgrace. A far cry more than her father suffered.

"Ye waste my time," she gritted. "I nay desire foolish games."

"Ah. Then what is it ye *do* desire alone in the darkness?" he drawled.

"Merely to be on my way."

Silently Bane shifted through the trees, coming ever closer. "On yer way to where?"

She frowned, sensing his movement but unable to see him through the darkness.

"That is my business and my business alone."

"Should ye not be safely tucked in yer virginal blankets at such an hour? The dark is a dangerous place for such a beautiful lassie."

"I have no fear." With a determined motion she lifted the dirk to brandish it at the shadows.

Bane offered a rasping laugh. "Ye believe that ye are protected by that slender blade? Or is it that shrill tongue ye depend upon to keep the demons at bay?"

Her lips thinned. "I am protected by my father and his men. Should any harm befall me, there would be nowhere safe enough for ye to hide."

Bane stilled, his age-old fury flowing through his body. Twas in this very spot that he had been surrounded by Foster warriors and brutally attacked.

And all for the love of a woman.

"Ah, the same father who drinks in his hall and waits to toss his daughter to the Beast of MacDonnell?" he mocked. "I tremble in terror."

Her color deepened. As much in anger as in shame.

"Saints above, I will not talk to shadows," she gritted. "Show yerself or be on yer way."

Bane hesitated. He should be on his way. To return either to the castle and his waiting sacrifice, or to the comfort of his lair. To linger implied more than a passing curiosity.

Oddly, as the thought brushed through his mind, he already had made his decision. He would be lingering. It had been near two centuries since he had considered a lassie more than a source of revenge.

Or dinner.

He was not as anxious as he should be to return to his solitary brooding.

Ignoring the prickle of warning in the back of his mind, Bane stepped forward, allowing the moonlight to reveal his cloaked form.

"As ye wish."

Isobella was not daft. Indeed, most claimed she was cursed to have been born with wits more suited to a man than a maid.

From the moment she had left the castle, she had known she was on a fool's errand.

For centuries the Beast had plagued her family, claiming the eldest Foster daughter in each generation without mercy. And for centuries not one laird or warrior had managed to do more than mutter beneath his breath and shake his fists in futile frustration.

None could enter the mist where the Beast lay in wait. Not without certain death. And not even the most fearsome warrior was willing to brave the dark when a chill settled in the air and whispers of the Beast echoed through the garrison.

What could a lassie with no more than a small dirk do?

Twas a question that she had no answer for. Not even as she had commanded her nurse back to the castle and she had forced her reluctant feet toward the distant glen.

All she knew for certain was that watching her father and his warriors drink themselves into a stupor while poor Katherine awaited death was more than she could bear.

God's teeth, she was no coward. Let the others hide away and blame Katherine's loss on destiny.

She would at least make an effort to save her.

With only a vague hope of stumbling over the Beast and somehow halting it, she had ignored the thick chill in the air that had made her skin prickle in fear. The lair was not far from the castle. Surely she could maintain her courage for such a short span of time?

Intent upon recalling how to breathe, Isobella did not note the foreboding sense she was being watched. Not until she had entered the dark forest.

Twas not that she actually heard the intruder. Or caught sight of a lurking form. Twas more the menacing awareness that lodged deep in her heart.

Too far from the castle to call out, Isobella was forced to

settle for the small clearing, where she could attempt to bluster the stranger away.

It had been a reasonable plan.

Until the intruder had stepped from the trees.

The fear clawing at her belly had suddenly been replaced with sharp disbelief.

By all saints, he was . . .

Beautiful.

Taller even than her father, who was considered a brawny man, he was lean and hard muscled beneath the silk cloak. In the moonlight his long hair was as dark and glossy as a raven wing and flowed well past his shoulders. His countenance was angular with flawless alabaster skin and features that made her breath catch in her throat. Perhaps his brow was a bit too broad and his mouth too sensually full, but such tedious flaws did not alter the impression of unearthly male beauty.

Swallowing the odd lump in her throat, Isobella at last forced herself to meet his watchful gaze. Her heart gave yet another leap.

Och. Never in all her years had she seen such eyes.

Silver in color, they shimmered with a cold fire, like the flash of hardened steel. And just as lethal.

A beautiful man, a voice whispered in the back of her mind, but dangerous.

Perhaps as dangerous as the Beast itself.

Holding the dirk high in an obvious threat, Isobella forced herself to take a breath.

"Who are ye?"

"A passing traveler," he murmured, his voice silky and edged with a peculiar lilt.

He was not of her father's clan. Nor any other clan they warred against. Not with that dark hair and strange silver eyes. Still, he had known too much of her to be a simple traveler.

"I dinnae believe ye."

"Nay?"

"A traveler would not pass through Foster land without halting at the castle to seek my father's favor."

"Favor?" His glittered with a dangerous fire. "I seek no man's favor. I walk where I desire and none stand in my way."

"Ye are very sure of yer courage before a mere maid. I doubt ye would be so brave if my father's warriors were to appear."

A raven brow arched as he stepped toward her with a fluid grace. "Should yer father's warriors appear, they will die."

She clutched the dirk until her knuckles whitened. "Stand back or I swear I shall make ye bleed."

He offered a passing glance toward the sharpened blade before he casually reached out to knock it from her hand.

"Dinnae seek to threaten me, wench." He was standing so close Isobella was forced to tilt back her head to look at him. In the moonlight he appeared breathtakingly handsome as he reached out to capture a stray curl that lay against her cheek. Isobella's mouth went dry and her heart missed several beats. She told herself it was fear. What maid of sense would not be terrified? But there was a warm, magical tingle feathering down her spine that she suspected had nothing to do with terror. "Ye have not the look of a Foster. I have not seen hair such as this. Nor eyes that have been kissed by gold. Tis peculiar."

She swallowed heavily. "If ye imply I am a bastard . . ."

"Did I not tell ye that I smell the stench of yer father's blood? Nay, ye are a Foster, more's the pity." His fingers drifted down her cheek to linger upon the pulse racing at the base of her throat. "But beautiful for all yer sins."

For an embarrassing moment Isobella feared her knees might give way. His flesh was chilled as ice, but there was nothing cold in the searing heat that flared at his light touch. It was like being struck by lightning, and Isobella savagely bit her bottom lip to keep from moaning.

Bones of Saint Mark, dinnae be a dolt, Isobella Foster, she sternly chided herself. The man was obviously an enemy of her father.

He could be there to take her captive and hold her for ransom. Or dishonor her. Or even kill her.

And all she could think to do was flutter over his male countenance.

Some warrior she was proving to be.

"And ye are overly bold, traveler," she gritted.

A slow smile curved his lips. "I feel yer heart quicken. Are ye frightened?"

"Nay."

"Tell me what ye seek in the dark."

His silky voice was weaving a spell about Isobella. With a frown she sought to shake off the strange lethargy seeping through her.

"Leave me be."

"Tell me."

She had no intention of telling the stranger anything of her business. What she sought in the dark was no one's concern but her own. Besides which, she was the laird's daughter. She answered only to her father.

So why were her lips opening and her gaze helplessly locked with the piercing silver eyes?

"I seek . . . the Beast."

"The Beast?"

"Aye, a fierce creature who has cursed my clan for generations."

"Ah." There was a faint pause as his lips seemed to twitch. "Ye have seen this Beast?"

"Och, of course not. He skulks in the fog nay showing himself, although 'tis rumored that he hunts during the light of the moon. And soon he intends to come for my sister. I shall be waiting for him to reveal himself."

The slender fingers abruptly shifted to grasp her chin, tilting her face upward so that he could study her features in the silver light.

"Ye, my sweeting, are most daring, or most foolish," he muttered in rather odd tones. "Surely ye cannae believe to kill a creature of legend?" His gaze slowly drifted down to her parted lips. "Or perhaps ye hope to seduce him to yer will?"

She sucked in a rasping breath. This man. He was befuddling her in a manner she could not explain.

"If he lives, he can be killed. I will find the means to do so."

His grip loosened, allowing his fingers to gently stroke the line of her lips. In the dim shadows of Isobella's mind she knew she should protest, but the bewitching spell held her captive. Her hands lifted to rest against his chest. Beneath her palms she could feel the cool silk of his cloak and hard steel of his muscles. A dark fire sparked deep within her.

"Should it not be yer father and brave warriors who hunt for the curse to his clan?" he murmured.

"Tis my choice."

The silver eyes darkened to a smoky gray. The austere features seemed to soften as his head began to lower.

"Nay, my beauty. Tis mine," he whispered against her lips.

A fierce shock of pleasure kicked through Isobella as he offered a featherlight kiss. Och, but she had dreamed of this moment. Longed for it, if truth be told. What maid did not dwell upon her first kiss?

And yet it still caught her off guard.

The men in her clan did not softly seduce women with their lips. They did not allow their fingers to tenderly sweep over a maid's countenance as if she were a rare and delicate object or murmur tantalizing words that made a woman shiver with longing. They were as likely to grab a woman and take their pleasure without once considering the lady in their arms.

Isobella leaned into his hard form, lost in his scent of mist and smoke. This was the magic she had dreamed of. The searing heat that flared through her blood. The sharp, aching excitement that settled in the cradle of her thighs.

His lips molded to her own, gently tasting of her before pulling back. Over and over he teased her with his tender touch until Isobella was ready to howl with frustration.

With a low growl deep in her throat she thrust her fingers into the thick satin of his hair, arching her body until there was not a breath between them. She possessed a craving she could not explain. A craving only he could fulfill.

As if he had been awaiting that precise moment, his kiss abruptly deepened, his tongue stroking over her lips. Isobella gasped, uncertain what he desired.

"Open for me, Isobella," he muttered, his hands grasping her hips and pressing them urgently into his hardening thighs.

Tentatively she parted her lips and moaned as his tongue invaded her mouth. Her old nurse had never said anything of such doings when explaining what occurred between men and maids in the darkness of night. Nor just how pleasurable such . . . intimacy could be.

Her fingers tightened in his hair, her body shivering. She was as close to the man as was possible, but it was still not close enough. She was yearning for something. Something just out of reach.

With a faint hiss the man was scattering fierce kisses over her upturned countenance then down the length of her arched neck. There was a pause, almost as if he were inwardly battling with himself, and then Isobella felt a sharp fire at the base of her throat.

"Forgive me," she heard him whisper as his teeth sank deep into her flesh and a thick blanket of darkness descended over her.

She knew no more.

Two

Isobella battled her way through the clinging darkness.

For long moments she lay still as she attempted to recall where she was and why her head ached like the very devil.

It did not take long to realize she was in her own quarters. There was no mistaking the scent of dried flowers she kept in bowls beside her bed or the fresh linens she demanded be changed daily beneath her.

A relief, she acknowledged, but it did not offer enlightenment as to why she felt as if someone had used her head to batten down the castle gates.

Grimly she sought to dredge up memories of the previous eve.

She recalled the celebration for her sister. She had forced herself to remain through the endless supper and drunken toasts until her teeth had ached. And then . . . what?

There was a vague memory of speaking with her old nurse and walking through the forest, but it all seemed like more of a dream than truth. A tattered nightmare that was created out of the worry preying upon her mind.

Isobella stirred uneasily. There had been something more.

A fear that had haunted her as she had walked through the dark and then . . . a man.

Blessed Mary. Her heart nearly halted.

Aye. There had been a man.

A beautiful, dangerous man who had stolen her wits and very nearly her heart when his lips had so softly touched her own.

And he had been no dream. Nor a nightmare.

Even now she could vividly feel the cool touch of his fingers and the heat flowing through her blood. It had been magical as he had kissed her in the moonlight and then . . . everything had gone black.

What had he done to her? And how had he returned her to her own bed with no one the wiser?

"Does she still sleep?" The soft, lilting voice of her sister abruptly intruded into Isobella's confused thoughts.

"Aye, mistress," her old nurse retorted close to Isobella's ear, her voice rough with worry. "I sorely fear she is ill."

A slender hand descended onto Isobella's forehead. "She has no fever, no wounds. Mayhap she is just weary from the night of revelry. I dinnae believe any slept well with such noise coming from the hall."

"Och, 'twas not the revelry. The lassie took herself—"

Stiffening at the realization the servant was about to reveal her foolishness of last eve, Isobella forced open her heavy lids.

"Enough, Janet," she rasped, flashing her nurse a warning frown. She had no desire to have her sister fretting over her. "Prepare my bath, I feel in dire need of a hot soak."

The thin lips nearly disappeared in disapproval, but she dared no more than a loud sniff as she straightened from the bed.

"Aye."

Waiting until they were alone, Katherine gently smoothed back the hair from Isobella's cheek. Unlike her younger sister, Katherine was tall with shapely curves and the golden hair of their father. A beautiful maid who should be wed and surrounded by children, not awaiting her death.

Isobella's heart clenched with a familiar ache.

"Oh, Isobella, Janet had me so concerned," her sister murmured. "She said that ye would not waken and that she feared ye had been injured."

Isobella forced a stiff smile to her lips. "Och, the old fool is always fussing o'er some bit of nonsense."

Katherine was not so easily fooled. "Is it nonsense? Ye're very pale. And cold to the touch. It seems an odd malady."

"I am very well, Katherine, merely tired." She grimaced, keeping as close to the truth as possible. Her sister would easily sense a blatant lie. "The night proved to be a long one."

Her sister sighed. "Aye. For me as well."

"Come." Shifting on the bed, Isobella tugged her sister down beside her. She held her tightly in her arms, laying her cheek upon the top of her head.

"I came to speak with ye last eve but could not find ye," Katherine murmured.

"I fear I could not sleep."

"Where did ye go?"

"Merely for a walk upon the grounds."

"Isobella." Her sister leaned back to regard her with a stern expression. "Ye went for a walk in the midst of the night? What if the Beast—"

"I am not the one who need fear the Beast," Isobella retorted in edged tones.

"There are other dangers in the dark."

The memory of a lean alabaster countenance and silver eyes filled her mind.

"Yes, so I have discovered."

Easily sensing the tension in Isobella, her sister offered a small frown. "Did something occur?"

"Nay."

The frown deepened. "Isobella?"

"Aye?"

Katherine sighed. "I wish yer promise ye will take better care. Soon I will be gone and—"

Isobella caught her breath as a pain twisted her heart. "Nay, dinnae say it, Katherine."

"I must. I love ye with all my heart, but ye're far too stubborn and inclined to rush into trouble with no regard for yerself. Father will not attempt to halt yer reckless follies, nor will any other man." A rueful smile softened the beautiful features. "I ofttimes believe they fear ye more than the Beast."

"And well they should," Isobella retorted fiercely. "I have no stomach for men who claim the bravery of warriors and then cower behind these walls when we most have need of them."

A hint of sadness entered Katherine's green eyes. "That is not fair, Isobella. There is nothing brave in hunting a beast who moves upon the wind and cannae be touched by steel. Tis the way of the clan, and there is nay sense in blaming our menfolk on what cannae be altered."

It was a familiar argument, but Isobella refused to be swayed. "How do they know it cannae be altered if they are not even willing to try?"

Katherine lightly touched her cheek. "Hush, my love, such bitterness is unseemly. Soon ye will have to take one of the men as husband. He will not thank ye for having branded him a coward."

"Husband?" Isobella widened her gaze in astonishment. "Katherine, ye must be daft. All ken that none of our brave and honorable clansmen are willing to have me, no matter how tempting the dowry. Indeed, 'tis a common jest among the men that it would be more comforting to share a bed with a wild boar than the laird's youngest daughter."

"Ye should not listen to such talk. Tis only the jealous mutters of lesser maids."

"Nay, 'tis the truth and I assure ye that it bothers me not a wit. Tis for the best that I become a spinster. I have no talent in bending my will to another and even less talent in pandering to the whims of a husband. I should only be miserable to be sold off as a broodmare and my husband even more so to have me."

"But—"

"Enough, Katherine." With a firm motion, Isobella crawled from the bed. She had no desire to argue with her sister. Besides, she needed a few moments alone to sift through her still foggy thoughts. Something had occurred last eve. Something strange and unexpected. She needed to determine what that might mean for Katherine. "I feel in dire need of my bath."

"I . . ." There was another sigh. No one attempted to gainsay Isobella when she used that precise tone. "Very well."

Bane's magnificent stone castle had been created by the same witch who had snatched him from the arms of death. It was a structure of mist and magic, but his artistic nature gloried in the flowing architecture and lush tapestries. Not even the King himself could boast such luxury. And most importantly, it remained constantly shrouded in a thick fog that protected him from the harsh glare of sunlight.

At any hour he could walk the battlements or stroll through the glen with no concern. It was his one source of peace in a very dark existence.

He was seated in the lavish comfort of his library when he felt a prickling awareness crawl over his skin.

With a smooth motion he was on his feet.

Isobella.

Despite the fact she had barely left the gates of her father's keep, he could sense her approach. As well as her determination.

But why?

He had taken care to use his powers to hide all memories of their encounter. It was the same power he used after feeding upon the stray travelers who passed by the glen. They would awaken, weakened and slightly dazed, never recalling they had encountered the notorious Beast of MacDonnell.

Was she simply so stubborn that she continued her foolish fight against her sister's doom? Or did she possess the rare ability to thrust through the barriers he had erected in her mind?

Or most disturbing of all, had he silently called to her despite his grim hold upon his instincts?

The questions plagued him as he discovered himself swiftly moving through the castle and out into the glen. He could, of course, allow the lassie to enter the mist. She would never stumble onto the castle. It was far too well protected. Instead she would simply wander in confusion for days until she at last died of hunger.

It would solve more than one problem. Including the fierce, biting desire that had haunted him since he had taken her in his arms last eve.

Still, his step never faltered.

The stirring of passions he had thought left in his grave were no doubt a worrisome distraction. For two centuries he had survived within a cloak of bleak loneliness. Only his lust for revenge was allowed to disturb his frozen calm.

But distraction or not, he had to concede that he was not yet prepared to banish the tantalizing heat that Isobella aroused deep within him.

It had been so long since he had experienced such sweet temptation.

So terribly long.

Moving with a flowing speed, Bane was out of the castle

and moving through the mist. In the distance he could sense Isobella coming ever closer.

He could sense it in the prickles that whispered over his skin and the odd warmth that battled the ice of his dead heart.

Reaching the edge of the mist, Bane was forced to halt and impatiently await the unexpected intruder. Although dusk had fallen, it was not yet dark enough for him to risk leaving the protection of his lair. A stark price he paid for his immortal existence.

Pacing with what he could only suppose was impatience, Bane counted the moments until he could at last hear the faint rustle of leaves as Isobella approached. Shifting until he was directly in her path, he was prepared as she abruptly appeared within the swirl of fog.

Lifting his hands, he placed them firmly upon her shoulders. "Come no farther," he commanded.

She stilled beneath his touch, her hazel gaze wide as she regarded him in silence for a long moment.

"So . . . ye are real," she at last breathed.

His lips twitched even as he silently warned himself to take care. This lassie clearly possessed the ability to pierce through his web of magic. Yet another reason to keep her at a distance, a warning voice whispered in the back of his mind.

A voice ignored by his hands, which compulsively smoothed over her shoulders and down her back. By all the fires of hell, it felt so wondrous to touch her.

"Not entirely," he conceded wryly.

Her brows tugged together, although he was relieved when she did not pull away in fear.

"Who are ye?" she demanded. "Or should I ask . . ." She swallowed heavily. "What are ye?"

Two questions he had no intention of answering. Bane allowed his features to tighten with disapproval.

"Why are ye here, Isobella? Tis beyond foolish to enter the mist. Unless ye desire death?"

Surprisingly an expression that might almost have been petulance settled on her lovely countenance.

"I dinnae wish to be here. I am not utterly daft."

Well, one of them was surely daft, he acknowledged with a slow shake of his head.

"Then why the devil are ye?"

"Because I could not halt myself," she muttered. "No matter how I battled, the need to come here was like a fever in my blood. It has plagued me all day." Her gaze narrowed with suspicion. "Have ye put a spell upon me?"

Bane's fingers abruptly tightened upon her back. Blood of the saints. Despite all his grim determination, his need had still managed to call for her.

Or had it?

Was it possible that there was something more to this overwhelming awareness that clawed within him? Something occurring between them that was beyond both of their understanding?

And which was the lesser of two evils?

He met her gaze steadily. "I wish it was such a simple matter."

"What do ye mean?"

"If it were a mere spell, then I could release the both of us. As it is . . . it appears we are both ensnared for the moment."

She caught her lower lip between her teeth. It was obviously not the reassurance that she sought. Indeed the suspicion in her eyes only deepened.

"Ye still have not told me who ye are."

Unable to halt himself, Bane stepped closer to her delicate form, allowing her sweet warmth to seep into his skin.

"Does it truly matter?" he husked.

"I . . . of course it does."

His hand shifted to the curve of her hips. They were narrow but perfectly formed and an enticement that made Bane clench his teeth.

"Why?"

There was a pause as if she were carefully considering her words.

"Because I believe ye have some knowledge of the Beast of MacDonnell," she accused. "Perhaps ye are even a servant of his."

His raven brows shot upward. "I am no servant."

"But ye do know of him?"

He bit back the urge to lie. What did he care if she feared him? Or fled from him in terror? Twas what he desired of all treacherous Fosters.

Was it not?

"Aye."

He refused to acknowledge his relief when the hazel eyes darkened with fury rather than the horror she should have revealed.

"And ye know of his plans to take my sister as his sacrifice."

He lifted a broad shoulder. "All know of the sacrifice."

"Ye did not answer my question," she gritted. "Are ye a threat to my sister?"

"Yer sister has belonged to the Beast since the day she was born."

Without warning, she was stepping from his light grasp, her countenance glowing with a fierce determination so lacking in her ancestors.

"Why? She has done nothing. She is an innocent."

Bane unconsciously tilted his head to an arrogant angle. He was unaccustomed to being challenged. At least not since his return to this world.

"She carries the sin of her forbearers. Tis justice."

"Nay, 'tis revenge being offered on one who is blameless. Has not enough Foster blood been shed?"

His features hardened with the bleakness echoed within his heart.

"Is there enough blood to heal the wounds of betrayal and treachery and murder?" he demanded.

She seemed to falter at the cutting edge in his voice and the sudden chill in the air. No doubt she was regretting the relentless desire that had led her to his lair.

"Ye speak of ancient legends," she at last retorted.

His gaze narrowed. "And what do ye know of them?"

She gave a restless shrug. "The story claims that a bard fell in love with the laird's wife, and when he attempted to kidnap her, the laird had him taken to the glen and killed. Or at least they attempted to kill him. Somehow he managed to crawl from his grave, and since that night he has taken the form of a beast and stolen away the first daughter of every Foster laird as a sacrifice."

A cold disdain made Bane's hands clench at his side. It seemed his enemies considered no sin too wretched or too cowardly to indulge in.

"Blood of the saints, I should have known that Fosters could speak nothing but lies," he rasped. "Honor has no meaning for them."

A flare of color touched her cheeks. As much for embarrassment at her family as in anger at his insult.

"I dinnae lie."

He gave an abrupt wave of his hand.

"I have already accepted that ye are a rare Foster. Yer clan cannae claim yer preference for the truth."

She regarded him for a long moment, as if attempting to see into his very heart.

"Ye say the story is false?"

His jaw clenched. For him the betrayal was not an ancient fable nearly forgotten in the mist of time. It was a cold ache that never faded, never healed, no matter how many years might pass.

"Of course 'tis false," he drawled in icy tones. "The bard was a simple man but he was no thief. The lassie was unwed and quite willing to be wooed by the bard, and even pleaded to be made his bride."

Isobella sent him a frown. "She was wed to the laird."

Bane gave a short, humorless laugh. "Not until the laird happened into the small village and caught sight of the maid," he corrected, an unwanted memory of the golden-haired beauty flaring through his mind. He had tumbled in love the moment he had caught sight of her. Unfortunately he had been young and foolish enough to believe she could return his love. "She was beautiful, of course, and capable of bewitching with a smile. The laird decided in a moment he would have her. No matter whom she might belong to."

Isobella took a stumbled step backward. "He . . . forced her?"

"Nothing so tragic," he admitted, his voice without emotion. "He wooed her with the promise of a life far more tempting than that of a bard. She would be the laird's wife with servants, and silks and spices. In truth, it took wee convincing. She was in his bed afore the sun had set."

She sucked in a sharp breath. "And what of the bard?"

Bane smiled coldly. It was difficult to recall how he had ever been so innocent, or so trusting. It had never entered his thoughts that his lover would be other than terrified by the laird's lusty intentions. Or that she might weigh the differences between marriage to a lowly bard and being wed to a laird.

Love and loyalty to him had been pure and unwavering. It could not be bought and sold with the toss of a coin.

"Being a fool, he had no notion he had been so easily betrayed by his beloved. When he was told she was awaiting him in the forest so that they might run away together and escape the laird, he eagerly sought her out. Of course, 'twas not his lover awaiting him."

Her face paled in shock. "He was killed."

"Quite brutally. Every warrior desired to return to the laird with blood on his sword. It assured them a fine reward."

Isobella pressed a hand to her breast, clearly disturbed by his blunt words.

"That is horrible."

"Aye . . . horrible."

Three

Isobella pressed her hands to her unsettled stomach as she turned from the burning silver of his gaze.

She should not have come here.

In all truth, she had not intended to do so.

Although she was still determined to find some means to rescue her sister from the curse, Isobella was not utterly witless.

Last eve she had been crazed with worry for her sister and incapable of thinking clearly. She had bolted into the darkness without considering just how foolish she was being.

She had had an entire day to consider the height of her folly.

And to dwell upon her encounter with the mysterious stranger.

Who had he been?

Or perhaps more importantly, what had he been?

Twas no natural man, of that she was certain. What man possessed such shocking beauty? Or moved with such fluid silence? Or could seduce a maid with a mere kiss?

And what man could so bewitch a lassie that she could not even recall returning to her bed?

Aye, she had been a fool. Twas only stupid luck that she hadn't been carried off to the Beast's lair. Or simply murdered in the woods and left for the scavengers to feast upon.

But even as she had gone about her duties overseeing the servants and chastising herself for having been so impulsive, she had been unable to banish the elegant male countenance and silver eyes.

It had not been the sweet moonings of a woman who had just had her first kiss. Or even fear at the realization that she had allowed herself to be near seduced by a . . . a creature of the night.

Twas more an itch that she couldn't get scratched.

An itch that became more bothersome and more intolerable with every passing hour.

As the sun had at last tilted toward the horizon, she could bear no more. She was uncertain what the stranger had done to her, but she did know that she could no more prevent herself from seeking him out than she could halt her heart from beating.

Slipping from the great hall, she had collected her cloak and was out of the castle before she could ever be missed.

A part of her had not expected to actually discover the creature. The entire eve still seemed more like an odd dream than reality.

But another part harbored a sense of inevitable doom.

He was out there, it whispered in the back of her mind. Just waiting for her.

And he had been.

Not only waiting, but just as wickedly beautiful and disturbing as she recalled.

Thank the heavens she had possessed enough sense to refrain from tossing herself into his arms. Although it was a task that became more difficult with every passing moment.

Every instinct urged her to abandon herself to the strange sensations he created deep in her heart.

Instead she forced herself to concentrate upon her sister.

Katherine was all that should matter to her.

Nothing else.

"Tis a tragic tale," she muttered at last, reluctantly moved in spite of herself by his words. "But the laird and his bride are long dead. What is the pleasure in punishing Katherine for a betrayal that was not her own?"

The hauntingly beautiful countenance hardened at her persistence. "It has naught to do with pleasure. The curse was given and it cannae be broken."

"There must be some means. I willnae accept that Katherine's death is inevitable." A pain wrenched her heart. "I cannae."

He regarded her for a long moment before slowly reaching out to gently touch a stray curl that lay upon her cheek.

"I begin to believe ye must be a changling."

Isobella was lost in the compelling silver gaze. "Why do ye say such a thing?"

"Because for all yer Foster blood, ye possess few of their traits."

His touch. So cold, and yet sending a violent heat surging through her.

"I . . . I have the look of my mother."

"Nay, 'tis not yer looks, although they are . . . exquisite. Tis yer courage, and fire and loyalty to yer sister," he murmured in silken tones that shivered down her spine. "None before ye have ever attempted to battle the Beast."

"My father would call it foolishness, not courage."

The thin nose flared with an increasingly familiar distaste. Whether servant or companion to the Beast, this creature obviously held her father in contempt.

"Because he is shamed, he cannae claim such an admirable spirit."

Isobella gave a restless shrug. She was not close to her father; indeed their relationship was prickly at best. But because he was her kin, she disliked having his faults so blatantly revealed.

"For all my spirit, I am not any closer to saving my sister. The Beast could appear any moment and I have no means to halt him."

His lips thinned with impatience, his fingers shifting to grasp her chin. "Even if he does not come, yer sister will still be beneath the curse. Eventually the compulsion to seek out his lair will overcome her. Naught can alter the inevitable."

Her entire body tingled at his touch, and Isobella struggled against the urge to melt against him.

Katherine, she sternly reminded herself. She could not forget Katherine.

"Unless I can bring an end to the Beast."

"Mayhap," he murmured, his tone distracted as his fingers traced the line of her jaw.

Her heart jolted. "Will ye take me to him?"

"Nay." The elegant features softened as a smoldering fire entered the silver eyes. "For all yer courage, ye are no match for the Beast."

Those slender fingers traced down her throat, lingering at the frantic pulse at the base of her neck. Och, she nearly purred with pleasure.

"There must be some means."

"None that ye possess."

"I am hardly likely to take yer word for it. Tis obvious ye are somehow connected to the monster."

Astonishingly his lips twitched at her fierce words. "And if I am? Do ye intend me harm?"

"If ye threaten my sister."

The twitch became a smile revealing strong, white teeth. "And how would ye accomplish such a mighty feat?"

Her gaze narrowed. "Are ye laughing at me?"

There was a moment of silence. Almost as if he was forced to consider her accusation. Then he gave a slow, disbelieving shake of his head.

"By all that is holy, I believe I am," he murmured. "Astonishing."

"Nay, 'tis not astonishing, 'tis insulting. I . . ." Her angry words became a shriek of surprise when he reached out to sweep her off her feet and cradled her high against his chest. "What are ye doing?"

He gazed down at her startled expression. Isobella's breath was wrenched from her throat at the searing heat in his gaze.

"I suddenly have wee desire to discuss curses, or beasts, or sisters," he rasped. "Ye are so lovely."

She trembled, her thoughts becoming clouded as pure desire flooded through her. His arms could crush her, and yet they cuddled her with a tender care. As if she were a fragile treasure rather than a shrill-tongued spinster. Perhaps, 'twas sinful, but nothing had ever felt so wondrous before.

"Nay, I am too skinny and my hair too red," she felt bound to protest.

His brows snapped together as he carried her deeper in the mist. "Who would tell ye such foolishness?"

"I need no one to tell me. I possess a mirror."

"It must be flawed." The silver gaze flared over her countenance, lingering upon her unsteady lips. "For an eternity I have collected the most rare and beautiful objects and none have satisfied my demanding taste as ye do."

She was burning from within, aching with a need she did not comprehend. It was a frightening sensation.

"Ye must put me down."

"If ye insist."

She was startled by his ready agreement. Creature or man, he did not take orders from anyone.

Too late she realized her mistake. Bending down he gently laid her upon a bed of moss and covered her with his hard body. It all happened so swiftly she was unable to roll away.

And then she had no desire to roll away.

Bane softly hissed in exquisite pleasure.

By the fires of hell, she felt good beneath him. So tiny, so delicate. Like a wood nymph that had strayed into his lair.

And so very warm.

His eyes slid closed as her heat cloaked about him. It had been so very long he had nearly forgotten the sheer pleasure of having a woman in his arms.

The softness of her curves, her sweet scent, the rasp of her breath as she quickened beneath him.

She was all that he had lost. And he ached for her with a fierce need that made him groan deep in his throat.

"Isobella."

Her hands gently fluttered to his chest, but much to his relief, she did not attempt to push him away.

"This is not what I meant," she breathed.

Bane regarded her from beneath his lowered lashes. "Yer heart races," he murmured. "Are ye frightened?"

She gave a rather bewildered shake of her head. "I should be. I dinnae know who or what ye are."

"If ye insist upon an introduction, ye may call me Bane."

"Bane." She considered a moment. "Tis an odd name, but it fits ye."

"Now what can ye mean by that, I wonder?"

Surprisingly she shifted her hand to lightly touch his cheek. "I suspect that ye are more than a mere man."

He gritted his teeth at the sharp bite of desire. Her touch was tentative, but it was enough to unleash the hunger burning through his body.

"Not at the moment. Ye have stirred feelings I thought forgotten forever." His head lowered to bury his face in the satin spill of her hair. "Ye smell so sweet. Like a field of flowers."

He felt her breath catch. "Och, this is madness."

"Madness, indeed." He turned his head to nuzzle his lips against her temple, his hands smoothing aside her heavy cloak and tugging at the ribbons at her bodice.

"Bane."

"I need to see ye. To touch ye. Tis a fever in my blood," he muttered, pulling back as he tugged down the loose material of her gown. A growl rumbled in his throat as he revealed the curve of her breasts. In the misty glow her skin was as perfect as a rare pearl, the small mounds of her breasts tipped with rose-hued nipples.

For a long moment he regarded her in stunned silence. It was not just the desire that held him motionless. Or the burning in his thighs that strained for release. Although it had been two centuries since he had enjoyed the delicious sensations, he recalled passion, and the need to brand a woman as his own. But there was something more in the fire racing through his body. A strange tenderness and fierce need to wrap her in his arms and never let her escape.

This woman was utterly unlike the maid who had betrayed him. She was brave and honorable and willing to risk everything for those she loved.

Slowly he lowered his head, brushing his lips over the swell of her breast. She gave a startled moan, then ramming her fingers roughly into his hair, she arched upward in silent demand.

Bane did not hesitate. Allowing the heat and scent of her to wash through him, he swept his tongue over the rosy nipple, teasing it to a straining peak before closing his lips about it to suckle with urgent insistence. She shivered with approval, and his hands ran an impatient path down the curve of her hips, tugging her legs apart so he could settle in the cradle of her thighs.

He was hard and straining as he gently rocked himself against her, damning the clothes that hampered his full possession.

"Oh." Isobella squeezed her eyes shut, her fingers pulling at Bane's hair. "What have ye done to me?"

Bane laughed softly as he continued to feast upon her sweet temptation. "Easy, sweeting, I will not harm ye."

"I have never felt such things. I didnae know . . ."

"Neither did I." A shudder wrenched through him, and Bane lifted his head to study her flushed features. She looked extraordinarily beautiful with her hair tangled about her pale countenance and her eyes more gold than green. And heartbreakingly innocent. His teeth snapped together. By the blood of the saints, what was he doing? He might be a creature of the night, but he was no monster. His honor had not been forgotten in the grave. He did not steal the virtue of young, untried maids. Even if they were Fosters. "Tis a dangerous thing."

Her rapid breath stirred the air. "Aye, most dangerous."

He grimly grasped command of his raging passions. Or at least he attempted to do so. It was a far more difficult task than he could ever have imagined.

"Ye should be tucked in yer chambers," he rasped. "This is no place for ye."

She offered him an accusing frown. "Tis where I would be if ye had not bewitched me."

He regarded her with a somber expression. "Ye must fight it. I cannae . . ."

"What?"

"I cannae be trusted," he forced himself to confess. "Tis been too long since I have desired a woman, and never one such as ye. I fear what I may do to ye."

Her eyes flashed with the stubborn spirit that so captivated him. "Ye think to harm me?"

He smiled ruefully. She had no notion of how easily he

could harm her. With the squeeze of his hands, he could crush her. Or sink his teeth into her and drain her blood dry. He could even enthrall her to the point she would become his willing slave.

"Not in the manner ye fear. But I would steal yer innocence. It calls to me like the song of a siren." His gaze lowered to where she lay beneath him, her skin still moist from his lips. A violent tremor wracked his body as he roughly tugged her bodice back into place and covered her with the heavy cloak. His limbs felt heavy as he forced himself to his feet and pulled her upright. Heavy and still aching with relentless need. "Go before I lose all honor."

She fussed with her cloak as a dark stain reddened her cheek. She did, however, manage to lift her chin and meet his gaze directly.

"I will not allow ye to hurt Katherine."

Catching her face between his hands, he pressed a fierce kiss to her lips.

"Go."

Isobella stumbled through the dark forest. Outwardly she had managed to straighten her clothing and smooth her tumble of curls, but within she still trembled with unfamiliar sensations and a lingering ache she very much feared would haunt her for far too long.

Twas a spell, she told herself for the hundredth time since leaving the mist-shrouded glen. Bane was obviously a creature of magic and he had managed to entrap her in some sort of bewitchment.

What else could explain her reckless need to seek him out despite all the danger? Or to be so strangely moved by his story of the simple bard when she should be outraged by the slander done to her clan?

Or to melt like the veriest tart the moment he touched her?

She bit her lip as she recalled the soft sweep of his hands, the feel of his lips on her breast, and the press of his hard body between her legs.

Oh aye, she had been a tart, but what maid could resist a man so handsome he stole her breath? Or one who could offer such exquisite pleasure?

Obviously not a shrewish spinster, she acknowledged wryly.

Still attempting to assure herself that it had all been no more than a strange spell cast upon her, Isobella came to a slow halt at the rustle of nearby leaves.

Abruptly she was aware of how alone she was in the darkness. And how vulnerable.

"Bane?" she called softly, even knowing that it was not her mysterious enchanter. He moved without sound, and more importantly, her entire body hummed with awareness when he was near. She glared at the nearby trees. "Who is there?"

With a shove of the branches, a large man stepped into view, his broad shoulders and shaggy mane of golden red hair all too familiar.

"Isobella," the man growled, folding his arms over his massive chest.

"Father?" A faint hint of unease trickled down her spine. Her father had an expression on his heavy countenance that never boded well. "What are ye doing here?"

"What am I doing here?" With a sharp motion he moved forward to grasp her arm, nearly lifting her off the ground. "I believe that is a question ye should be answering."

Isobella gritted her teeth. Few things infuriated her more than being bullied. Those who used their strength to force their will upon others were no more than brutes to her mind.

"Father, ye are hurting me."

"Tis nothing of the hurt ye will be feeling." Lifting his free hand, he slapped her across the face.

Isobella's head snapped backward, but with a grim stubbornness she met his baleful gaze steadily.

"I have done nothing."

The thick face flushed with fury. "Oh, nothing, is it? Ye dare to make a jest of me and my warriors?"

"A jest?" She frowned in confusion. "I dinnae ken what ye mean."

"Ye think the villagers and servants are not whispering of yer bold efforts to hunt down the Beast and rescue yer sister?"

Another tingle of unease raced through her. She could clearly smell the heavy scent of ale upon her father's breath. His temper was unpredictable at best, but it became frighteningly violent when he had been deep into his tankard.

"They dinnae even know."

"Oh aye, they know. They have been boasting of yer bravery and daring when they think I cannae hear them, and all the while sneering at me and my men." He gave her another backhand. Isobella stifled a cry as her lip began to bleed from the blow. "I willnae have it. I willnae be branded a coward by those beneath me."

Sensibly she knew that she should attempt to placate her furious father. Katherine could turn his anger with a few pretty tears and a tremble of her lip. Isobella, however, had never been capable of such feminine wiles. Her pride refused to allow her to play the role of the submissive daughter.

"Then mayhap it should be ye out here hunting the Beast," she retorted in fierce tones.

He gave her a rough shake. "Impertinent wench, I shall teach ye to use that sharp tongue on yer father . . ."

Braced for yet another blow, Isobella was caught off

guard when she discovered herself being abruptly released. Tumbling to the ground, she hastily brushed the hair out of her eyes in time to see her father tossed through the air as if he weighed no more than a feather. He hit a nearby tree with a dull thud and crumpled to the ground.

Stunned by the unexpected attack, Isobella scrambled to her feet, searching the darkness for the attacker. Not that she could hope to battle whatever had so easily defeated her burly father. She had not even thought to bring her dirk.

For a moment she could see nothing, and then a shadow flowed toward her father's unconscious form.

She could make out no features, but a familiar flare of heat warned her precisely who the intruder was.

"Bane," she croaked. "No."

The shadow stilled, almost as if determined to ignore her plea.

"He hit ye," Bane rasped.

Isobella caught her breath at the icy danger that pulsed in the air. She did not doubt that her father's life was hanging in the very balance.

"Twas nothing," she said softly.

"Nothing?" With unnerving swiftness, he was standing before her, his fingers cupping her chin to tilt her face upward. "Ye are bleeding."

"Nay. It has already stopped."

"He hurt ye, and I will kill him for that."

"No." She reached out to grasp his arms. "He is my father."

The silver eyes were flat with fury, his beautiful features set in lines that nearly made her heart stop.

"A father who raises a hand against his own daughter?"

"He believes that he was suitably provoked."

He hissed in disgust. "Bah . . . the man is a dog. Without honor and without courage."

Isobella lowered her gaze. How could she deny the

charges? Her father was a self-indulgent man who cared more for his own pleasures than tending to his duties. Or even his own daughters. Still, she could not stand aside and allow him to be slain.

"Say what ye will, he is still my father," she said in quiet tones.

A growl rumbled deep in Bane's throat. "Yer father he may be, but if he strikes ye again, I will see him in his grave."

Slowly she raised her lashes, meeting his fierce gaze with a frown. "Why?"

A heartbeat passed before his expression gentled and he cupped her face between his hands.

"I cannae bear to see ye in pain," he murmured, his thumb tracing over the deep cut in her lip.

There was the predictable tingle of pleasure at his touch, but there was something more. Reaching out her tongue, Isobella lightly touched her lip. Her breath caught in her throat. By all the saints, it was completely healed.

Her eyes widened. "Bane, how . . . ?"

He smiled faintly as he reached out to scoop her into his arms and hold her against his chest.

"It is too cold for ye to be out here."

She gave a choked gasp as he easily carried her through the heavy darkness. He never hesitated or stumbled as he weaved his way through the trees.

"What are ye doing?"

"Ensuring ye are returned to yer chambers safely." His gaze swept to her lips. "I will not have ye set upon again."

If it were any other man, she would have been loudly protesting being carried as a mere child. Her independent nature did not encourage others to fuss over her. But Bane was no mere man, and rather than the prickly annoyance she should have been feeling, a warm sense of peace flooded through her.

A peace she could not recall ever feeling before in her life.

Sweet Mary, she was obviously demented.

Isobella grimaced. "Tis becoming a familiar happenstance."

His lips thinned. "No longer. I assure ye that neither yer father nor any other man will lift a hand toward ye again."

Isobella did not doubt him. There was an edge of menace in his voice, assuring her that he would most certainly punish anyone foolish enough to trouble her. Which was absurd.

Was he not an enemy of her clan? Was he not here to assist the Beast in capturing her sister?

It made no sense for him to cuddle her against him as if she were his beloved. Or to threaten retribution on those who would offer her harm.

"Och, ye are the most devilish creature," she muttered in exasperation.

His gaze swept her countenance. "True enough, but surely I have done nothing to be so condemned by ye, Isobella?"

She furrowed her brows, cursing herself for the pleasure she discovered at simply being held so close to his large form.

"I ken very well ye're some sort of magical creature. And I suspect that ye have knowledge of the Beast. Why am I not attempting to kill ye?"

"Ye desire to kill me?"

Of course she had no desire to kill him. That was the problem, she acknowledged with a pang. When he was near, she could not convince herself that he was a monster.

Could a ruthless fiend treat her with such tender concern? Could his touch make her ache with such sweet longing?

It seemed impossible.

"Tis what I should desire."

The silver eyes abruptly shimmered. "Shall I reveal what I desire?"

The soft rasp of his voice sent a shiver of excitement through her. He did not have to tell her. She could feel it in the very air.

"Ye willnae distract me with yer kisses," she warned, hoping he could not sense the flutter of her heart. "I will discover what ye are."

He gave a slow shake of his head. "Nay, I shall not allow ye to do so."

"What do ye fear?"

His lips twisted in a humorless smile. "More than I should."

Coming to the halt at the edge of the forest, he slowly lowered her to her feet. He studied her countenance for a long moment, his dark thoughts unreadable. In silence he turned to leave, and Isobella felt her heart clench in disappointment.

Ye are daft, Isobella Foster, she told herself even as she heard Bane give a low curse. Before she could react, he had swiftly turned, and grasping her cloak, he tugged her roughly against him.

"Bane . . ." she breathed before his mouth caught her own in a kiss stark with hunger.

The world was still spinning when he lifted his head to regard her with glittering eyes.

"Return to yer chambers and lock the door," he husked. "And nay return to the glen. I dinnae possess the strength to let ye escape again."

Four

Isobella had always been stubborn, but she was not entirely daft. Bane had warned her to return to her chambers and lock the door, and that was precisely what she did.

Unfortunately a locked door did not bring an end to the fierce craving that continued to plague her. Nor ease the sharp pain that seared through her as she sensed him moving ever farther away.

For hours she paced the floor, battling every instinct that urged her to flee the protection of the castle and return to the misty glen and her silver-eyed stranger.

"A pox upon the man and his devious spells," she muttered, even as a renegade doubt settled in her heart.

What if it wasn't a spell? it whispered. What if this . . . magic was simply what happened between a man and a woman? What if it did not fade but continued to haunt her night after night?

It was that horrible thought that had led her to crawl beneath her sheets and cover her head with her pillow.

Nay. She would not allow the man to distract her from Katherine. She could not. Be it spell or female foolishness, she had to put him from her thoughts.

For all her determination, dawn was brushing the sky when at last Isobella tumbled into troubled sleep. And even then her dreams were a frustrating maze as she wandered through a vast castle, running down endless corridors that led to the same shadowed chamber. A chamber she knew harbored a monster with silver eyes.

Not surprisingly she awoke in the late afternoon feeling wearier than when she had taken to her bed.

Calling for her bath and dressing in a simple woolen gown, Isobella grimly left the smothering confines of her rooms. She was not so reckless as to risk returning to the glen, but that did not mean she could not attempt some other means of rescuing her sister.

There had to be some manner; it was all a matter of knowing where to search.

Collecting her cloak, she pulled open her door, only to discover her sister in the hall lying in wait for her.

"Isobella, I wish to speak with ye."

With a strained smile, Isobella tugged the cloak about her.

"Forgive me, Katherine, but I am in somewhat of a hurry."

Katherine remained firmly blocking the doorway, her arms crossed in an obvious display of stubborn determination.

"Nay, ye arenae leaving these chambers until ye tell me what occurred last eve."

"Last eve?"

"Isobella, I was in the great hall when they carried Father in," Katherine clarified. "They said they found him in the forest badly injured."

Isobella abruptly turned to hide her countenance. She recalled all too well her father's drunken fury and the manner in which Bane had rushed to her rescue.

"Not so badly. A few bruises 'tis all."

"They also say that he claimed he had gone to slay the Beast and was attacked."

Isobella gave a humorless laugh. By the saints, only her father could find a means to glorify his own spectacular defeat.

"He went to slay the Beast? How very courageous of him. I did not believe he possessed the spirit."

"He does not, as we both very well know," Katherine retorted dryly. "If he were in the forest, it was not to slay any beast."

Isobella bit her lip, already suspecting where her sister was leading her.

"Perhaps he was in his cups and lost his way," she muttered.

"He was in search of ye."

"Of me? Why would ye think such a daft thing?"

Stepping into the room, Katherine tugged Isobella about to meet her searching gaze.

"Because he stormed through the halls last eve bellowing for ye in a drunken fury. He nearly tore apart yer chambers when ye could not be found. Janet at last confessed she had seen ye leaving the grounds just before dusk."

"Janet," Isobella breathed. The elderly servant was no doubt also responsible for spreading rumors among the castle that she was on the hunt of the Beast. "I should have known."

"She is concerned for ye."

"Aye. I know."

"As am I." With a frown, Katherine tightly grasped her shoulders. "Isobella, what were ye doing in the forest?"

Isobella closed her eyes as she heaved a weary sigh. "In truth, I am not entirely certain."

Katherine gave her a slight shake. "Ye were searching for the Beast, were ye not?"

Lifting her lashes, Isobella smiled wryly. She could only

wish that her motives had been so pure and noble. Unfortunately she very much feared that it was the dark desire that had lured her to the mist. And the memory of Bane's searing kisses and lingering touch.

Her thoughts had not been on Katherine or the Beast or anything else in that moment.

"That is what I am attempting to convince myself."

"Why must ye be so stubborn? Do ye truly believe allowing yerself to be slain will save me from my destiny?"

"As ye see, I was not slain."

"None of yer jests." Her sister's anger abruptly faded as she regarded Isobella with a heartrending concern. "I will not have it, Isobella. I could not bear anything to happen to ye."

Isobella reached up to grasp her sister's hands and squeezed them tightly.

"Do ye believe I feel any differently?" she demanded. "Ye are the most precious thing in the world to me. I will not lose ye without a fight." She abruptly grimaced. "Not that I have managed to do more than make a fool of myself."

"A fool?"

"'Tis nothing." Isobella blew a stray curl from her forehead, regarding her sister with a hint of uncertainty. At last she squared her shoulders. "Katherine?"

"Aye?"

"Have ye ever been in love?"

Not surprisingly, her sister was caught off guard by the abrupt question.

"What?"

Isobella shifted uneasily. She had never been one to dwell upon romantic notions or flutter over a handsome man. It had all seemed a foolish sort of business to a woman of sound wits.

Now she felt as awkward as if she were walking blind-folded through a bog.

"Is there a man that causes yer heart to leap when he walks into the room?"

Astonishingly, a pretty blush touched Katherine's cheeks. "I have always thought Douglas a fine man."

"Douglas?" It took a moment for Isobella's eyes to widen in disbelief. "The blacksmith?"

The blush deepened. "I ken he is not of our station, and that father would never allow him to court me, but he is gentle and kind and he only has to walk into a room to touch my very heart."

Touch my very heart . . .

Isobella's breath was wrenched from her throat. That was it. That was what Bane had managed to do with one glance, one softly spoken word, one caress.

It should be impossible. She was not even sure who or what he was. But she could not deny the truth.

"Have ye allowed him to kiss ye?"

"Isobella," Katherine breathed in embarrassment.

"Well?"

Dropping her gaze, her sister allowed a mysterious smile to curve her lips.

"Only once. It was after the spring fair and he escorted me back to the castle."

"And ye enjoyed it?"

Her smile widened. "It was the most wonderful moment in my life."

Och, yes. So wondrous that it stole a woman's very wits.

"What did ye feel?"

"My heart was beating so swiftly I thought it might leap from my chest and my palms became sweaty. And . . ."

"What?"

Katherine pressed her hands to her flushed cheeks. "I

possessed the most embarrassing urge to rip off my clothes so that I could feel his hands upon my skin," she confessed in low tones. "Shocking, is it not?"

Isobella smiled wryly, recalling precisely how magical it had been to have Bane's hands upon her bare skin. And how she still ached with unfulfilled desire.

"Not so shocking," she muttered.

A frown touched her sister's brow as she slowly lowered her hands.

"Isobella, have ye discovered some man whom ye desire?"

Isobella clenched her hands at her sides. She had wanted to believe the power Bane held over her was a spell. Some bewitchment that could steal her will and force her to do his bidding.

It would be far easier to forgive herself for her treacherous feelings.

"I wish it were so simple," she admitted in weary tones.

Katherine eyed her with open concern. "My love, what is it?"

Squaring her shoulders, Isobella gave a shake of her head. Time was slipping away. She could waste no more.

"I really must go, Katherine."

"Where are ye going?"

"To the village." Moving forward, Isobella gently kissed her sister before hurrying toward the door. "I shall return as soon as I am able."

Pausing only long enough to gather a wedge of cheese from the kitchens to ease her hunger, Isobella hurried from the castle and traveled the well-worn path to the village. Her hurried pace was predictably slowed as she came to the tightly packed shops and cottages.

She had devoted a considerable amount of her own wealth and efforts to helping the various merchants and craftsmen establish their various trades. It was difficult to walk down the street without being pulled aside to admire a newly fired urn or taste of a freshly baked pie. Or to remark upon a baby's new tooth.

As a rule, she enjoyed her visits to the village. She enjoyed being among those who valued her opinion and did not consider her strong will an embarrassing fault, but rather something to be rejoiced.

Today, however, she found herself increasingly impatient with those who crowded about her. She needed to be left in peace so she could be about her business. She needed to be done before night fell and she might risk encountering Bane once again.

At last having greeted all who approached and promised to consider the handful of problems that were always brought to her, Isobella was able to slip away and continue her path to the jagged hills beyond the cottages.

Silence cloaked about her as the moorland was left behind and she climbed ever upward. The surroundings were harsh but beautiful in their simple way, and Isobella paused for a moment to appreciate the sight of her father's castle below and the distant loch.

The untamed wilderness appealed to her Scots blood, but it was rare that she ever traveled beyond the village. As with the misty glen, these hills were shadowed by the Beast, and only the most daring would linger among the heather.

Giving a small shake of her head, Isobella returned her straying attention to the matter at hand. Above her she could make out the ancient stone cottage that clung to the hard ground.

It was the cottage that had once belonged to the betrayed bard.

And the place she hoped would hold the answer to the ghastly curse.

Not allowing herself to consider the fear trickling down

her spine, Isobella clambered over the large rocks that now blocked the path and forced herself to push open the wooden door barring her entrance.

Just for a moment she nearly bolted. However, there was nothing in the simple room with its scrubbed table, chairs, and narrow bed in the corner to send a chill over her skin. In truth, it was astonishingly well tended for a cottage that had been abandoned near two hundred years before.

But there was no denying the unmistakable chill in the air or the haunting sadness that seemed nearly tangible.

Sucking in a deep breath, she at last forced her heavy feet to enter. Once inside she briefly faltered, but when no horrid Beast charged from the shadows and the thatched roof remained firmly in place, she cautiously moved forward.

She was not certain what it was she searched for. Something mystical, she supposed. Something that would reveal the soul and heart of the Beast.

Whatever the blazes that might be, she wryly acknowledged, crossing toward the shelves that held a few pieces of crockery and neatly stacked tunics that had long been forgotten. Nothing mystic there, or in the deep chest that held an exquisitely carved Lude harp lovingly wrapped in silk.

Carefully Isobella stroked the glossy wood of the instrument, startled by the odd tingle that raced through her fingers.

This had once belonged to the bard. A simple man who had loved so deeply and passionately that his beloved's betrayal could echo through all eternity.

Against her will the image of a young, innocent man joyfully playing upon his harp rose to her mind. When he had left this cottage, he could have no notion that he was heading into a villainous trap devised by her ancestors. Or that his beloved was already plotting to betray him.

Her heart grew heavy. Such terrible sadness. Such grief. She could feel it in every part of her.

"Lady Isobella."

The soft, rasping voice had Isobella abruptly turning about, her hand pressed to her leaping heart.

Thankfully she swiftly discovered the intruder was no frightening monster come to devour her. Or even a ghost she had unwittingly stirred into existence.

Instead an elderly woman with a deeply lined countenance and stooped form regarded her with glittering black eyes.

"Forgive me," Isobella murmured with a shaky smile. "I thought this cottage deserted."

The woman waved a gnarled hand. "I tend to it on occasion. Twould be a shame to watch it crumble to dust."

"Ah, I did wonder how it remained so tidy," Isobella confessed.

"Most would tell ye 'tis because of the curse." The black gaze peered at Isobella with discomforting intensity. "This was once the home of the bard."

"Yes, I ken as much."

"What is it ye seek?"

Caught off guard by the abrupt question, Isobella discovered herself unable to conjure a suitable story to explain her presence. Although she was uncertain that she would even attempt a lie. Not with that unnerving gaze seeming to pierce to her very heart.

"The truth, I suppose."

The tiny head tilted to one side, her expression one of curiosity.

"Of the bard?"

Isobella briefly glanced toward the forgotten harp before attempting to harden her heart. By all that was holy, she did not want to pity the man who had once called this cottage home. Not at the cost of losing Katherine.

"Of the monster who will take my sister," she corrected in stern tones.

"He wasnae always a monster, ye ken," the woman said gently. "Once he was a simple man who loved a maid and was betrayed."

She clenched her hands at her side. "He possesses my sympathy, but those that betrayed him are long dead."

"There are some wounds more difficult to heal than others."

Isobella gave a restless shake of her head. "I dinnae have the time for his wounds to heal."

There was a long pause as the woman regarded Isobella with a strange expression. "So ye will kill the Beast?"

"Can he be killed?"

"Aye." The woman stepped closer, bringing with her the faint scent of roses. "Sunlight or a wooden stake to the heart would be the end of him."

Isobella'a heart gave a sudden jerk. For her entire life she had been warned that the Beast could not be killed. At least not by a mere mortal being. It was a creature of magic, her father had blustered, and would slay any who would dare to hunt it.

Even when Isobella had at last given in to her inner urgings and sought out the Beast, she had not truly believed she could best it. She had simply come to a place where she could no longer bear to stand aside and await fate.

Now she was not at all certain what she felt. Elation? Dread? Utter terror?

"A wooden stake?" she breathed. "And he would . . . stay dead?"

"For all eternity." The woman reached out to lightly touch Isobella's cheek. Her fingers were cold, but oddly comforting. "Tell me, Lady Isobella, what would ye do for love?"

Isobella blinked in confusion. "What do ye mean?"

"Would ye kill for love?"

An icy sensation clutched at her heart. A few days ago

she would not have hesitated with her answer. She would have sworn to do anything to keep her sister alive. Including killing whatever threatened her.

Suddenly she was not nearly so certain.

The Foster laird had slain the bard without mercy and without conscience, cursing his clan for all eternity.

Could further death truly bring an end to the suffering?

She gave a slow shake of her head. "I thought I could, but now I dinnae know."

"Would ye offer sacrifice?" the old woman rasped.

"Sacrifice? Sacrifice what?"

"Whatever ye must, even yer own life."

Isobella met the glittering gaze squarely. "Aye, that I would do," she said without hesitation.

The old woman smiled. "Such love has the power to alter destiny. That is the only weapon ye shall need."

Clasping Isobella's hands with her own, the woman whispered beneath her breath, and Isobella felt something pressing into her palm. Glancing down, she realized that she now held two miniature portraits. One of a pretty maiden with golden red hair and the other a handsome, dark-haired man with silver eyes.

Her breath caught in shock as she realized she was look-ing at the images of the bard and his treacherous lover.

An image of Bane . . .

The Beast of MacDonnell.

Lifting her head, she was not at all surprised to discover the old woman had disappeared from the cottage.

She had given Isobella the answers she had sought.

It was now up to her to decide if she possessed the courage to do what must be done.

Indifferent to the fear he was spreading throughout the countryside, Bane charged his way through the darkness. It had been agony awaiting the sun to set so he could leave the protection of the mist and search out the woman who refused to leave him in peace.

He had sensed the precise moment she had entered his cottage. He had been curious but not overly concerned by her intrusion into his long-lost home. There was nothing there to harm her, and at least she was not torturing him by seeking him out once again.

But then the mysterious witch had appeared at her side and his curiosity had altered to wary unease.

Throughout the centuries he had been visited by the witch who had taken him from his grave.

She had never offered her reasons for snatching him from death. Nothing beyond her hatred for the laird that had cast her out of his clan. Nor had she ever spoken of the curse that he had placed upon the Fosters.

Instead she had remained enigmatic and inclined to speak in riddles that held no sense.

He did not trust her. Not at least with Isobella.

Reaching the cottage that had once held his youthful dreams, Bane slipped through the door and prepared himself for battle.

It took only a moment to realize the witch had already disappeared and that Isobella was alone. She was seated on the edge of his bed, her head bent and her face hidden by the thick fall of her fiery curls.

He should leave, he told himself. It was obvious she was in no danger.

But even as he commanded himself to return to the mist, his feet were carrying him forward and his hand was reaching out to lightly stroke her hair.

He could physically feel the pain in her heart. The witch had clearly troubled her. How could he leave without attempting to offer her comfort?

"Isobella?" he murmured softly.

Her head abruptly lifted, but there was no surprise upon

her countenance. She had obviously sensed his presence the moment he had arrived.

"Bane."

He felt a jolt of pain at the shadows in her eyes. "Are ye harmed?"

"Nay, I am fine."

"Ye are certain?"

"Of course." A frown tugged at her brows. "What is it?"

"I sensed . . ." Bane abruptly broke off his words. Perhaps the witch had not made her presence known to Isobella. There was no need to frighten the poor lassie if she had not been bothered. "I thought ye might be in danger."

"There is nothing here to harm me." She met his gaze squarely. "Or at least there was not until now."

Bane flinched at the truth in her words. Despite every part of him that rebelled in horror at ever harming this woman, there was no denying the curse that would take her sister.

There was no means to halt it.

He would hurt her, no matter how it might destroy him to do so.

Bane bit back a low curse. "What are ye doing here?"

A humorless smile twisted her lips. "I was seeking answers."

He glanced about the familiar surroundings, easily able to summon up the memory of his mother stirring a pot over the fire, and his father carving the elegant lutes that the bards came from all over the land to purchase.

"Answers to what?"

"The Beast."

"Ye think he is hidden in this cottage?"

"Nay, but this was once the home of the bard."

Bane's lips twisted at the unexpected flare of pain. "He has been dead and forgotten a long time."

Slowly rising to her feet, Isobella held out her hands to

reveal the miniatures that Bane had commissioned to be painted two centuries before.

"Not so very forgotten," she rasped.

Bane stilled as he met her glittering gaze.

She knew the truth.

There was no longer any doubt that he was the Beast of MacDonnell.

Her most hated enemy.

Five

Bane barely controlled the urge to snatch the portraits from her hands and crush them beneath his heels. They were reminders of a past he now wanted only to forget.

"I thought those lost," he at last gritted.

She remained silent a long moment before she lifted her head to regard him with a somber expression.

"This was the maid ye intended to wed?"

He grimaced. "Aye."

"She looks very much like Katherine."

"As do all Foster women." Unable to halt the movement, he reached out to touch a fiery curl. "All but ye."

"She was very beautiful."

"Very beautiful," he agreed in flat tones. "And she possessed the voice of an angel when she would sing. She entranced me."

The hazel eyes narrowed. "Ye loved her."

"Nay, I loved only the woman I imagined her to be." Taking the miniatures from her hands, Bane tossed them onto the bed. The faces in the portraits were strangers to him. "She was never that woman."

Her gaze swept over his countenance, as if seeking some hidden truth.

"What did ye imagine her to be?"

Bane trailed his fingers down the firm line of her jaw. "Bold, courageous, and above all, loyal." His nose flared with ancient fury. "Instead she was quite eager to betray me for a soft bed and glittering jewels. I was a fool nay to have sensed the truth of her."

Her eyes darkened, as if sensing his suppressed emotions. "I suppose that hurts more than her betrayal."

Bane blinked in confusion. "What?"

"Ye allowed yerself to be deceived by a pretty countenance and sweet voice. It must be difficult to forgive."

"Forgive?" he growled. "I will never forgive the wench."

"Nay," she said softly. "I meant it must be difficult to forgive yerself."

Bane snapped his brows together in disbelief. "Ye dinnae know what ye speak of."

Her gaze was far too knowing. "Ye dinnae blame yerself for having been so mistaken in yer heart?"

"I have no heart," he rasped, reaching to grasp her hand and place it against his chest, which did not move. "It died the night I was murdered by the Foster laird."

Her fingers curled into the silk of his cloak. "I dinnae believe that. Ye would not have rushed to protect me from my father if yer heart was dead. Ye feel."

Bane held himself motionless, willing himself to master the surge of emotions that battered through him. An impossible task, of course. For centuries he had lived with an aching, hollow emptiness. Now he could no more halt the tide of sensations than he could halt the moon from rising.

He shuddered at the unfamiliar force. Lust, tenderness, and above all, an overwhelming need to take this woman in his arms and hold her for all eternity.

She was what he had always desired, his heart whispered. She was the woman he had dreamed of when he had been a young, romantic bard. Her purity, her courage, and her generous heart called to him. This woman would never betray those she loved. She would walk through the fires of hell before she would trade her soul for riches.

"By the blood of the saints . . . aye, I feel," he rasped, cupping her face in his hands. "Ye have made me feel again."

The very air thickened with the hunger he could not hide, but she did not pull away in horror. Instead her hand slowly lifted to gently stroke his cheek.

"Just as ye have made me feel," she whispered. "I tried to convince myself that it was a spell ye had put upon me, but I ken it isnae. Tis ye. Just ye."

Bane's gaze warily narrowed even as her gentle touch roused the predator in him. "Ye know who I am. What I am."

"Aye."

"Then why do ye not fight me?" he demanded. "Ye wish me dead."

Her eyes darkened with sadness. "Tis what I thought I wished, but no longer."

"Why?"

"The curse was made in betrayal and violence. How could it be broken by the same means?"

Bane flinched at her stark question. In truth, he had no answer. The curse had been created out of his vicious need for revenge. He possessed no knowledge of how to bring it to an end. He could not even be certain his death would lift the enchantment.

His muscles tightened as he realized the direction of his thoughts. Fires of hell. Did he desire to break the curse? Was his thirst for justice truly sated?

His gaze seared over Isobella's countenance. Despite the darkness, he could see every feature with heartrending clarity. The wide brow, the delicately carved features, the sensuous lips that made him shiver with longing. And above all, the hazel eyes that revealed a soul that was untarnished by greed or hatred.

Aye, for this woman he would give up all, including his very life.

Lowering his head, he pressed his lips to her temple. "Isobella, I cannae alter the past."

She leaned into him, cloaking him in the heat he craved.

"Neither can I, and in truth, at the moment it does not matter. I dinnae want to think of the past or the future."

Bane shuddered as the dark hunger flared through him. To have her so near, so intimately pressed against him, was the sweetest torture.

"What is it that ye do want, Isobella?"

Isobella wavered.

It was not that she doubted the choice she had made sitting here in the dark. The old woman had offered her a means to save Katherine and she would take it. No matter what the cost.

Nor did she regret the selfish need that had kept her at the cottage as dusk had fallen.

She had known Bane would come to her. She had known it in the very depths of her heart.

And she wanted to be here for him. Just for this night she wanted to grasp the happiness offered. Tomorrow she would do what had to be done.

Still, she could not deny a measure of uncertainty as Bane's fierce presence surrounded her. It was one thing to imagine the pleasure of offering herself to the man who had stolen her heart. It was quite another to have her body shuddering with excitement and her blood racing so swiftly it made her head dizzy.

Sucking in a deep breath, Isobella thrust aside her bout of nerves. She would never have this opportunity again. She would not allow maidenly fears to halt her.

"I want to know what it is to be held in yer arms," she at last admitted with a boldness she was far from feeling. "I want to feel ye close to me."

His gaze narrowed even as she sensed his body harden in response.

"Isobella . . ."

She lifted her hand to stroke his cheek. His skin was smooth and cool to the touch.

"Do ye desire me, Bane?"

His hands abruptly clutched her shoulders as his eyes flared with a stark need.

"Desire? I wish it were so simple. Then perhaps I could fight against this," he growled. "I hunger for ye, Isobella. I ache for ye until I fear I might go mad."

Isobella struggled to breathe. Hunger. Aye. She did hunger. And ache.

She twined her arms around his neck and pressed herself fiercely to his hard body.

"Then make me yers, Bane."

His arms lashed around her, but the silver gaze remained wary. As if he feared to trust in her eager response.

"Ye know that cannae be, my love," he rasped in a pained voice. "I am the monster ye have hated all yer life. I am the Beast of MacDonnell."

"Not tonight." She caught and held his smoldering gaze. "Tonight ye are a bard and I am a simple maid."

He groaned low in his throat as his eyes squeezed shut in frustration.

"A maid who is innocent. Ye must give yerself to yer husband."

"Nay, I shall never wed," she swore. "Besides which, my innocence is mine to give . . . and I have chosen ye. Tis my right."

"Isobella."

She could sense his struggle as passion warred with his

deeply held honor. For a moment she feared he might thrust her away. His arms tightened about her, and his muscles hardened until he shuddered with the strain.

Then with a harsh moan, his head swooped downward and he claimed her lips with a searing possession.

"Sweeting . . . my love," he muttered against her swollen mouth. "For so long I have been alone. Alone and cold beyond bearing. Ye have awakened me."

Her heart squeezed at his words. Her clan had not been alone in their suffering over the years. For as long as the curse held, Bane's wounds would never heal.

Lifting herself onto her toes, Isobella gently placed a kiss upon his lips.

For a moment he held perfectly still, as if savoring her soft caress. Then with one swift motion he swept her off her feet and carried her to the narrow bed.

Isobella nestled into the softness of the feather mattress as he hovered over her, her lips curving into a smile as he reached to slowly remove the ivory combs from her hair.

With meticulous care he fanned her curls across the pillow, the heat in his gaze sending a chill of excitement through her.

Beneath that gaze she felt beautiful in a manner she had never before experienced.

Suddenly she was not the shrill-tongued daughter of the laird. She was not an object of fear or pity.

She was a desirable woman.

A woman with the power to bewitch a man.

The realization banished her lingering hesitation, and with a growing urgency, she reached up to thrust aside his cloak even as his own hands moved to tug on the ribbons of her bodice.

Their lips met and clung as Bane swept aside her clothing and then his own. Isobella raked her fingers through his long hair, sighing in sweet relief when he at last slid his naked form over her own.

Och, but he was perfect, she acknowledged.

His alabaster skin was exquisitely smooth, his body honed to lean, fluid muscle. A beautiful, deadly predator, with the gentle touch of an angel.

She eagerly ran her hands over his broad shoulders and down the length of his back as his lips nuzzled her cheek and blazed a path down the curve of her neck.

She heard him whisper soft words in an ancient language as he brushed his fingers over the tips of her breasts. Isobella gasped at the fierce pleasure that shot through her. Her nipples hardened as he teased them to tight nubs, her back arching in an instinctive plea for more.

"So beautiful," he whispered against her skin. "So warm."

"Bane . . . please."

She was uncertain what she was pleading for until his lips closed over her aching nipple to suckle her with a fierce tenderness.

Her eyes squeezed closed with near unbearable pleasure. His fingers were cold as they traced over her skin, but his touch made her burn with a fever she had never felt before. She ran her fingers restlessly through his hair as he turned to nuzzle her other breast, barely able to hold still beneath his relentless caresses.

There was something stirring within her. An aching pleasure that demanded more.

Raising himself onto his elbows, Bane traced her lips with a delicate touch.

"I feel ye so soft and warm beneath me, but I fear ye are a dream that will suddenly be stolen from me."

"I am no dream," Isobella husked, her hands skimming over the fluid muscles of his back.

"Ye will not fade with the sunrise?" he demanded, his lips scorching a path down her neck to her collarbone.

Isobella caught her breath. Nay. She did not wish to think about the sunrise. Or what it might bring.

There was only tonight . . . and this man.

"Love me, Bane," she pleaded. "Please, love me."

"More than life itself," he moaned, his kisses becoming fiercely demanding as he licked and nipped his way over her breasts and down her stomach.

Isobella caught her bottom lip between her teeth to keep from screaming as those searching lips blazed down the curve of her hip, brushing tantalizingly close to the moist heat between her legs before continuing down her thigh to the very tip of her toes.

His touch was sheer bliss, but the sensations coiled within her demanded more. She desired . . . och . . . she did not know, but it was forcing her to arch her back off the mattress and her teeth to clench in frustration.

"I cannae bear any more," she moaned.

His soft laugh whispered over her skin as he continued his torment, nibbling her toes until they curled in pleasure. Only then did he turn his attention to her neglected leg, on this occasion pausing at her thigh to nudge her legs apart.

"Open for me, Isobella."

She forgot to breathe as his mouth shifted to taste her with an intimacy she had never imagined.

Isobella gave a soft shriek as his tongue stroked through her dampness. Her fingers clutched the sheets beneath her as her muscles became rigid beneath that insistent caress.

"Bane."

"Aye," he murmured, his tongue discovering a tender nub that he teased with merciless care.

She had opened her lips to protest, but the words died in

her throat. Oh my, how could anything feel so . . . wondrous? Her hips lifted off the mattress as he gently suckled her, her soft moans filling the cottage. His hands cupped her thighs, holding her still beneath the relentless pleasure taking her to the very edge of fulfillment over and over.

Panting with a need she did not even comprehend, she shifted to grasp his silken hair.

"Bane . . . please."

Thankfully sensing she could bear no more, Bane lifted himself to cover her trembling body, his hips settling between her parted legs.

"Isobella, ye are certain?" he whispered softly.

She lifted her gaze, regarding the man poised above her. In the shadows he appeared dangerous and untamed with his long hair tangled about the impossibly handsome countenance and his eyes glittering with a feral hunger. Even his fangs were visible in the moonlight.

She should be terrified.

Instead she slid her hands over his smooth chest, knowing that she wanted this more than she had wanted anything in her life.

"I am certain."

"Thank the gods," he muttered, his head swooping downward to devour her lips. With a slow, deliberate motion, he began to press his manhood into the very center of her heat.

Isobella instinctively tensed. She knew little of what occurred beneath a man and a woman, but she had heard the stories of the pain a virgin must endure.

"Be at ease, sweeting," Bane whispered close to her ear, his voice oddly strained as he lowered his hands to grasp her hips. "My powers will ensure that ye feel no pain."

She opened her mouth to demand what powers he spoke of, only to give a gasp as a tingling sensation rushed through her body and his thick manhood pressed relentlessly into her.

Her nails sank into his back as she moaned in delight. As he had promised, she felt no pain as he stretched and filled her. Only . . . what?

There were no words to express the pleasure she felt at having him so deeply embedded in her. She felt complete in a manner she could not explain.

With care, he gently withdrew, and Isobella's nails dug even deeper into his skin.

Surely this could not be all? She was still reaching for that wondrous pinnacle that remained frustratingly elusive.

"Nay . . ." she moaned.

"Patience, my love," he urged, flexing his hips to plunge himself back into her. "I promise we will find paradise together."

Her breath came in short pants as he rode her with a steady rhythm, his chest brushing her tightened nipples with every thrust. Instinctively she curled her legs about his hips, meeting his thrusts as the coiling pressure threatened to consume her.

And then, just as she was certain she was going to shatter, she reached that astonishing peak.

The world halted as her entire body became rigid and then began to convulse with shocking force.

She cried out as Bane cradled her face in his hands, his hips pumping frantically into her until he gave his own rasping shout and collapsed onto her sated body.

Rolling onto his side, Bane held Isobella tightly in his arms. Over and over he pressed his lips to her tousled curls, allowing the sweet scent of her to fill him.

A part of him knew he should release her so that she could dress. Unlike him, she must feel the chill in the air.

But a greater part of him refused to allow her out of his arms.

What if she were a dream? What if he loosened his grip and she disappeared into the shadows?

It had taken an eternity to discover this woman who filled his heart with such love. He would truly die if he lost her now.

For long moments they lay in silence, both struggling to recover from the powerful force of their desire. Then, with an obvious reluctance, Isobella pulled back to regard him with a haunted expression.

"Bane, ye must go."

His arms instinctively tightened about her. "Nay. I will not leave ye."

She brushed her fingers over his cheek, her tenderness soothing wounds he had harbored for an eternity.

"It will soon be dawn. Ye must return to the glen."

Bane's features hardened. She was right, of course. He could already sense the coming dawn. But for once he did not care. He would not return to his castle alone. Not after he had tasted the happiness Isobella could offer.

"Come with me," he abruptly demanded.

Not surprisingly, she blinked in shock at his words. "What?"

"Come with me." Cupping her cheek in his hand, he regarded her with the love that burned in his heart. "I need ye, Isobella. I need yer touch, yer smile, yer warmth. I cannae bear to be alone any longer."

Much to his dismay, a stricken expression flared over her delicate features.

"Bane . . . 'tis impossible."

Something very close to panic clutched at him. He knew he was being selfish. She deserved what every woman desired. A man who could offer her a family, and friends, and

272 / Deborah Raleigh

the promise of growing old together. Things he could not possibly give her.

And yet she had sworn she would never wed, he reminded himself fiercely.

Surely the love and devotion he would offer her would be preferable to becoming a spinster vulnerable to her father's violent temper?

If nothing else, he could offer all the luxury any woman could desire.

"Why? Ye shall want for nothing," he urged. "I promise I can offer ye more than ye ever dreamed possible."

A sad smile curved her lips. "Ye have already given me more than I dreamed possible."

"Isobella, I have waited an eternity to find ye." He lifted his hand to savor the soft skin of her cheek, knowing with absolute certainty that he would never have enough of this woman. He had been lost and alone in the darkness for so long. She was his salvation. "Dinnae ask me to let ye go. I cannae."

"I—"

"I will beg if I must," he interrupted in ragged tones, revealing the depth of his emotions. "I will stay here until the sun rises and I am reduced to ash if that is what I must do to convince ye I cannae exist without ye."

The hazel eyes widened in dismay. "Nay. Dinnae even say such a thing."

He pressed his lips to her forehead. "Then return to my home with me. Be my wife."

She gave a strangled moan as she clutched him with shaking fingers. "Please, I must return before I am missed. My sister will be concerned."

Pulling back, he slid his fingers beneath her chin, tilting her face upward. "Isobella, look at me." He patiently waited until the thick black lashes lifted to reveal her wary gaze. "Do ye love me?"

He could feel her stiffen at his blunt question, her heart pounding so loudly he feared it might burst. He silently willed her to speak the truth. To admit what she had already confessed with every eager touch.

"Aye, I love ye," she at last whispered.

"Will ye join me?"

Their gazes locked and held. Bane found himself growing frustrated at the knowledge she was hiding her innermost thoughts from him.

There was something troubling her. Something beyond the thought of offering her future to the Beast of MacDonnell.

"Before I leave my family, I must see my sister. I wish to say good-bye."

Bane briefly closed his eyes. The damnable curse.

No matter how deeply they might love one another, it would always lie between them. It made him long to howl in regret.

He gently brushed his thumb over her swollen lips. "Ye know I would change her fate if I could."

He heard her soft sigh whisper in the darkness. "Aye, I ken." She pressed her hands firmly to his chest. "Now go before it is too late."

With grudging reluctance, Bane rose from the bed and swiftly pulled his clothes on. The last thing he desired was to leave Isobella, but he could hesitate no longer. The dawn was dangerously close. He already risked not being able to return to the mist in time.

Pausing to admire the sight of her still flushed and tousled from their lovemaking, Bane bent down to gently press his lips to her own.

"I shall be waiting for ye," he pledged before turning to slip out of the cottage.

Cloaking his presence to ensure he was not sensed by the slumbering villagers, Bane rushed swiftly through the thinning darkness. The prickles upon his skin assured him that his hesitation in the cottage had nearly cost him his existence.

Still, he could not regret a single moment in Isobella's presence.

Slipping into the welcome mist, he came to a halt and allowed a smile to curve his lips.

Isobella. By the fires of hell, she had given him so much more than just her innocence.

She had offered her trust, her warmth, and above all, her love.

It was that which had managed to dispel the cold emptiness that had plagued him for so long.

And he would make certain she never regretted leaving her clan to join him, he silently swore.

Absently his hand lifted to touch the torc about his neck, his gaze narrowing in shock. Glancing downward, it took only a moment to realize that the priceless golden ornament was missing.

Impossible. The torc had been an ancient artifact of his family. It had been given as a betrothal gift for centuries and he had not broken tradition. He had offered the torc to his beloved when she had agreed to become his wife.

She had still possessed it when she had crawled into the bed of her laird, but the moment he had uttered his curse, it had magically appeared about his neck.

He paced along the edge of the mist, his thoughts racing.

The torc was connected to the curse. Of that he was certain. And its disappearance could only mean one thing.

The curse was lifted.

Isobella had once again performed a miracle.

Cursing at the morning sunlight he could sense outside the mist, Bane continued his pacing.

He desperately wished to make his way to Isobella and reveal the glorious truth. Nothing could stand between them now.

They would be together.

For all eternity.

Six

Isobella remained on the narrow bed for several long moments after Bane's departure.

Despite the pounding urgency to be done with her awaiting task, she could not deny herself the pleasure of savoring the night spent in Bane's arms.

The hungry passion had not come as a surprise. She had sensed the brooding desire from her first encounter with Bane. Nor had she been particularly amazed by his skill. He obviously possessed powers far beyond a mere man. Powers he had readily used to assure her intense pleasure.

What had caught her off guard had been his tenderness.

His every touch had made her feel cherished. As if she meant more than the very world to him.

Despite her innocence, she knew that few women experienced such devoted care. Certainly the few snatches of conversation she had overheard from the various Foster wives had not revealed the contentment she felt.

Indeed, they were more often heard to complain that their husbands considered a bedding something to be done with great speed and little concern for the woman beneath him.

Bane had not taken her simply to ease his lust. He had pleasured her in a manner that only a man in love could offer.

Remembering every touch, every soft moan, Isobella was at last wrenched from her reverie by the biting chill in the air. She had lingered long enough, she silently chastised herself. The dawn had arrived and her duty was clear.

Hastily pulling on her dress, Isobella was halted as she felt the unfamiliar weight about her neck. Glancing down, she discovered a golden torc.

She frowned as she tentatively stroked the glowing metal. Even her untrained eye could detect the exquisite workmanship of the strange engravings, but the obvious worth of the torc was not what brought a frown to her brow. It was the disturbing thought of how it came to be upon her.

She recognized it as belonging to Bane. She had seen it glittering beneath his silken cloak. But how had he managed to place it upon her without her knowledge?

And why had he done so?

They were questions she could not answer, and with a faint shake she grimly pulled her cloak about her and left the silence of the small cottage. The torc was the least of her concerns at the moment.

She did not allow herself to glance back as she scrambled down the steep hill and crept through the still-sleeping village. She had never been one to wallow in regrets.

She would not begin now.

The sun had crested the horizon when Isobella at last reached the castle, and she was forced to creep past the rising servants as she made her way toward the upper chambers. Thankfully none took note of her slender form and she gained his sister's room without interruption.

Quietly she crossed the floor and perched upon the edge of the mattress. Reaching out, she lightly touched her sister's golden red hair. She appeared young and heartbreakingly vulnerable in sleep, but Isobella knew there was a hidden strength within Katherine.

A strength she would need.

Stirring in her sleep, Katherine turned onto her back and opened her eyes. It took a moment for her gaze to focus upon her sister perched next to her, but then with a frown of concern, she abruptly raised herself to a sitting position.

"Isobella? What is it? Has something occurred?" she demanded in a voice still thick with sleep.

Isobella conjured a comforting smile. "Nothing for ye to fret over."

Katherine glanced toward the windows barely lit with a rosy glow. "There must be something to have ye abroad at such an hour. Tis barely past the break of day."

"I have an errand that must be done."

"An errand?" Katherine's expression was one of skepticism. "What errand?"

"Tis nothing for ye to fret about. I merely wished to ensure ye would not worry when ye awoke and found me gone."

Although inclined to ignore that which she found unpleasant or distasteful, Katherine was no fool. She was well aware that Isobella would not be about at such an hour unless her errand was pressing indeed.

"I dinnae like this, Isobella. What business could ye possibly have so early?"

"Tis a simple matter that will soon be over."

Katherine reached out to grasp her fingers in a near painful grip.

"Does it have to do with the Beast?"

Isobella paused a moment, debating how best to answer the direct question. She had no desire to worry Katherine. But then again, she possessed a need to ensure her sister would not seek to interfere.

"Aye."

A dark flush stained Katherine's cheeks as she struggled to contain her flare of anger.

"Och, Isobella, I will not have it. Ye are not to risk yerself in such a manner. Who knows what the Beast might do if he were to have ye in his clutches?"

Isobella choked back an embarrassed laugh at her sister's unwitting words. By all the saints, she knew precisely what the Beast did when he had her in his clutches.

And it had been the most extraordinary experience of her life.

"Dinnae fear," she muttered as her sister's gaze narrowed in suspicion. "The Beast will not harm me."

"Ye cannot know that."

"But I do," Isobella retorted in tones that defied argument. "I have discovered the means to bring an end to the curse."

Silence filled the chamber as Katherine regarded her with a stunned disbelief.

"What did ye say?"

Isobella reached out to lightly touch her cheek. "The curse is to be lifted."

"Nay." Katherine gave a shake of her head, clearly too frightened to allow herself hope. "The curse cannae be broken. Father swore that—"

"Father never made the effort to discover if the curse could be ended," Isobella interrupted in disdainful tones. "It was far easier to cower in his castle and proclaim that yer sacrifice was inevitable than to risk his own neck."

"Ye must not be so hard upon him, Isobella. He has never possessed yer courage." She smiled sadly. "Few of us do."

Isobella gave a dismissive wave of her hand. She was not about to waste her last few moments with her sister discussing a man who would have condemned his own flesh and blood to death.

"It no longer matters." Leaning forward, she regarded her sister with a somber expression, willing her to believe the truth. "Ye are free of the curse."

Katherine blinked in confusion, still unable to accept that the threat that had haunted her for her entire life was at an end.

"Sweet saints, Isobella, are ye certain?" she breathed.

"Quite, quite certain, my love."

"I . . ." She swallowed heavily. "I can barely believe it."

"I assure ye that it is true."

"But what must be done?"

Isobella smiled as she squeezed her sister's hand. "There is nothing for ye to do. I shall take care of everything."

Still stunned, Katherine gave a slow nod of her head. Isobella was thankful for her bemusement. Had her wits been clear, her sister would never have accepted such a vague assurance. She would have badgered Isobella until she was certain of every gruesome detail.

"It seems an impossible dream."

A warmth flowed through Isobella as she watched the dawning joy light her sister's countenance. Although Katherine had never complained or bemoaned her fate, it had always hovered like a dark cloud over both their lives.

Now a hope that Isobella had never dared possible bloomed to life in the green eyes.

And reminded Isobella that time was swiftly passing.

As long as the curse still existed, there was the danger Katherine could be enchanted. Bane himself claimed his sacrifice would come to him whether he called or not.

She would not risk failure now.

Squaring her shoulders, she rose to her feet. "Katherine, before I leave, I have a boon to ask of ye."

"Of course. Ye know I would do anything for ye, Isobella. Ye have only to ask."

"I wish yer pledge that ye will tell Douglas of yer feelings."

Katherine's eyes widened at the unexpected request. "What?"

"No matter what our father or anyone else might say, ye should not settle for any man less than one who loves ye," Isobella said with steady conviction of a woman who knew precisely what she spoke of. "Riches and power are meaningless when compared to true devotion."

Katherine gave a slow shake of her head, a hint of wonder dawning in her eyes.

"I have never before given myself leave to even consider a future with a man. Or a family."

"Ye may do so now."

"Aye." Katherine pressed a hand to her heart. "Oh, Isobella, how can I thank ye?"

"Just be happy no matter what the future may hold."

"How could I not be?"

Satisfied she had done all that was possible to ensure her sister would have the future she deserved, Isobella reached down to brush her lips over Katherine's cheek.

"I must go."

Without warning, her sister reached out to grab Isobella's cloak, forcing her to a halt.

"Isobella."

Turning back, she gave a lift of her brows. "Aye?"

"Ye will take care?"

"All shall be well." Isobella gently removed the cloak from her sister's grasp. "Good-bye, Katherine."

Hurrying from the chamber before she could be halted again, Isobella slipped into her own rooms to retrieve the dirk she had left near her bed. She did not bother with the leather sheath as she held it tightly in her fingers and made her way back out of the castle.

More than one servant attempted to halt her progress, but Isobella did not even note their calls of greeting and occasional request for advice.

Her thoughts were utterly concentrated upon placing one foot before the other as she crossed the courtyard and headed through the gates. Once on the main path she turned toward the nearby forest.

All too soon she arrived at the clearing she sought.

With a silent prayer she slipped off the heavy cloak and lowered herself to her knees.

Only when she was fully prepared did she allow herself to glance toward the mist that hovered so close.

"Forgive me, Bane," she whispered, lifting the dirk and plunging it toward her heart.

Bane cursed beneath his breath as he paced the edges of the mist.

By the fires of hell. He could feel Isobella. He had felt her the moment she had left the protection of her father's castle and entered the forest.

At first he had been nearly consumed by a rush of relief as she neared. Despite her assurance that she would come to him, a part of him had still harbored a biting doubt.

What if she came to her senses and realized that she could easily wed a man who could offer her a family and place within her clan? Or concluded she could not bear to accept the monster who would soon take her sister?

She did not yet know the curse was broken. And he had no means of revealing the truth until night once more descended.

Who could blame her for concluding her feelings for him were not worthy of the sacrifices she would be forced to endure?

Certainly not him.

But then his fears had been dispelled as she hurried in his direction. Indeed, he had nearly fallen to his knees in gratified relief.

She was coming to him.

Bless the heavens above, he was not to be condemned to an eternity of aching loneliness.

Anxious to greet her, he had gone as far as he dared in the fringes of the mist. And there he had waited, a growing hollowness filling his heart as she had halted in the clearing, just out of his reach.

What was she doing?

He could sense no one about to halt her passage. Not even a stray animal that might have frightened her.

Why did she linger?

"Isobella . . ." he at last called out, any thought of pride long forgotten. "Isobella."

"I fear she cannae hear ye." Appearing in the mist, the old witch regarded him with a glittering gaze. "At least not at the moment."

"Ye." Bane narrowed his gaze, his every instinct tingling with warning. "What have ye done?"

With a rattle of her carved bracelets, the witch calmly adjusted the plaid about her shoulders.

"Done?"

Bane took a step forward, his hands clenched at his side. He was in no humor for her riddles. Not when Isobella was behaving so oddly.

"Ye were with Isobella in the cottage. What did ye do to her?"

The witch shrugged, not at all intimidated by his dangerous tone.

"I did nothing but offer her what she most wished."

"And what was that?"

"The answers she sought."

Bane stiffened in annoyance. He should have suspected that there had been more than ill fate that had allowed Isobella to discover the truth of him.

"Ye gave her the portraits and revealed that I am the Beast of MacDonnell," he accused.

"Aye."

"Did ye hope to frighten her away from me?"

A smile touched her lips. "She is a woman of courage. I knew she would not be so easily frightened."

Bane's brows snapped together. This woman might very well have driven Isobella away from him. He would not forget.

"And that is all ye revealed?"

"She demanded the means to break the curse."

"She was the one to break the curse?"

She gave a slow nod of her head. "For a price."

The ghastly tingle once again flooded through his body. "What was the price?"

"A sacrifice willingly given."

"Nay." Reaching out, Bane grasped the witch and glared into her wrinkled countenance. He did not care if she returned him to his grave. All that mattered was that Isobella did not pay for his sins. "Fires of hell, I will not allow it. If a sacrifice is what ye demand, then ye will take me, not Isobella."

"The sacrifice must come from the daughter of a Foster."

"Never. I will—"

Bane's desperate words were brought to a sharp halt as a piercing pain flooded through his chest. For a moment he thought the witch must have struck him with a spell. It would not be beyond her to punish him in such a manner. But as he pressed a hand to what must be a mortal wound, he realized he was untouched. His eyes widened as he accepted that the pain was not his own. It was Isobella's.

Without conscious thought, Bane tossed the witch aside and charged out of the mist. The morning sun would surely kill him, but he had to try and reach Isobella. He had to do something to save her.

Stepping directly into the forest, he raced through the shadows, barely aware of the mist that continued to shroud about him or the witch who easily kept pace with his swift motion.

It was her magic no doubt protecting him from the sun, but he felt no gratitude. Not when he could see Isobella crumpled on the ground, her dirk stuck directly in her heart.

Falling onto his knees beside her, Bane tenderly pulled her into his lap, his hand compulsively smoothing back her tangled curls.

"Blood of the saints . . . Isobella," he whispered in broken tones, his tortured gaze lifting to plead with the witch at his side. "Return the curse."

A deep sadness settled on the lined countenance. "Tis not possible. The curse was broken the moment she offered ye her love."

Bane grappled to know what she was saying. "Her love?"

"Aye." With gentle care the old woman removed the dirk from Isobella's chest and lowered her shawl to cover the bloodstained body. "Hatred conjured the curse. Only love could end it."

"Then why has she done this?"

"She thought this the only means to save her sister as well as ye."

Fury far beyond anything he had ever experienced before raced through Bane. He had done this. His selfish need to punish those who had hurt him had led to this moment. Now he would truly comprehend the meaning of hell.

Gritting his teeth, he cradled Isobella to his chest, willing to barter with the devil to save his beloved.

"Ye can save her," he growled, holding the witch's gaze with a lethal intensity. "Ye possess the powers."

She gave a slow shake of her head. "Nay, the powers are not mine."

"What do ye mean?"

She reached out to lightly touch his cheek. "The powers are yers. They always have been."

Bane flinched as if he had been struck. "Mine? That is ridiculous. I am nothing more than a simple bard. I have no powers."

"Aye, ye do. Twas yer will that brought ye from the grave, I only assisted ye to focus that need."

His lips parted to deny her charge, only to close when he forced himself to recall that brutal eve.

There had been pain and anger and overall an aching sense of loss.

But even as the darkness and cold had closed about him, he had refused to accept defeat. With fierce concentration, he had wrenched and molded it into a weapon of his own. Like his father carving music from a piece of wood, he had created life out of death.

"My powers," he whispered.

"Ye must believe in them, just as Isobella believed in ye. If ye cannae, she will die."

With a last pat upon his cheek, the witch turned to disappear in a swirl of mist.

Frantically Bane glanced down at the pale woman he held in his arms.

He could save her. But only if she was willing to share the existence he had chosen.

He would not force it upon her.

"Isobella?"

For a moment there was no response, and he desperately feared he was too late. Then at last her heavy lashes fluttered upward.

"Bane?" Her voice was terrifyingly weak. "Ye must not be here. The sun . . ."

His muscles knotted. Had there ever been such a lassie? Even now her concern was for him rather than herself.

"Be at ease," he soothed. "We are in the mist."

"In the mist? But how?"

"It does not matter."

With an obvious effort she lifted her hand to touch his arm. "I am happy ye are here. I feared I would not be able to say good-bye to ye."

Pain greater than any dirk to the heart could cause lanced through Bane.

"Damn ye, Isobella. How could ye be so foolish?"

A strained smile curved her lips at his furious tone. "I am sorry, but it had to be done."

He briefly closed his eyes. "Nay, Isobella, it dinnae."

"Katherine . . ."

"Katherine was in nay danger," he softly confessed. "The curse was broken. Ye ended it the moment ye offered me yer love. This torc about yer neck was proof of that."

Her lips parted in shock, the hazel eyes darkening with disbelief. "My love?"

"Aye."

"Och . . ." Her lashes briefly lowered before she raised her gaze to regard him with a weary amusement. "I was so determined to be a martyr. In truth, I was very proud of myself. Now even that is denied to me."

Bane's nose flared with fierce emotion. Hellfire. He thought her a woman of intelligence. An obvious mistake if she thought he could allow her to sacrifice herself for him and not ken he would soon join her in the grave.

"Do ye believe that either Katherine or I desired ye to be

a martyr?" he rasped. "We would both rather die than lose ye."

She shivered in his arms. "Tis too late now."

His grip tightened as he leaned over her. "Nay, it is not too late, my love."

"Bane, I can feel the truth." She struggled to speak, her delicate features etched with pain. "I am dying."

He gazed deep into her shadowed eyes, battling his instinct that demanded he simply use his powers upon her before it was too late.

"I can keep ye from death if ye will let me."

Her fingers briefly tightened upon his arm before she sucked in a ragged breath. "Nay. That is not possible."

His lips twisted at her ridiculous words. "I am proof it is possible," he reminded her softly, pausing as he forced himself to confess the stark truth. "But such a life doesnae come without cost, my love."

"Cost?" She frowned, her thoughts clearly becoming more confused. "Ah . . . the sunlight."

"Aye. I cannae bear the sunlight, nor fire." He instinctively squared his shoulders as he prepared himself for her predictable horror. "And to survive I must drink the blood of others."

Her eyes widened in shock. "Blood?"

"Tis the only means."

He could see the struggle waging deep within her, and he sternly resisted the urge to dismiss the price of immortality. He might be capable of swaying her decision, but he could not force her to accept what such a decision would mean to her future.

"Ye kill others to stay alive?" she at last demanded in a faint voice.

He gave a sharp shake of his head. "Nay, 'tis not necessary to kill. Indeed, those I choose dinnae even ken I have fed upon them."

Her brows drew together as her hand lifted to lightly touch her neck.

"Ye fed upon me . . . that first night."

"I dinnae feed, but I did use my magic to make ye forget our encounter," he corrected with a wry smile, easily able to recall every moment of that first eve. He had ken from the beginning this woman was destined to rattle his peaceful life. "Not that it proved to be successful. Ye are clearly more stubborn than most."

That brought a small smile to her lips. "So I have been told."

It was that smile that was Bane's undoing. With a choked moan he buried his face in her hair. He could not survive without her. Not even for a moment.

"I would do anything to have ye with me, Isobella, but the choice must be yers," he whispered against her cheek. "I cannae force this existence upon ye."

He felt her fingers gently stroke his hair. "We will be together?"

"For all eternity," he swore.

"Do ye know, Bane, I am not certain if that is long enough."

Bane stiffened before slowly raising his head to regard her with a searching gaze.

"Ye agree? Ye accept the cost?"

"Nay cost is too great to be with ye."

Heady relief rushed through Bane as he pressed frantic kisses to her upturned face. Thank the heavens above he was not to lose her.

"Isobella."

"What must I do?"

Pulling away, Bane tossed back his cloak and shoved up his sleeve to reveal his bare wrist. Then steadily holding her gaze, he allowed his fangs to lengthen.

He did not miss the sound of her breath catching at the sight of his true form, but she never flinched as he raised his arm and sank his fangs deep into his flesh.

Waiting until the blood ran freely, he lowered his arm and pressed his wrist to her lips.

"Feed," he urged gently.

Holding his gaze, she opened her mouth to allow the blood to trickle past her lips. It took less than a heartbeat for her pallor to be tinged with a hint of color and the horrid rasping of her breath to ease.

Bane stroked her cheek as his power raced through her, healing the wounds and altering her from within. She trembled with the force of the change, but Bane knew there was no pain. Soon enough she would become accustomed to the sensations flowing through her body.

At last she gathered her composure and regarded him with wide eyes.

"That is all?"

"Nay. I must feed as well."

Without hesitation, she reached up to scoop her hair away from her neck, her expression one of calm acceptance.

"Very well."

Lowering his head, Bane ran his tongue along the curve of her neck before pressing his fangs into her skin.

"Bane," she gasped, arching her body upward as her fingers tangled in his hair.

Just for a moment he desperately feared he had hurt her and he began to jerk back in horror.

"Nay, dinnae halt," she demanded, her hands pressing his fangs deeper into her flesh. "Tis the most extraordinary thing."

He tasted her blood in his mouth and abruptly comprehended her startled shock.

By the fires of hell, it *was* extraordinary.

Searing heat blazed through him, stirring his passions to a fever pitch. He could feel her very essence seep into him. An evasion that was more intimate than his possession the eve before.

Closing his eyes, he allowed the astonishing miracle to sweep through him. Isobella was now more than his wife and lover, he accepted with a sense of joy. She had become a part of him that could never be banished.

Bane quivered, awaiting the rush of fulfillment to ease before slowly pulling back to place a gentle kiss upon her lips.

"Ye are mine," he muttered in rich satisfaction.

Her fingers brushed his cheek. "Aye, just as ye are mine."

With an effort, Bane lifted his head to study her pale features.

"How do ye feel?"

"I . . ." Her eyes abruptly widened. "Blessed saints."

His hands urgently cupped her face. "What is it?"

"The pain . . ." she whispered, " 'tis gone."

Bane briefly closed his eyes, sending a prayer of thanks to the heavens above.

He was far from certain that he deserved this wondrous woman. Indeed, after the past two centuries he was quite certain that he did not.

But then again, who was he to argue with the kindly fates that had blessed him? Few men were allowed the chance for true happiness.

He was not about to toss it aside.

With a rumbling laugh, Bane scooped her slender form next to his chest and rose to his feet.

"Come, sweeting."

Her brows lifted, but she made no protest as her arms willingly wrapped about his neck.

"Whate'er are ye doing, Bane?"

He glanced down at the hazel eyes that held his salvation.

"Taking ye home. Where ye belong."

"Home." She tasted the word upon her tongue before a glorious smile curved her lips. "Aye, that is precisely where I belong."